# LOW LIFE

## A SHACKELFORD INVESTIGATIONS
### Book 1

## KRISTY ROLAND

D1059342

LOW LIFE, Shackelford Investigations Book 1
Copyright ©2022 by Kristy Roland. All rights reserved.

ISBN: 9798789036853


This is a work of fiction. Names, characters, places, or incidents
are either the product of the author's imagination or are used
fictitiously. Any resemblance to actual events, places,
organizations, or persons, living or dead, is entirely coincidental.

All rights reserved. No part of this book may be reproduced,
scanned, or transferred in any form by any electronic or
mechanical means, including information storage and retrieval
systems without written permission from the author except for
brief quotes for review purposes.
Front cover images made with Deposit photos license.


First edition, 2022

To Jorge, Lance, and Liliana:
Thank you for your love and support

Author's Notes:

If you are familiar with the Fayette and surrounding counties in Georgia, you will notice that I have taken great liberties in describing these areas. It was done in an intentional manner to fit the story as needed. All representations in police procedures may or may not have been altered for the story.

# Chapter 1

**Sidra Shackelford said** into her wireless comm link, "He's at the Tavern on 6th," once she'd spotted the target her brother lost. This bar was one of four on Holliday Street in Griffin, where people could bar hop all night.

"I'll be right there," Daley said.

"I got it."

Mitchell was in his surveillance minivan, doing his usual job of monitoring the outside, while Sidra and Daley did the hard work. He said, "You got this, Sidra. Be yourself."

Daley laughed. "When you send an alcoholic into a bar..."

"Hey, I told you it was a bad idea," Mitchell said.

"You two are assholes." Sidra made her way through the crowd. Her two brothers had a full conversation over the comm while she kept her eye on the target. Walburn and Privet hired Shackelford Investigations to find Diane Hutchinson, but they'd

1

found Benny Valentino instead. A known associate of hers. This should be interesting.

Sidra asked the bartender for a water, handed him a five. "Can you put that in a martini glass for me?" She offered him her best smile and gave him a wink. He poured the water into a martini glass, added an olive, and slid the drink toward her.

Damn, he looked good behind the bar.

"Flirty Bird," Daley said. "Stop drooling over the bartender and get your eyes on Valentino."

Sidra turned, spotted Daley at the other end of the bar, between two people. He leaned an elbow on the bar and took watch as Benny Valentino sat at one of the high-top tables past the dance floor. The music here ranged from country to rap, and the only thing frowned upon was topless dancing. Everything else was balls to the walls acceptable.

Sidra had on tight jeans, a flimsy black blouse and her long brown hair pulled back into a loose French braid. The purple glasses she wore were fake. She looked around like a lost dog and made her way to Benny and accidentally bumped into him.

"Sorry," she said, adjusting the glasses and continuing with the drunk klutz charade. "Have you seen, like, a couple of drunk girls running around?"

"You're in a bar."

"I mean. One of them's this tall—" She held her hand up to show him. "The other one has bleach-blonde hair."

2

"No," he said with a laugh. "But I'll be happy to help you find them." Stuck out his hand. "Name's Benny."

"I'm Bianca." His big, sweaty hand felt like a dog's tongue in her palm. Benny didn't let go for a minute, and Sidra tried not to pull away. "So anyway..." She finally got her hand back.

Benny's plaid shirt pulled tight across his round belly like an elastic, the buttons about to pop off and hit her in the eye. She resisted the urge to wipe her hand on her jeans. "Have a seat," he said, "while you wait for your friends."

"Okay."

"Tell me a little about yourself," he said, a big smile on his baby round face. Like she was at a job interview.

"I'm an Aquarius," she said. "I like to take gigantic risks. But I don't like outdoorsy stuff, you know, with bugs and stuff. One time, I hiked up Stone Mountain and broke my ankle. I like to cook, sometimes. Not all the time though." She nodded like an idiot. "I do filing at an accountant's office. Real boring stuff. What about you?"

Benny smiled, all interested. She liked that. "I'm a headhunter," he said, and she heard his northern accent.

"Headhunter? I've never heard it called that before." Benny let out a big laugh. She said, "And you're so upfront about it, too. How many dates do you get being so open about what you want?"

"You're funny." He looked around the bar.

3

"Come on, tell me. What do you do?"

"Do you live around here?" Benny said.

"Not really."

"Let me buy you another drink." He took her glass and hopped off his seat. Sidra followed him to the bar where Benny ordered more drinks. Sidra gave the bartender a look and he made her another martini with a wink. Martinis weren't her choice of drink; just straight up whiskey would do. But right now, she had to focus on Benny Valentino.

They walked back to the little table. "I think my friends ditched me," Sidra said, and sounded a little disappointed. With no response from her brothers, she hoped like hell they had eyes and ears on her, it's the only thing that kept her focused. "What were you going to tell me?"

"Okay, so a headhunter is a person who finds employees for businesses."

"Oh."

"I work with temp agencies. Contact various people. Find workers in places like this. I help grow businesses. Are you looking for a job?"

"A fun one. You ever get involved in any crazy stuff?"

"Like what?"

"You know, like you think someone is normal and you find out they're crazy."

Benny laughed. "Aren't we all crazy?"

"Nope. Not me."

Benny leaned in close, the beer on his breath had fermented like a trapped skunk in his mouth. "I'm gonna keep my eye on you."

"You're not from around here."

"Oh?"

"You talk like you're from Canada or something."

This made him laugh. "I'm not from that far north, and Canadians don't talk like this. Guess where I'm from?"

"I just said Canada and you laughed at me."

Benny said, "I was born in Chicago. I lived in New Jersey and then Boston. Lived in Texas for six years, moved to Tampa, and now I'm here."

"That's a lot." Sidra tried to give Benny her best The-Booze-Is-Working stare. "What else? What else do you do?"

"Tell me, Brandy," Benny said.

Mitchell and Daley said in unison: "Bianca."

"My name's Bianca," she said.

"Oh, sorry. I'm terrible with names. How about I just call you Sweetheart?"

"I bet you say that to all the girls."

And Benny Valentino laughed again.

"I think my friends are hiding out around here somewhere. One of them has this big, scary boyfriend. If you had to hide from someone, where would you go?"

"There's nowhere to hide from anyone these days, Sweetheart. Not with all these phones and tracking devices."

"But if you knew someone who was going to run away and hideout, where do you think they'd go?"

"I don't know. Canada?"

She playfully slapped his arm. "I mean here, in Georgia. If my friend needed a place to hide, where could she go? Like, if her big scary boyfriend was a bad drug dealer, or something like that. If you're a headhunter, you should know these things."

Benny sipped his beer. "Introduce me to your friend, and I'll see what I can do to help out. You ever do any modeling or acting? That shit's becoming huge right now in Georgia. I bet you could make a lot of money trying to be on TV. I know a guy who'd love to talk to you about it."

"If you give me his phone number," Sidra said. "I'll call him. I'm going to run to the restroom. Hope you're here when I get back."

"Oh, I'll be here," Benny said, a sleezy smile on his face.

On her way to the restroom, Sidra said into her comm, "I'm not getting anything from him. And for clarity, I remembered my own fucking name, okay?"

"Another martini and you won't remember anyone's name," Mitchell said.

"You're doing great," Daley said.

"It's not like I haven't done this before." She looked like she was talking to herself as she yelled over the bar crowd. She only stepped away from Benny to collaborate and made her way in a circle through the dance floor.

"We might not get everything right now. Ask him if he has any contacts at Omega. You can play the angle that way. Hold on. Benny just got up. He's making a phone call. Walking out the door."

Sidra made her way through the crowd of dancing, drunk people. It was nearly midnight and people still poured in.

Daley said, "I'm going into Fat Boys. Sidra, you take the Saloon."

Outside, she took a right and made her way to a bar called Southern Saloon, this one geared toward the country crowd, but they didn't care who walked in without cowboy boots.

"Don't see him in the parking lot," Mitchell said. "He hasn't exited from the south end." Mitchell breathed hard, on the move now.

"Damn," Daley said. "Benny slipped out quick. Mitchell, get eyes on his vehicle and report your status. Sidra, anything?"

"No. I'm still making my way through the Saloon." She looked around, desperately trying to find him and a little mad that they'd lost Benny Valentino twice. What kind of detectives were they?

7

A guy grabbed her from behind, and Sidra spun around, but the young cowboy wanted her to do a two-step. She sidled off the dance floor and kept her eyes on the bar in case Benny had his eye on her. When Sidra stepped outside, she said, "I don't see him. Did we get burned?"

"These guys are always sharp," Daley said.

"There's an alley past the Saloon." The dark alley was a cut through from bars to a back parking lot, with a side exit out of Fat Boy's. Daley caught up to her and they walked the length of the alley. A handful of drunk people stood past the end where it exited into the lot.

Mitchell said, "Hey, Valentino's car is gone."

"Great," Daley said. They waited a few minutes, each taking their time to make their way back to Mitchell, who'd been parallel parked on Holliday Street. Sidra got in after Daley and slid the door shut.

"You were supposed to be watching him," Sidra said to Daley. "You lost our man twice."

"I couldn't hear over the music," he said. "You stood up and I thought Benny was following you, but he went in the other direction. You're the one who doesn't know how to entertain a man long enough to keep him at the table."

"Did we learn anything valuable?" Sidra said.

"Still don't have a clue where Diane Hutchinson is," Mitchell said. He looked down at his cell phone, his biceps stretching his black t-shirt. Sidra grabbed her cell phone and turned off the Bluetooth for the comm link. Pulled the microphone from around her neck where she had the speaker tucked into her bra. Daley handed her a little black box, and Sidra grabbed a small black magnetic stylus which she used to take the earpiece out of her ear.

The disappointment of not getting what they wanted filled the air, but they weren't mad at each other. This was the name of the game.

Mitchell said, "There was a lot of noise interference inside the Tavern, but I heard most of your conversation. Calls himself a 'headhunter'. Is that how they kidnap people? Recruit them?"

"He may not even have anything to do with Diane," Daley said. "We could be working a dead end here." Daley turned around and faced Sidra. "Where'd you park?"

"The big lot." Sidra put the little black box and her purple glasses in the duffel bag. Mitchell dropped her off at her own surveillance minivan. A silver Toyota Sienna with the back seats removed.

"See y'all tomorrow morning," she said to her brothers as she got out, then Mitchell took Daley to his own vehicle. Sidra had every intention of going home, but the need for a drink pulled her in. Not just a need. The liquor spoke to her like a familiar friend. *Feel my warmth. I'll take care of you.* She grabbed twenty bucks out of her wallet, the last of her cash, and stuffed her purse into the portable toilet in the back of her van she used when she was out on a long day of surveillance.

The Tavern on 6th hadn't slowed down since they'd walked in hours ago. Red Hot Chili Peppers blasted from the speakers, the walls vibrating with the bass. Sidra ordered a drink at the bar. "Whiskey sour."

John said, "Start a tab?"

Sidra handed him the twenty. "One more after this, and you can keep the change."

He smiled, gave her a salute, and made his way to fill more drinks. She spent plenty of time in her life bar hopping, and she loved a good dance club, but this wasn't her scene anymore. She thought about all the work from the last five days that had gotten them this far, and still they had no tangible clues. So, she sat there contemplating her life. How'd she'd gotten this far in the last two years of being a private investigator with Dad and her brothers. While business was flourishing, Sidra was broke.

Life's just peachy, she thought when John brought her the second drink.

Sweaty people surrounded her, and she wasn't drunk enough for this obnoxious music. After a quick stop to the restroom, she made her way back through the crowd. Diane Hutchinson could be dancing in this very room, and Sidra wouldn't know it. The woman was supposed to testify against the Marquez family, and disappeared instead.

Back in her van, Sidra slid into the driver's seat. The dash read 1:04 a.m. Tired, she thought about her work meeting at seven o'clock tomorrow morning.

There was a tap on the window.

Sidra looked left. It was Benny Valentino. Of course it was Benny.

"Hey," he said. "Why'd you ditch me?"

Pulling herself together, she said, "Oh, sorry. The music was too—"

"Come on. Let's go get another drink. You been to the Saloon yet? Lot'sa dancin'." He wiggled his butt to show her.

"I can't," she said. Was their cover blown?

"That's too bad," Benny said. She thought he was giving her something. A napkin with his phone number, maybe. A towel? Benny Valentino was fast. Calculated. He reached his arm through the half open window and pressed the towel against her face with one hand, then grabbed her hair with the other. Sidra remembered pressing the minivan's horn, but after one deep breath to scream, she was out.

# Chapter 2

**Sidra woke up** partially naked and chained to a concrete floor. The overhead fluorescent lighting had multiple busted bulbs, but she could see a wall covered in graffiti and paint splatter. No idea where she was. Every bone and muscle hurt when she rolled to her side. She tasted blood in her mouth. Her head felt like it was going to explode.

Shouldn't have gone in for the drink.

*Where's your warmth now, asshole.*

She looked around the stifling little warehouse, now certain this was the old indoor paintball range on Experiment Street. She sat up and felt a wave of nausea. The room spun, all that graffiti blending into fuzzy images. Her wrist was in a handcuff attached to a three-foot chain. The bolt in the concrete wasn't budging. In the corner sat a metal folding chair and a little blue wooden train, she recognized as Thomas.

"Hello?"

She didn't hear anything. Was Benny coming back or did he leave her here to die? Spray paint covered the windows, but she caught little slivers of moonlight through the slim gaps in the graffiti on the windows.

Sweat dripped down her back, and her long braid stuck to her neck. The warehouse was about 15,000 square feet, with an open second level for shooting paint balls below. She couldn't see because of all the ten-foot walls that looked like a maze for hiding. Footsteps pounded on metal stairs, then the sound of someone walking across concrete.

"Oh, you're awake," Benny said. He squatted down to look at her. "You okay? I didn't hit you too hard, did I? Let me see." He moved closer, his eyes staring into hers, and she swung a leg out and kicked him hard enough that he fell on his butt. "Hey." He got to his feet and dusted off his pants. "No need for that. I'm not going to hurt you."

"I'm naked and chained to the floor."

"But how bad are you hurt? Sometimes I forget how strong I am."

"You have a fancy way of impressing women. You mind taking this off?" She held up her wrist.

"Can't." Benny whipped out a cell phone. "Smile. No, not like that. That's more of a scowl."

"What are you doing?"

"Trying to figure out who you are. I'm sure I could get a pretty penny for you. Maybe Tanner Wells would like you. Couldn't find your ID, which I found strange considering you were in a bar, and I realized you hadn't been drinking. That's something else. How you can drink water and get tipsy? Flirtin' with me like that.

13

Weird. I'm certain I've never seen you before. No cell phone. You lost your friends." Benny shrugged.

"And here I was," Sidra said, "thinking that I was meeting this swell guy and going to get laid." She pressed a hand to her head where he'd hit her and felt blood. "I thought you were rich, with that diamond earring in your ear and that gold Rolex. Boy, I had you pegged wrong."

"You can still get laid," Benny said.

"Won't enjoy it as much knowing how you treat women."

Benny put his hand to his chest. "I happen to be a really nice guy. I'm just misunderstood. So who was the guy?"

"What guy?"

"The guy you were walking around with after you ditched me." Benny cocked his head sideways. "What'd he do, ditch you?"

She wanted to ask him about Diane Hutchinson, but she didn't want him to learn who she was. Right now, she needed to remain a nobody. And figure out how to get the hell out of here. The bolt in the concrete was long, and it wasn't budging. She'd been trying to work it the whole time she sat there talking to Benny.

"Where are my clothes?"

"Somewhere." Benny waved his hand but didn't take his eyes off of his phone.

"So, this is headhunting?"

"Yep." Benny looked at her, his face serious. "You see, my father didn't have custody of me when I was growing up, and me and my mom moved around a lot. She taught me everything I know about headhunting. God rest her soul. You sure you're okay? You got some blood going into your eye. You need a towel or something?"

"No, I'm not okay, you asshole. How about the key to this cuff?"

Benny shook his head, and rubbed his chest. "Beer really messes me up. When I eat too much and drink beer, I feel like I'm about to have a hawdattack."

"Are you going to let me go?"

"No," Benny said, rubbing his swollen belly.

"Then what are you going to do with me?"

"I'm waiting."

"For what?"

Just then, there was a sound. A door opening, and then a loud, "Mr. Valentino?"

"Room in the corner," Benny called.

A moment later, a guy walked in. She noticed right away his pinky and ring finger on his left hand was missing.

"Why do you always take their clothes?" the man said.

"Bruce, I told you this. It helps me remember how soft and fragile they are. So I won't hurt them when I'm not supposed to. Now, do you want her or not?"

15

Every warning sign Dad ever gave her was going off like a thousand red flashing lights. The silence between these two was deafening. Her heart slammed into her chest as cold sweats hit her skin in this hot box of a warehouse. This tall man, Bruce, sized her up and rubbed his chin between his finger and thumb.

"People are going to be looking for me," she said, in an attempt to impede whatever was going on. "And when they find me, you're going to die."

This made Bruce laugh. "Yeah, I'll take her. Delores'll love this one."

"Nacho and his crew will pay, too. Cameo's having a feud with him right now."

Another sound came from the back of the warehouse. Benny and Bruce looked at one another, and Benny said, "I said come alone."

"I did."

Not sure whether to scream for help or just pretend she wasn't there, Sidra continued to wiggle the bolt in the concrete. The damn thing was barely moving. Had her dad and brothers come to save her? She wasn't sure if she was relieved to be saved, or pissed that she needed saving.

Benny and Bruce pulled out their guns and separated. Sidra was a sitting duck. How could she have gotten herself into this situation? Lesson learned, she thought and decided to yell, "Help!"

A gun shot sounded. Then, "Where's my son?" Three more shots fired. Sidra jumped every time and her heart pounded a million miles a minute. Benny somewhere talking about a boy. Never gonna see him again. Something hit a wall, more shots, and she got off her ass and frantically pulled at the chain. The concrete finally chipped away, then the lights shut off, and she was in the dark.

Sidra couldn't see her hand in front of her face until her eyes adjusted.

Silence enveloped her.

She tried to steady her breathing. As she moved, the only noise was the chain attached to her wrist, and she felt herself shake. She settled back down to the floor. No weapon except for an out of reach chair in the corner. There were no more voices, no more gunshots.

The beam of a flashlight hit the ceiling. Disappeared, then she saw it again. Quietly, Sidra worked the bolt in the concrete. But it wasn't enough time. A man walked into the doorway of the little room. Not Benny or Bruce.

This guy put the bright light right in her eyes to blind her. Sidra held up her hand to block the light.

The light stayed on her face, and then a second later, the guy walked to the chair, and she assumed he picked up the toy train. He said, his voice gruff, "Where's my son?"

"That was already here when—"

The guy turned and walked out. "Wait. They mentioned some names."

17

He stopped, turned, and put the flashlight back in her eyes. "Talk."

"No. Not until you get me out of here."

He shot a bullet into the floor next to her and she screamed. Sidra swallowed, looked down at the floor, away from the light. Away from the gun this stranger aimed at her. She was nowhere close to being free. Five, six shots fired. How long until the police showed up? "Don't shoot me," she said, and thought about her job. "I met Benny tonight because I was looking for information on a woman named Diane Hutchinson. And you're obviously looking for a boy."

"Who are you?"

"Nobody."

That flashlight didn't feel good against her skull.

***

Sidra woke up wrapped in a net of some sort, and this new guy stood over her like a hulking figure ready to pounce. She was in a bed, her body cold, her hands bound to something at her sides. The net trapped her and her vision blurred again and she swallowed down bile that kept coming up. He held her hands down, and she saw big scissors. He was trying to cut her fingers off. Her hands and wrists hurt so badly. What was wrong with these people? She screamed then, because he was really hurting her and when he put his hand near her face, she tried to bite him. She scratched and clawed at him, lifted her leg through the afghan, not a

18

net, and kicked him in the stomach. Something clattered to the floor. The chain attached to her wrist wasn't attached to anything, and she flew up out of the bed so fast, but he saw it coming, flipped her around and put her in a choke hold.

When she woke up again, she was alone, in the same small bed, in the same small cabin. Her wrist no longer had the cuff and chain attached to it. Pain shot straight through her back when she pulled her knees up. Glimpsing down, she still didn't have on any clothes, but the blue and green afghan covered her again. The cabin was little. Little enough that the twin sized bed was in the living room. A wood-burning stove sat in a corner next to a brown couch. All the walls were wood paneling, and it made the place dark. The front door had a dirty yellow curtain hanging from a broken rod. In the kitchen, a green Formica table sat pushed against the side of a rusted ice box, the table cluttered with a bunch of junk.

It was dark outside; the only light came from the kitchen. Boots were by the front door next to a pair of little boy's shoes. A small lamp on a nearby table. A Coke can next to some magazines. An Easter basket full of spent bullet shells. She wrapped the afghan around her body and winced. She needed to get out of here. Past the bed was a tiny room filled with boxes throughout and a dresser and lots of junk. It was as though someone had taken an entire house and tried fitting everything in this tiny cabin. There were boxes and crates everywhere. On the left was a small bathroom where she peed fast and found a dirty t-shirt on the floor. Through the front door window, she spotted a black SUV outside and wondered where the guy was. She had no idea where *she* was.

Private Investigators usually had real boring lives. Stuff like this didn't happen. She'd gotten more action working at a grocery store, with kids stealing from the candy aisle than working at Shackelford. So this? She didn't know what was going on.

She'd fucked up in a bad way.

Sidra looked for keys. On the kitchen counter she found some medical papers, some phone records. A Georgia map hung on the wall between the fridge and stove, with several cities marked with various colored push pins like marking vacation destinations. Some cities had numbers next to them, some had names. In one drawer, she found silverware and pulled out a big knife. Wallets, various IDs, and dead cell phones were in another drawer. And keys. But which set belonged to the SUV outside? This guy was crazy. Possibly a serial killer.

Sidra stood in the middle of the tiny kitchen wearing this guy's dirty t-shirt and held a knife and shook with nerves because she would stab him if she had to. She knew self-defense tactics, but that would only get her so far. She could hit a target at the gun range from twenty yards with complete accuracy, and further than that outdoors. But now, all she thought about doing was running.

Out of the corner of her eye, she saw him walk past the window but she wouldn't make it out in time, so she stepped back to the tiny cluttered bedroom just as the front door opened and closed.

When she stepped from the room with the knife, the guy was looking at the bed, then looked at her.

"I want to leave," she said, and even though she told herself not to cry, she could feel it start in her throat.

The guy held up his hands in surrender. "Okay." He had day old scruff on his face, a dirty t-shirt that matched the one she had on, and blue eyes that looked as cold as the blade was sharp.

The knife shook as she walked past him, but he didn't move. "Where are the keys?"

He pointed to a small rack next to the door, and she wanted to slap herself because she hadn't even seen it. "Don't follow me." She backed out of the door.

She walked to the Explorer, jumped inside, and locked the doors. Near the front door, he stood with his hands on his hips, not looking like he was about to stop her. Sidra took the keys and tried to put it in. It wouldn't go in right. "Come on." She looked at the key and the ignition. Maybe the key went in teeth up? Noticed the H. Explorers weren't Honda—

The crazy guy was right there, and Sidra screamed. Before she could grab the knife, he'd unlocked the car door. Grabbed her, and yanked her out of the vehicle.

21

She kicked and he deflected. When she got an arm free, she punched him in the chest, felt the shock through her elbow and knew it was a good one. Just like her brothers taught her. Punched him in the diaphragm, but it felt like she'd hit a wall. He slapped her fists away like she was a gnat, and then he used his leg to catch her off balance, but she caught him in the kidney with an elbow and he backed himself into the open doorway of the vehicle.

He reached in and grabbed the knife. "Enough. I don't want to hurt you."

"Go ahead. Kill me now because I refuse to stay here and be your captive."

"I just might do that. But this is my best kitchen knife. Can't have you running off with my best kitchen knife."

Great. A psycho with a sense of humor.

"I thought we were going to have a talk," he said. "If I got you out of there, you said—"

"What's that?" Sidra had turned her head to the scent of a sickening smell mixed with smoke in the air, but she didn't see a full fire. What she saw in the dark distance was what looked like a large smoker built into the ground with smoke billowing out of the sides.

"Don't worry about that. Tell me what they said. Look at me."

Sidra ignored the smoke for now, still wondering what was burning as she looked at him.

He said, "I swear I won't hurt you. I just want to find my son. As soon as you tell me what you know, I'll take you wherever you need to go."

With the desperation in his voice, she actually felt sorry for him. "Okay," she said.

"Let's go inside."

"I don't want to."

"Fine by me." He walked off. "I'll keep the door open in case you change your mind."

For a minute she stood there, the warm night air nipped at her legs along with the mosquitos. Fine, she thought, and followed him inside. He dug around in the back bedroom and came out with a small box of clothes. "You can clean up in there."

The bathroom didn't have a door. While she went inside the bathroom, he went into the kitchen. Sidra looked at the tiny window above the shower and wondered if she could fit through it. A blue washrag covered a hole in the corner of the window, and she wanted to climb out, but he'd catch her before she could get far. She caught her reflection in the mirror and winced. A small gash on her browbone, dried blood on her left eye, a bruise on her cheek.

The water from the sink looked okay, so she cupped her hand and drank, kept on until what felt like sand in her throat had disappeared. She used a sour smelling rag to wipe her face and arms. Whatever Benny used to knock her out, left her dizzy and nauseous. It was as if he hurt her, then seemed concerned that it was too much.

None of the clothes were her size. They were small and extra small and fear prickled her skin. Where the hell did this guy get them? The panties were all lace and thongs. Sidra didn't even want to go there. She tossed on a pair of banana yellow sweat pants that came to her calves, and a tiny white shirt with a butterfly on it, both small enough to fit her thirteen-year-old niece. She found one pink sock with hearts and one lime green with clovers.

When she sat down at the table, he offered her something purple from an old jelly jar. "No thank you," she said, leery of what was in the drink. "What time is it?"

He stood near the sink, and moved some papers to look at a clock. "3:52. You hungry?"

"Not really."

He began dishing out something from an old butter dish into a small saucepan, flicked on the flame and heated it up. Whatever it was, smelled delicious.

Sadly, Sidra's family wouldn't come looking for her unless she didn't report back at least by late morning. Not feeling one hundred percent safe, she wanted to give this guy the names he needed and get home.

"What's your name?" she asked.

"What's yours?" He dumped whatever he'd warmed onto a plate.

"Daisy Carmichael."

"No, it's not," he said, and sat down. He wasn't a small guy, seemed even bigger in the tiny space. He had tattoos on his arms, mostly above his elbows, couldn't quite make out all of them. "You wouldn't give me your real name that fast. You've spent too much time trying to get away and you feel a need to protect yourself."

"Okay," she said, his food wafting into her nose.

"And," he said. "I've met the real Daisy Carmichael. You're not her."

"No, you haven't, I just made that up."

He pointed his fork at her. "Told you. I can spot a liar from a mile away."

"My family will come looking for me."

"You're not my prisoner." He put his left arm around his plate, almost as if to protect it.

"So who are you?"

"Ford Lincoln Mercury."

"Very funny." When she stood up, he turned so fast into a defensive position that he hit his leg on the table. Half the stuff on the table fell off. Sidra held up her hands. "Is the offer still open for the drink?"

He nodded, but didn't turn his back to her. Sidra poured herself a glass of the purple stuff from the fridge, sat down, and took a sip. It was grape Kool-Aid. After she eyed what he was eating long enough, he pushed his plate to her, said, "Finish it," and grabbed a clean fork out of a drawer. Sidra didn't know if he had the creepin' crud but she took the fork and finished the stew. "It's rabbit," he said, and she tried not to think about it.

When she finished, she set the fork down and looked at him as exhaustion from the adrenaline rush set in.

"How'd you end up chained to the floor?"

"I underestimated Benny Valentino. He was an asshole." The thought of this guy being like Benny crossed her mind, and even though she didn't fully trust him, there was something about him that seemed righteous enough to put her at ease. "My name's Sidra. My dad got a case to find Diane Hutchinson because she's a witness who was supposed to testify in court and she disappeared. She was affiliated with the Marquez family. They're some local drug dealers. Have you heard of them? And Benny Valentino is associated with them and he's known for committing crimes for the family, so we'd been watching him for a few days hoping to find Diane."

"I'm Casey Lincoln." He put his elbows on the table and leaned in. "You won't find Diane Hutchinson because I'm the one who nabbed her. She's dead, I burned her body in my backyard."

Sidra leaned back in her seat but couldn't get away. Her pulse quickened, and she didn't know what to say. "You killed her?"

"Yes."

"Why?"

Casey Lincoln took a deep breath. "Because Diane Hutchinson kidnapped my son four months ago."

"Why did she kidnap your son?"

"Don't start asking questions you don't really want the answers to."

Sidra nodded. He was right. The bottom line was that Shackelford Investigations was hired to find Diane Hutchinson. This guy says she's dead, then the case is closed. "You have proof Diane is dead?"

Casey pushed his chair back and dug around in the kitchen drawer with all the IDs in them. He pulled out Diane's driver's license, then fished around through the pile of phones.

Sidra looked at the picture. It was definitely the same one they'd had on file at Shackelford. She pushed the ID back to him. "So you killed her and burned her?"

"Yeah," Casey said, matter of fact. "Benny too. You said so yourself. He was an asshole."

This guy just burned people?

"What about the other guy?" Sidra asked. "Bruce?"

Casey shook his head. "Don't know a Bruce."

"He was there when you showed up. If you didn't shoot him, then he got away. Apparently Benny was selling me to Bruce, and Bruce was going to sell me to Delores."

"Delores is a pimp. You would have ended up in Savannah at the Port of Entry on a shipment to God knows where."

Sidra let that sink in. "Benny said that a Nacho would pay well for me, and that he and Cameo were having a feud."

Casey tilted his head back. He closed his eyes, clenched his jaw and squeezed his fists tight. When he opened his eyes, he said, "Cameo is one of Nacho Marquez's street dogs. Human trafficking is her specialty."

"How do you know so much about these people?"

"Because I used to work for Nacho Marquez, and a long time ago, Cameo was my partner."

# Chapter 3

**Sidra had fallen** asleep at the table with her head resting on her arm. The sun was coming up now and shining through the window. Unless Casey Lincoln was hiding in a box somewhere, he wasn't in the cabin. The black Ford Explorer still sat parked out front. Sidra opened the front door and stepped outside, listened for a moment to the sounds of the birds chirping. Off to the left of the cabin, before the woods, three deer stood grazing on grass.

She walked out from under the little porch to where she'd seen the smoke last night, and sure enough, Casey Lincoln sat in a folding chair in front of what looked like a BBQ pit built into the ground. It was about fifty yards from the cabin and her socks became wet with dew as she walked to him.

Casey turned slightly when she approached. He had the Thomas train in his hand, spinning the wheels with his thumb.

"How long have you been out here?"

"Spend a lot of time out here." Casey pocketed the blue wooden train.

The fire pit he'd created was about six feet long and four feet wide. All Sidra saw was the metal dome cover sticking out of the ground. The cover had slats near the top to let out smoke. There was a handle on one of the short sides.

When Casey stood, Sidra noticed two cell phones in a bucket next to his chair. He grabbed thick, heat-resistant gloves, the kind that looked like they could withstand the heat of lava.

"Back up," he said. Casey moved to the side of the pit, grabbed the handle, and walked backwards as he slid the cover off.

Sidra was afraid of what she'd see in there, but she couldn't look away. There was a distinct shape of what could only be a burned, charred body in that pit. He used a shovel, and Sidra stepped back and looked away, as he broke up whatever remains were on a large grate. Smoke plumed out with a smell of something strange. Not like the fire's dad made when they were kids.

"Who was that?"

Casey stopped with the shovel and looked at her for a moment, and Sidra thought it would be nothing for him to shove her in there too and close the lid. But he ignored her, then continued breaking up the remnants with the shovel. "When all this cools, I shovel it out into a wheelbarrow and spread it out in the woods. It was Benny."

She wanted to throw up. "How many people have you killed?"

"These people took my son. And I'll kill whoever gets in my way of finding him." Casey put the shovel down, grabbed a cell phone and thumbed through it. "Benny sent out a couple of photos of you."

Sidra took the phone. It was the photos he'd taken last night. She looked like a helpless teenager. In the recent messages, Benny had texted Bruce, and a guy named Mark. Bruce responded first.

"Bruce was going to pay three grand for me, depending on my condition. And Benny wrote back that he was trying to figure out who I was, and they could work something out with D for more money. I looked good and would make her a nice profit." Chills when down her spine. Benny deserved to be dead. That was one less low life on the streets.

Sidra looked through his contact list, then checked through the call logs on his phone, didn't find any from last night when she'd left him at the table. Did he erase the call log, or had she been played?

"Bruce is still out there," Sidra said.

"The Marquez family is going to be quiet for a few days until they figure out who got Diane and Benny. That Bruce guy? I never even saw him last night. Doesn't mean he didn't see me. You probably won't mean anything to him, just the girl that got away, but I'd keep my eyes open if I were you, especially if he has your photo."

"I will."

Casey took the cell phone from her hand. "I'll drive you back when you're ready."

She was more than ready. Beyond ready. Never want to see this place again ready.

***

The Toyota Sienna was where she left it in the parking lot. Benny was probably going to sell it after he sold her. Shackelford Investigations was near the Fayetteville square on Highway 85, a few blocks down from the city complex and library. The house was a renovated Victorian farmhouse with a wraparound porch that was not only used for the office, this had been her parents' home for the last ten years.

Fayetteville was less than twenty-five miles south of Atlanta, depending on the route. The city was safe and all for the most part, but it wasn't perfect. Crime was growing. That was obvious with the ever-growing population. There were layers to it, though. The allure of a city made people stay, but the hidden agendas made them leave. Pull the sheet back and expose all the ugly colors like a bad photo developing. Fayetteville had its fair share of crime, but this town wasn't the only place the Shackelfords made their money doing investigating.

The driveway on the left was for Mom and Dad. Sidra parked in a small parking lot to the right that was shared with a realty company, and she walked around to the back of the house to the porch. The back door led into the kitchen, and when she walked in, Mom stuck her head around the corner and said, "Thank God."

Sidra walked into the room and looked around the table at her three brothers, her sister, and Mom and Dad. The room was large enough to accommodate a table for twelve and still hold a hutch and a liquor cabinet.

"We were about to call the police," Mom said.

Sidra walked behind Dad, to her own chair. Two boxes of donuts sat on the table. Sidra helped herself to one as they bombarded her with questions, and Daley handed Mitchell a twenty. "Told you she went home with someone," Mitchell said.

Her brothers. The funny guys.

Sidra inhaled the donut. Her hands were dirty. She still had blood on her arms. The clothes she wore looked like they belonged to a preschooler and she wasn't wearing any shoes. Not to mention the bruise on her cheek and the small gash on her forehead. Sidra looked at Mitchell. "Does this look like I went home with someone?"

"I don't know what you do in your spare time," Mitchell said. "All we know is that you weren't here on time."

"What happened?" Dad said. He sat at the head of the table in a nice pressed shirt. They would be late to church this morning. Her parents never missed church on Sunday. Even during the summer Dad kept his beard trimmed. Still not old enough for full gray, but it was starting to show.

"I went back to the Tavern for a drink. Benny found me later. I woke up at two different times with two different men."

"Good Lord," Mom said, and gave Mitchell and Daley a look like it was their fault.

With the look on Dad's face, Sidra touched his arm. "I'm fine now." She ate another donut in silence. Savored the whole damn thing. "Can I get some water or vodka or something?"

Amy jumped up, but Sidra knew her older sister was looking for an opportunity to leave. Her family was too much for her sometimes. She'd been kidnapped at fourteen and had never been the same since. Amy returned with a glass of water and a cup of coffee. She kept her hair in a short pixie cut and looked like a typical soccer mom in her jeans and summer cardigan.

"Thanks."

Amy smiled, a smile that was very similar to Sidra's. Amy said, "I'm going to go finish up the website revamp," and everyone nodded because Amy was the quiet one.

"Did you get anything?" Daley said.

Sidra sipped her coffee and nodded. Mitchell groaned and handed Daley his money back. "What was the bet?"

"That you'd go back in and look for Benny," Mitchell said.

"Wrong. I didn't go looking for Benny."

Daley handed Mitchell the money back.

Mom said, "You two are the biggest children I've ever seen."

Woolsey, the youngest at twenty-nine, sat at the end of the table with a laptop in front of him. He said, "According to social media, there was a shooting on Holliday Street last night in Griffin. Were you involved in that?"

"No. But can you look up a paintball warehouse on Experiment Street and tell me who owns it?"

A second later he said, "GT Greater Atlanta Property Management. Let me do a history search."

To Mom, Sidra said, "And if you were just now going to call the police, you'd have been about seven hours too late. Because sometime in the middle of the night I was about to be sold to a guy named Bruce for three thousand dollars, and I'd probably be halfway to Miami by now."

Mom put her hand to her mouth as she looked at Dad. "She can't do this anymore."

"I'm thirty-one years old, Mom. I know what I signed up for."

Daley said, "Who would pay three grand for you?"

Sidra gave him a look. If she had something to throw at him, she would.

Mitchell laughed. "We're in the wrong business. We could go down to Atlanta, pickup a couple of hookers with way more experience than her."

"We can close the case," Sidra said. "Diane Hutchinson is dead."

Dad said, "You two knock it off." To Sidra: "How did Diane die? Benny kill her?"

"Are you going to report this all to Walburn and Privet?" They were the criminal defense attorneys who hired Shackelford Investigations in the first place.

"Yes," Dad said. "That's how this business works."

"Then yes, Benny killed her. And he died, too, but I don't know who killed him."

"You didn't do it, did you?" Dad said.

Sidra picked up her third donut. A blueberry cake. She pondered Dad's question. Did he really think she was capable of killing someone? She thought about Casey Lincoln all alone in the woods, secluded to burn people as he needed to get away with crime in order to find his son. What lengths would she go to protect her family? To protect herself?

"I've never killed anyone in my life, Dad. The Marquez family are drug dealers and human traffickers. Benny Valentino scoped out bars looking for young women to kidnap so he could make money. Diane Hutchinson did the same thing. I'm glad they're dead."

# Chapter 4

**Sidra went home** to her crappy rental on Tulip Street, took a hot shower and washed her hair, careful with the small gash on her head that she was sure Casey Lincoln had given her when he hit her with a flashlight. It was too late for all that medical nonsense now. She tossed the clothes into the trash. She put on some cotton shorts and a t-shirt and curled into a ball on the sofa and fell asleep.

The next morning, she woke up with a sore neck and the sound of hammering next door. Not just hammering, a nail gun, POP POP POP, and it wouldn't stop. Her rental was a small, outdated bungalow that was built in the seventies. All the rentals down this street were the same, complete with vintage wallpaper and linoleum. The bathroom was a Hodge-Podge of avocado green and baby pink tile. When she'd moved in, Mr. Elbert said she could paint and make changes at her own expense. Six months later, the only thing Sidra had done was break the porcelain towel rack one night when she'd come home drunk.

Mr. Elbert was having the place next door renovated. He'd told Sidra she could move in for a settled rent amount until he was ready to renovate the house she rented. Then she could renew her lease for a higher amount or find a new place to live. She paid $500 a month for this dump. Now he's trying to charge these new tenants over a grand. Screw that.

Sidra pulled on a pair of jeans and braided her long hair into a loose French braid again. In the kitchen, she looked around the messy house. Dishes piled in the sink. Stacks of mail and junk spread all over the floor because she'd taken the table outside under the carport so she could paint it. That was days ago. Before they got caught up in tailing Benny. All of her thrift store junk cluttered the house. Reminded her of Casey Lincoln's cabin.

Something smelled terrible, but she couldn't figure what it was or where it came from. She opened an old pizza box and found moldy leftover pizza, crawling with ants. The raid choked her as she sprayed the hell out of it like an air raid on an enemy.

She shoved her feet into the black doc marten boots and knew she should have chosen better shoes for where she was going.

***

The District Attorney's office for the Spalding region was in Griffin on Main Street, inside the Government building. Griffin was one of those old mill towns with brick buildings dating back over a hundred years. Now, if a person lived in Griffin, they were either old money rich, or just plain poor. The middle class was gray because the middle class still struggled to live. Four major families owned everything in Griffin, and if you weren't part of those families, you were a nobody.

Sidra entered the building, stopped for a security check, and then took the stairs to the third floor. Through large wooden doors, she found the District Attorney's office, complete with navy and gold ornamental rugs and high ceilings. At the receptionist's desk, Sidra said, "Hi, I'd like to speak with Tanner Wells, please." He was a senior assistant, his father a prominent figure in Atlanta. Probably how he got so far in life.

"Do you have an appointment?" The receptionist was in her fifties, and wore perfume strong enough to make a scent dog die. The plaque on her desk said her name was Jolene Pike.

"No, ma'am, I don't. But if you'd please let Mr. Wells know that Sidra Shackelford is here, that would be great." Sidra turned and coughed, but it was mostly to suck in a breath of fresh air.

"Oh. Are you related to Harvey Shackelford?"

Sidra nodded. "He's my dad."

"I've known your dad a long time," Ms. Pike said. "Give me just a moment. Tanner's leaving soon for court."

Sidra looked around while Ms. Pike disappeared. Phones rang. Another assistant was making copies, endless amounts of files piled up everywhere. An elevator dinged somewhere down the marble hallway. Ms. Pike poked her head around a corner and waved Sidra over. She followed her down a carpeted hallway until they arrived at Tanner Wells's tiny office. A paper pusher, Sidra thought.

"Thank you," Sidra said, her voice all Southern politeness. Ms. Pike smiled and left.

Tanner Wells came around his desk. "What can I do for you, Sidra? Is that right? And you're Harvey's daughter? Yes?"

Sidra smiled and shook Tanner Wells's hand. A lot more handsome and a lot younger than she'd expected. His sandy blonde hair and blue eyes gave him a good-boy look.

Sidra looked down at her dirty boots. A person could tell a lot about someone by their shoes. Tanner's shoes were spotless. She had a nice suit, why hadn't she worn it?

Sidra let go of Tanner's hand, and said, "Yes, my name is Sidra and I'm Harvey's daughter."

Tanner smiled and gestured to a chair, then took the one across from her.

"Sidra? I've never heard that name before."

"To be honest, Mom thought she'd made it up. A great aunt on my dad's side the family was named Sidney, and a great-grandmother on my Mom's side was named Drea." Sidra smiled because the only reason she was being nice was because she needed something from him. And he was cute. "Anyway, in

Latin, it means like a star. Tilda Shackelford swears she made it up, though."

"Interesting," he said, and sounded bored. "What can I do for you?"

"Arthur Walburn hired Shackelford Investigations to find Diane Hutchinson. And while we were looking for her, Benny Valentino mentioned your name."

"Is that so?"

"He kidnapped me and said you'd like me. I don't know what that means—"

"Benny Valentino is a criminal. I work for the DA's office." Tanner held his hands wide as if that should explain enough. "Have you filed a complaint? What happened?"

Sidra didn't want to go into details about that, considering Benny was dead. "Why would he say that?"

"I don't know. A lot of the Marquez cartel is being investigated. We're doing everything we can to stop what they're doing. We know Diane's missing. Do you have anything on that?"

"Benny said he killed her."

She had to hold her cards close, laying each one down as needed. With no reason not to trust Tanner, the only thing she didn't want him to know about was Casey Lincoln. They'd made a deal. He didn't want the police to know about him in order to continue looking for his son. If the police knew about Casey and his affiliation with the Marquez family, they'd pick him up in a heartbeat. She'd tell Tanner that Benny kidnapped

41

and killed Diane Hutchinson. Bruce was the wild card that had gotten away.

"I overheard Benny talking to a man named Bruce. They were going to sell me to a woman named Delores, or someone named Cameo. Human trafficking is their business. Do you know anyone named Bruce?"

His brows narrowed as he thought about that. "I know of a Bruce Carpenter that was associated with them, but he died a few years ago in a car accident."

"This guy had a scar on his lip and was missing his pinky and ring finger on his left hand."

"New players show up in this business all the time. I'll definitely want his name and description for the local Drug and Gang Task Force. We can send it out to surrounding counties and see what they come up with."

"I'd appreciate that Mr. Wells—"

"Tanner, please." He sat back in his chair and pulled his foot up over his knee. "Did Benny mention anything about a body, location, anything like that?"

Sidra pretended to think for a minute. "I was nervous, and I wasn't in the same room as them. I just heard him say that he took care of her and they don't have anything to worry about." According to Casey, Diane Hutchinson was dust in the ground, and Sidra prayed he was being reliable about what he'd done. In her lifetime, though, she'd never come across a reliable drug dealer.

Tanner looked at Sidra for a moment. "Tell me more about Benny."

"We were doing our surveillance, and we lost Benny. He must have been watching me because when I went to my van, he showed up. He must have used chloroform—"

All the color from Tanner's face disappeared. "Are you sure about that?"

"No," she said. "But he used something. I ended up at that old paintball warehouse over in Experiment not too far from here."

"That's where you heard them talking?"

"Vaguely. The walls are high."

"Did Benny know who you were?"

"Didn't seem like it." She tried to keep her answers short and not give too much away.

"And how did you get away?"

"I think they got spooked. They just left me there."

Tanner thought about this, pulled his foot off his leg, and leaned forward. In her mind, she went back over everything she said, hoping nothing stood out. Diane Hutchinson was going to be a star witness for a money laundering case against Hector Marquez, but Diane also had charges against her. Once the depositions were made, the case involved the whole Marquez family. Someone screwed up because Diane Hutchinson should have been in protective custody. Without Diane's testimony, the defense's case fell apart. Right now, Tanner had another problem. Benny killed Diane and was loose on the streets.

Sidra kept her voice casual, like she wasn't trying to dig into anything. "Trafficking in Georgia is at an all-time high, especially for children and women. I can go on and on about statistics if you'd like. Diane Hutchinson took part in organized kidnapping. I'd be curious to know how many women have gone missing in this area in the last few years."

Tanner was confident in his next words. "My job is to help prosecute any criminal activity and I can assure you that what you're getting at is inaccurate."

"I don't think it's your job to tell me what's inaccurate when the criminals in this area—the entire state, even—are getting smarter than the police can handle. Strange stuff happens and these people are pretty slick."

"I agree. And I think we'll have to have a talk about that another day." Tanner stood up, held out his hand. "Until then, Ms. Shackelford."

"Sidra," she said. "I'd hate to cause a panic in the area about the local bars being pickups for human trafficking."

"I'd hate for that too," he said. "I'd be careful what rocks you go looking under."

Sidra left with Tanner's precautionary warning and drove over to the Tavern on 6th. Which was weird because the Tavern was on Holliday Street. The bar wasn't open yet, but she spotted John in the dark bar, wiping down tables. She knocked on the window and he walked over to unlock the door.

"We're not open yet," he said, and leaned against the frame.

"I was wondering if I could bother you for five minutes."

"Suppose so." John stepped aside and let her in.

"What happened Saturday night?"

"A fight broke out at Fat Boys and everybody dipped out in a panic."

Sidra thought back to what Woolsey told them. "I heard it was a shooting."

"The media always gets it wrong. The fight started and there were gunshots down the street, but not around here."

Could that have been the same time Casey went into the paintball warehouse?

"You want a drink?" John asked.

"I thought you were closed."

"I mean, if you're paying, I'll pour you one." John stepped behind the bar and poured her a malt whiskey on the rocks.

"You know that guy I was talking to—short, big belly, earring in his ear? You ever seen him around here before?"

"A couple of times but not enough to pay attention." John stacked beer glasses upside down behind the bar. He had a casualness to his work, like he could do it in his sleep.

Sidra sipped the drink. "A weird question. Anybody ever go missing around here, girls who were out partying on Holliday, and later reported missing?"

John thought about it for a minute. "The only thing I remember hearing about was that woman a year ago, Michelle Waites, I think, but they found her a few days later."

"I remember that," Sidra said with a nod.

"What's going on?"

"I'm not sure," she said.

"Doesn't the city have a missing person's page? You can check there. All the people who work in the bars talk about stuff like that, gotta keep our eye out for business purposes. Can't sell drinks if people don't think they're safe."

True, and she'd never find herself alone on Holliday Street again. Well, not at night anyway. Sidra couldn't have been the first person Benny Valentino had done this shit too, but she was his last.

# Chapter 5

**Sidra left Griffin** and drove to Clemmie's because she was starving. The diner was about a half a mile from the Fayetteville square. It was family owned, and what gave the place its good name was the home-style southern food. Clemmie's had been around since her dad was a kid and the diner was known to some as a staple in the city. It was a white wooden restaurant with a wide front porch, and sometimes she'd catch the owners out here chatting with customers. The diner was shaped like an L, and Sidra opted for a booth near the front windows.

She walked in, surrounded by familiar faces, and people said hello, gave friendly waves, and nods. They all knew Harvey Shackelford's family.

Penny, the owner's wife, said, "Sidra, where have you been hiding?" as she poured coffee for Mr. Freddy at the counter.

Mr. Freddy Calloway turned on his stool. "You still trying to keep up with those boys of yours?"

"They're trying to keep up with *me*." Sidra leaned on the counter between two stools as Penny and Mr.

Freddy laughed. Mr. Freddy was her old middle school principal who finally retired a few years ago.

Penny said, "What do you want?"

"Coffee—" She looked over at Mr. Freddy's plate filled with scrambled eggs, grits, bacon, and two buttered biscuits. "The usual."

Sidra grabbed the hot mug of coffee and sat down at a booth in front of the windows. Clemmie's was as comfortable as a person was going to get in a town. This was old school when people raised their kids right. She remembered coming to Clemmie's every Friday night for ice cream. Nothing fancy, just chocolate or vanilla. It was all Harvey could afford back then. Fifty cents for an ice cream cone.

Clemmie's wasn't too busy, but that would change in about an hour when the lunch rush hit. Sidra spotted Val making her rounds to all the tables. Earrings covered her ears, her arms sleeved in tattoos. She'd been working here since high school and never left. If Val ever quit, the place would shut down.

"Where you been?" Val said, with the same tone as Penny.

Before Sidra could answer, Penny slid a plate across the counter and Val set it on the table. Smelled delicious.

Val said, "Heard anything more about Mary Beth James? I swear that woman went flying in the air. I ain't never seen anything like that in my life."

"She died."

"I know."

Mary Beth James was a middle-aged woman who had been eating at Clemmie's when a teenager stole her purse out of her car. Mary Beth chased the guy down, ran into traffic on Highway 54 where a driver hit her at seventy miles an hour.

"Here comes trouble," Penny said, and Sidra looked out the window. Harvey Shackelford walked fast, on a mission to get his $6.99 heart attack plate. But Sidra knew that look. Apparently Val did, too.

"What's he pissed off about? Let me get out of here." Val moved down the tables and refilled more coffee.

When Harvey walked in, he got the same cheery hellos, but he waved people off. That wasn't like him. He was friendly and people liked him. They couldn't go anywhere without him having a conversation with somebody. He set his sights on Sidra and stormed over.

"I had to track you down." He squeezed himself in the booth across from her. He gave Val a lift of his finger, but kept his eyes on his daughter.

"Why didn't you call?" Sidra picked up her cell phone. "Oh, you did. Sorry. What's wrong?"

"Don't 'what's wrong' me." His face was tight. "You went to see Tanner Wells. You can't do that, Sidra. Not without my knowing."

Sidra shrugged, said, "Okay."

Val brought over a coffee and orange juice. Harvey said, "I'll do a usual plate, but with fried eggs. Can I get some sausage gravy on the side?"

"You're not getting any of that. How about some scrambled egg whites with a side of wheat toast?"

"Val," Harvey said, and gave her a look.

"Don't yell at me because you had a heart attack six months ago. You can't just have what you want because Mrs. Tilda's not here. How about some oatmeal?"

Harvey sighed and tried to hand Val the orange juice since he wasn't getting breakfast. "Next you're going to offer me a plain turkey sandwich."

"Are you mad at me, or are you mad at her?"

Harvey took back his orange juice. "You know what? I already ate breakfast. This'll be fine."

Val patted Harvey on the shoulder. He'd known these people for way too long. He turned back to Sidra. "We agreed I would talk to Arthur Walburn. You mentioned nothing about Tanner Wells. He just called Walburn and Privet to inform them he learned from one Sidra Shackelford that his client was dead. That's not how things work."

"Then Tanner should have kept his mouth shut."

"He's a Senior Assistant. They want a body."

Well, they weren't going to get one.

"While I need you to learn how to do these things," Dad said, "because I won't be around forever, you can't go asking questions, making it look like you're going behind my back."

"Tanner Wells is being dramatic."

"Tanner also felt as though you were being accusatory about the failure of efforts in human trafficking in the area."

Sidra bit into the homemade buttermilk biscuit. She chewed and looked at Dad. A minute passed and then he slammed his hand down on the table, startled her enough to make her jump and Mr. Freddy turn around. Dad didn't say anything, just embarrassed the hell out of her.

"What?" she said.

"I don't think you're telling me everything."

"Why would I lie to you?"

"Because that's what you do. Maybe not outright, but you're damn sneaky about stuff. I need you to keep it clean when the business is coming from an attorney's office."

For twenty years, Harvey Shackelford had been with the Atlanta Police Department, first as a patrol cop, then a detective. Her sister Amy got kidnapped and Dad screwed up when he put his job on the line to get his daughter back from a deranged killer. The killer got away, and his partner nearly died. Harvey Shackelford retired early, per the APD.

He started Shackelford Investigations shortly after. He knew a lot of people in various counties, good guys and bad. Shackelfords got the job done. They weren't above the law, but sometimes, people looked the other way when it came to their investigations. Harvey didn't talk about this. He tried hard to keep everything on the up and up.

"I'm going to stand by what I said," Sidra said.

"On a scale of one to ten, how bad are you pissing down my leg?"

"Dad, I don't want you to be liable for anything I do."

He leaned in close. "You have a license and a gun and you work under my name. Anything you do, my business and my name are liable."

"I'm a Shackelford too. I can be responsible for the business."

"Oh," Dad said, and leaned back. "Miss Smarty Pants, with no college degree. Miss Valedictorian of Fayetteville High School, who ran away and gave up a full soccer scholarship. Miss Sixteen-Jobs-In-Ten-Years. I think you set the world record for worst work ethics in the history of the United States."

"The whole United States? That's something," she said, pissed off because the word *unsuccessful* came to mind.

Dad started ticking off on his fingers. "The dog pound. The cleaners. The tire shop. The florist. The bakery. Medical clinic. Marco's Big Tacos." He tapped his finger on their table. "Clemmie's. Where else?"

"I know how to do a lot of things, Dad. All those jobs I had gave me skills that I use every day to do my job."

"And the drinking?"

Sidra looked around Clemmie's, everyone acting like they weren't listening to the drama. "I'm not drinking as much, okay?"

"Not as much still means too much. How many you had today so far?"

She narrowed her gaze at him, a little pissed off that he was right. One malt whiskey at ten o'clock in the morning seemed more like a punishment now rather than a drink to start her day.

"Okay." Sidra put her fork down. "Even if I was drunk, I could change a tire on a car faster than Mitchell and Daley put together sober."

Dad tried not to smile. "You're right about that, but it doesn't change anything."

Sidra felt her throat catch, tired of feeling like Dad's biggest disappointment.

"I trust you, but don't go behind my back asking questions about things, okay?"

"Okay."

"Are you going to eat that?"

***

At the crappy rental, Mr. Elbert's official eviction notice was in her mailbox. Thirty days from now, she needed to empty the house, or her belongings would be condemned. She balled up the paper and threw it across the room. Thought for sure she'd have longer than that.

Frustrated, Sidra started painting the kitchen table she'd left outside under the carport. The sound of the construction next door was wearing on her nerves. The old table she'd gotten from a thrift store for twenty dollars was one of those old circular wooden things that everyone had in the seventies. The paint she used was named *Peacock yellow*, a drab mess up from the hardware store that she'd gotten for eighty percent off. The color was fine with her. It would look nice with the wooden chairs she was going to paint in an avocado green. Or, as the paint swatch called it, *Alligator pear*.

Across the street, a Jack Russell terrier named Bruno had been barking at anything that moved. His owner, Mrs. Applebaum, was an older, overweight woman who rarely left her house except to get the mail and yell at any kids who rode their bikes in her driveway and made Bruno bark. The woman never walked Bruno, so he did the next best thing. He climbed the fence and took himself on a stroll.

Sidra brushed paint on the legs of the table and thought about all the lies people told. *I trust you*, Dad said. No, he didn't. Sidra had screwed up so much she'd become a joke. Lies and secrets. That's what her whole family was about.

They all had their secrets.

Sweat poured down her back as she finished with the first coat of paint. That's what life felt like. Layers of paint piled on to cover stuff up. She watched a construction van back up next door, the driver nearly backing into the concrete steps.

Sidra could hear Bruno coming down the sidewalk, he barked the whole time. When he got to her driveway, he walked up to her, sniffed around the paint and the brushes, walked in a few circles smelling everything, his tail wagging high. Then he started barking at her.

"You're high strung." Sidra put down her paintbrush and walked inside the air-conditioned house. Bruno followed. In the fridge, she found a leftover BBQ rib and handed it to the dog. He happily took the bone and left. As she got back to the table, she watched Bruno climb back over the fence.

Sidra bent down for the paintbrush, stood up and startled. Casey Lincoln stood there on the other side of the table. He held a metal Batman lunch box in his hand.

"How did you find me?" she said.

"Wasn't hard."

She pointed at the lunch box. "Cute. You brought your lunch."

"Can we talk?"

"I thought you were in hiding?"

Casey looked around. "So can we go inside?"

Sidra let him in, said, "I would have cleaned up if I'd known company was coming over." Casey's t-shirt fit him tight across the chest and arms. She spotted more of his tattoos, believing a couple were gang or cartel related.

"I want you to do me a favor," he said. "I can pay you." He handed Sidra the lunch box. "It's three grand."

"That's how much Bruce was going to pay for me. It's a lot lighter than I thought." Sidra popped open the latch, and sure enough, there was cash wrapped into little bundles. "I'm sure whatever you want me to do; this won't be enough."

Casey surprised her when he pulled a gun. "I told you my son is missing. I just need you to put on something nice and try to get into this party. I don't have anyone else to help me."

Sidra closed the lunch box and set it on the coffee table. Then she kicked Casey Lincoln in the nuts. Casey wasn't a small guy, not by a long shot. But he underestimated her. She grabbed his gun, or maybe he let her take it. "If you want out of the drug business, pulling a gun on people to get what you want needs to stop. Don't do that shit again."

He looked up at her.

She said, "I'm assuming you've gone a little crazy because you're stressed out?" He was down on one knee, still catching his breath. Sidra held out her hand. Not because he really needed help but as an olive branch. Casey took her hand, nodded by way of apologizing, then Sidra set the gun down on top of the Batman lunch box.

"I'm not making any deals with you, but tell me."

"He's four years old."

"Where's his mother?"

Casey sighed. "Can I sit down? Jesus, what's wrong with you?" He limped over to the sofa, sat down, and sighed again. He said, "I know I'm in over my head with this, but I know these people. I used to work for them. This is what happens when you want out. They do unbelievable things to you and kidnap your son." Casey put his head in his hands for a moment then looked at her. "Forget it." He got up.

"I don't know what you want me to do. Nacho Marquez is a big-time drug dealer in the south."

"He's not a drug dealer, he's a *businessman*. He gets everyone else to do the dirty work for him. That's how it works. It's a whole organization."

"And you want me to get involved? No, thank you. I like my life." Sidra went into the kitchen for a glass of water. She never heard him follow her.

He said, "His name's Brandon, and he's four years old." Sidra turned, and he stood there in the kitchen. "All you have to do is go to this party and be a lookout. It's at his house. I'll back you up the whole time."

\*\*\*

"Ask him for more money," Daley said.

"Is the money really that important?"

Sidra called an emergency meeting at Shackelford. Dad, Mitchell, and Daley sat in the office with her as she told them what was going on. Woolsey was on speakerphone. "How do you even get into this party?"

"I don't know. Dress pretty and walk in?"

Daley laughed. "Will they let drag queens in?"

"Screw you, Daley."

"Does he think the kid is there?" Dad said.

"I don't think Nacho Marquez would keep a kidnapped boy at his house."

"Then what's the point?" Dad asked. "Snooping around a drug dealer's house is not a good idea. And whoever this Casey Lincoln is, he's bad news."

"Y'all do stuff like this all the time."

"No, we don't," Dad said. "Everything people think we do is made up on TV."

"Most exciting thing I do," Mitchell said, "is when I catch some cheater having sex in the back of the car. And I get to record it."

Dad slapped Mitchell with the back of his hand. "Don't start."

"This Saturday night," Sidra said. "I'll find out more about this party and let you know."

# Chapter 6

**The next day**, Sidra got a text message with a photo of an invitation. It wasn't a party Casey wanted her to attend; it was a fancy wedding. *La Sombra del Caballo* was a venue in Monroe County with rolling pastures and a full restaurant. The place was huge, with rental cabins and horseback riding, two lakes and the Towaliga River west of the property. With a proper setup, upcoming musical artists held concerts at La Sombra.

First homework assignment was gathering information on the bride and groom. Abigail Cortez was a beautiful Hispanic girl, twenty-four who'd graduated from the University of Georgia two years prior and went by the name Abi. The groom was a white American guy, also twenty-four and also a UGA grad. His name was Tyler Honeycutt. People and their social media fame. The couple had lots of photos of themselves on Facebook and Instagram.

Abi was Nacho Marquez's niece. There were only three photos on Abi's social media with him. These drug dealers—*businessmen*—didn't like to be seen. One photo was of Abi as a young girl in a swimsuit standing next to a trim and fit "Tio Nacho." Not bad looking. The second was of Abi dressed in her UGA cap and gown, her mother which from Sidra's research looked to be Nacho's only sister, and Nacho himself with a big smile on his face. The third was Abi, Nacho, and Tyler with a caption: I can't wait for our big day, Thank you, Tio Nacho, *el padre que nunca tuve.*

Next, Sidra hit a dress consignment shop in Peachtree City, where she found a shit ton of options because it was June and prom was over. These dresses had changed so much from her prom days. Not that she was old, but damn, these girls were wearing slits to the crotch like red carpet movie stars.

With it being wedding season, the store was having a twenty percent off sale. Still, these price tags were ridiculous. Maybe she could return the dress? Ten dresses later, she found a chiffon, spaghetti strap dress that didn't reveal too much and stopped above the knee. It was elegant and flowy, but the color was taupe, which was great because she didn't want to stick out too much at this shindig.

The next day, her brothers nearly blew up her plan. They weren't moving forward with this until they met Casey Lincoln. "I don't know this guy," Daley said. With his military experience, it was no wonder he was hesitant. Not only that, all three of them, Dad, Mitchell, and Daley, didn't trust why Casey needed someone to have eyes on Nacho Marquez at his niece's wedding. What was this guy's deal?

They stood outside the Sac-O-Suds in Jackson.

"Where are you going?" Harvey said to Mitchell when he walked off.

"To pee."

"Get me some tuna," Daley said.

It was after eight, and Casey wasn't there yet. Of course, they'd agreed to meet half-passed, and they were there early. Sidra walked over to the railing and looked out to the Ocmulgee River; the night so dark she couldn't see anything but the moon shining on the smooth river rocks below. The smell of fishy water was in the air. Sidra enjoyed fishing. Hadn't been in a long time. It was the perfect place, out on the quiet water to think. So much to think about.

"This guy gonna show up?" Daley shouted.

Sidra looked at her phone. Nothing yet from Casey.

Mitchell walked out of the Sac-O-Suds wearing a yellow Two Yutes Tuna t-shirt. "They were all out of tuna."

Sidra checked her phone again, sent Casey a quick text.

She looked over at her guys. Dad stood there, all six-foot-one, his hands tucked in his pockets. He'd done this a thousand times... waiting to talk to someone. Mitchell was thirty-eight years old, and he stood there flexing his chest in his new tight t-shirt. While he was a goof-ball at times, Mitchell was a hothead. He'd get in someone's face and had the muscle to back it up. A wife and three kids, he protected his family like a bear.

61

While Daley didn't have the muscle like Mitchell, he had a good-looking, chiseled face. Daley had to grow up fast. He had a thirteen-year-old daughter to take care of. Mitchell was the muscle, but Daley would put a bullet in someone and feed the body to wild hogs.

Guess they weren't any different from Casey Lincoln.

They just didn't talk about it.

Someone dressed in black stepped out of the woods and they all turned.

"That's him," Sidra said. "Don't shoot him."

When Casey approached them, Daley said, "Why are you sneaking up on people?"

"I was making sure you were alone."

After all the introductions, Mitchell, Daley, and Casey sized each other up like three gorillas circling a nesting ground. Who was going to be in charge here? Sidra hadn't told them anything about Casey except that his son was missing and he was paying cash. They knew he killed Diane Hutchinson, but they didn't know he'd also killed Benny.

"Is the money stolen?" Harvey asked Casey. "Is that why they took your son?"

Sidra hadn't thought of that. Even if Casey looked like he was about to punch Harvey, he didn't show it. Not with Mitchell and Daley standing next to him.

"You have to understand," Harvey said, "that we're not going to get involved in anything illegal."

"I'll be the one doing the illegal work, Mr. Shackelford," Casey said. "Sidra said she feels comfortable being at the party and keeping eyes on Nacho Marquez and his family. Would you like to know what I'm doing, or no?"

Harvey shook his head.

Daley said, "Three grand ain't much when it comes to kidnapped kids and staking out drug dealers."

"I told Sidra three more after the job was complete."

Harvey said to Sidra, "You already negotiated this?"

"Negotiated?" Casey said. "She said if I didn't hand over more money she'd go to the police."

"That's extortion," Mitchell blurted out, like he was so honest.

Sidra looked at Casey. "We settled this."

"Settled?" Harvey said. "How'd you settle it?"

"Come on, Dad. Have a little bit more respect for me?"

Casey said, "I just need a favor, Mr. Shackelford. My son is four years old. I fucked up real bad, and I need eyes on Nacho Marquez for this one night. And I swear, you and your family will never see me again."

***

From the outside, when La Sombra was set up for a wedding, it was beautiful. They were parked in an enormous field roped off with designated parking spots because they opted out of the valet. They were in

63

Mitchell's minivan. Him up front, Sidra and Daley in the back, Daley chewing gum, his ball cap on backwards like he was going to a frat party after this.

Sidra had her long hair twisted into a loose bun on her head, and she'd put on a ton of makeup to cover the gash on her brow and the faint yellow of the bruise under her eye.

Daley was prepping the equipment, talking to Sidra about what to do and not do. "It's not like I've never done this before."

"Not with people like this," Daley said. "Stay away from the photographers and videographers." He handed her the micro comm for her ear. "It should link to your phone in a second."

"Can you two stop with the chatter when we go live?"

Mitchell turned, said, "Sorry, Sis. I don't have anyone to talk to when I'm in here all alone."

"We're all on comm links," Daley said. "If you have any problems, just say so." Daley held up a flashlight, pushed Sidra's head to make sure her ear looked normal. "Perfect." No sense of personal space in this family. She tucked the wireless microphone into her bra and hoped no one would notice it.

Mitchell held up his cell phone to Daley. "Look at this." It was a stupid video of some guy parkouring and falling. Daley cracked up. These two were the future of Shackelford Investigations. They were supposed to be her communication and protection for tonight. Jesus.

"Sidra," Daley said, his voice serious. "Whatever you do, do not leave the premises. Do you understand?"

She didn't say anything, was a little confused about why he'd say that. When she didn't answer, Daley put his hand on her head and nodded it for her. "Stop it." She swatted his hand away. "You'll mess up my hair."

Mitchell mocked, "You'll mess up *mah hayyer*." All exaggerated Southern drawl. "Do not go off comm, either. You're just surveillancing."

"It's surveilling."

"That's what I said," Mitchell said.

"Whatever. I got this, okay?"

***

The good news was that Sidra fit in perfectly with the young twenty-something wedding attendees. The bad news was that she didn't have a date or anyone to talk to except her brothers on comm. She kept her cell phone handy to make it look like she was talking on the phone as she gave them information about what was happening. The plan, according to Casey, was that Sidra would text him as soon as she spotted Nacho Marquez because Casey would be busy at two separate locations, breaking into Nacho's warehouse and a safe house to look for his son's whereabouts or get whatever information he could.

The outdoor venue was beautifully arranged for the dream wedding of a princess. Everything was

65

decorated with white lights and white chiffon draping over everything. The chairs were cushioned in white with gold backs. Sidra made her way down a paved walkway to where the ceremony would take place, and found a seat on the groom's side of the family, and sat next to four young ladies who could not believe Tyler was getting married. Eek!

Before the wedding started, Sidra spotted Nacho, dressed in a tuxedo, talking to a couple of men who looked just like him. Sons or brothers. They were definitely Marquez. Sidra sent Casey a text to let him know Nacho was there. She snapped a photo of him and sent that, too.

He sent her a thumbs up.

Sidra put her phone to her mouth, said as low as she could, "Eyes on the Cheese. Text sent. We're a go." If Nacho got wind that someone was breaking into his properties, or if Sidra saw him sending people off, she was to text Casey right away.

About ten minutes later, Sidra watched Daley, dressed in a suit, sit down in a chair three rows behind her. More eyes on Nacho.

This place was not only beautiful, but it was enormous. La Sombra had a lake about a hundred yards in front of them, and there were golf carts set up to chauffer guests to where the reception was located.

The ceremony started with Nacho walking Abi down the aisle and it was the longest wedding Sidra had ever been to in her life.

"You owe me," Daley said.

"Me too," Mitchell said, because he was stuck in the van again.

Sidra didn't respond. She was feeling claustrophobic sitting in a crowd of at least three-hundred guests. How much did this wedding cost? Oh, it was cheap considering it was paid for by a *Businessman*.

When it finally ended, Sidra kept her eye on Nacho and followed him to a golf cart. He was laughing and smiling and hugging people, so proud of his little Abi. Sidra hopped on a golf cart with some other people and took the ride along the concrete path to the reception. She would have walked, but didn't want to lose Nacho.

"I've got eyes on the Big Cheese," she said into her phone.

The lady next to her said, "Oh, I'm starvin' too. I know they're Mexican, but I hope they have some fried chicken. I'm Tyler's Aunt June." She held out her hand and Sidra shook it. "Are you a friend of Tyler's?"

"Yes, ma'am," she said, throwing on the charm. "I went to school with him and Abi."

"Oh, I'm so excited," Aunt June said. That's all she said, and Sidra didn't know if it was because of the wedding or anticipation of fried chicken.

They stopped at a big pavilion set up next to the restaurant where everything was decorated with tables set for ten, complete with white table linens and more lights. There was an open bar to the left and past the pavilion, a dance floor, and a stage for the band. They'd already started with music and then the DJ was introducing the new Mr. and Mrs. Tyler Honeycutt.

Sidra and Daley avoided each other so they wouldn't be seen together, but she knew he was over at the hors d'oeuvres, because he said, "Ah, man, they got coconut shrimp over here."

"Bring me some," Mitchell said.

"Nah, man, come get your own. No one will suspect anything. They'll all be drunk in about thirty minutes."

While she kept her eye on Nacho, taking wedding photos, and dancing with Abi and Abi's mother, Sidra made friends with three young ladies who went to school with the bride and the groom. Abi and Tyler are *so cute. Look at them.*

Sidra was surrounded in a sea of white and muted neutrals that blended in perfectly, and watched as everyone seemed to have fun. They ate food and drank and laughed. Sidra, careful with her objective.

And while she kept her eye on Nacho, she noticed one man who'd been with him from the moment she'd arrived, now had his eye on her. She didn't know if he was family, a bodyguard. No, not a bodyguard, a little too old for that and not built for it. A chill passed through her spine as she locked eyes with the man. He'd probably noticed her staring at Nacho for the last few hours.

Sidra threw her arm over one of the girls' shoulders. Kelsey maybe. No, it was Kelly in pink. "I'm getting another drink." They all bounced off, Sidra and her new best friends, Kelly taking Sidra's hand the way girls do, and now they were laughing about how they pre-partied.

"You mean pre-weddy-inged? Weddinged."

"Wingdid."

"Wingdings. I got wingdinged."

And the three ladies laughed like it was the funniest thing ever.

"Please save me," Sidra said, and her brothers laughed because they heard every word.

"Sidra," Daley said. "Do not get wingdinged at this wedding."

She took a step away from the ladies. "Do you have eyes on the Cheese? I had to look away?"

"Yep, and some Silver Stud is approaching you."

Sidra stepped back to her new friends. "Whew, I love this song," she said as Nelly began singing about how hot it was. As they danced at the bar, the Silver Stud casually bumped into her.

"Oh, so sorry," he said, with a slight Hispanic accent.

"No problemo," Sidra said, and didn't stop dancing. He smiled at her, swung his hips, and Sidra nodded. The spaghetti strap on her dress fell off her shoulder and the Silver Stud brushed her shoulder as he put the little strap back in place.

"You take this song literal," he said, and Sidra smiled at him.

As the Silver Stud ordered a drink, her new friends began singing. Daley said something to Mitchell about intel, and Mitchell responded. "Nacho's brother. His name is Lorenzo."

Daley said, "I've got eyes on Nacho. Sidra, stay on Lorenzo."

Which wasn't a problem. Lorenzo sat down on a high stool at the bar and seemed to take a liking to watching her. He was probably checking her out because he wanted to kidnap her and sell her into sex trafficking. Or use her as his personal strip tease dancer.

Sidra waved herself with her hand as she walked up to the bar. "It is hot in here. Can I get a shot of tequila?"

The bartender said, "Mixed drinks only. No straight shots."

No shots? What the fuck?

Lorenzo said, "Let the girl have a shot," and the bartender obliged.

Daley said, "For real, Sidra, slow it down."

God, she wanted to kill him.

"Thanks," she said to Lorenzo and then threw back the shot and realized how stupid that was. This guy could have given her something to knock her out for the Silver Stud. Sidra held out her hand, "I'm Emily Smith."

He took her hand, kissed the top, and said, "Lorenzo." No last name.

"Nice to meet you. Such a beautiful wedding."

"Like every little girl's dream, eh?"

"Of course. Abi's such a lucky girl." Sidra smiled at him, trying to convey her innocence to the older guy. Schmuck.

"You go to school with Abi?"

"I recently met her. I know Tyler. We graduated together. I mean, we all graduated together. But I met Tyler years ago. I heard Abi's family owns this place? It's amazing."

"Yes," Lorenzo said. "Lots of horses, and the lake. Lots of parties out here. It's great for business."

"You work here?"

Lorenzo laughed. "Me, my brothers. We own it. All of it."

Sidra feigned surprise. "Wow, that's awesome. I'd love to talk to someone about the business plan here. I graduated with a degree in business communications and I want to open my own business as a consultant. I'd love to know how you and your family started this up."

"Lots of hard work," Lorenzo said, and brushed his finger on her shoulder. She smiled and really wanted to break his finger.

"And what are the horses for?"

This made him laugh. "For riding. You want to see?"

"Yes," Sidra said, and hopped off her stool.

Daley: "Sidra, do not leave."

71

Lorenzo took Sidra's hand. "This way," he said, and led her to a golf cart.

Daley: "Goddamn it, Sidra. Do not get in that golf cart."

Sidra ignored Daley, and then Mitchell said, "I'm tracking you with the phone."

She didn't feel too uncomfortable, she and Lorenzo had a driver. Of course, he could be the one hiding the bodies. To be extra flirty, Sidra held up her arms like she was on a roller coaster.

A minute later, they were at the stables. The driver stopped at the entrance, and the front of the barn was still open. Apparently, they were giving tours because they were not the only people here. Sidra let out a breath she'd been holding. There was an attendant making sure no one let the horses out.

"Good evening, Señor Lorenzo," the attendant said, and Lorenzo nodded at the young man.

"We have thirty horses here," Lorenzo said. They leaned against one of the horse stalls. "Takes lots of people to care for them. You look for a job?"

Sidra smiled. "Sorry, but I need more money than that. I'm a business consultant for a company in Atlanta but I'm always looking to make more money."

"What would you do, for more money?"

Sidra gave him a little shove. "Not like that."

Lorenzo laughed. "Got to do crazy things to keep up with the business, eh?"

"Oh, I know. And I'm willing to do what it takes to make it to the top. That's how I got through school. Sometimes you have to step on people to get what you want. I mean, I'm not a bad person, Señor Lorenzo. I just don't want to be left on the ground. Do you know what I'm saying?"

"Oh, yes. And please, call me Lorenzo."

"So, Lorenzo," she said. "What exactly does your family do?"

# Chapter 7

**They got out** of there as soon as Casey sent the text. He gave her no further information. Mitchell, Daley, and Sidra drove from Forsyth to Fayetteville.

"Stop at the gas station," Sidra said. Still in her dress, she ran inside and bought chips, cookies, candy, and drinks.

When she returned, Mitchell said, "What's all that?"

"Let's go to McCurry park. I've got this." Sidra pulled out a joint she'd gotten from Kelsey.

"Put that away." Mitchell backed the van out of the parking lot. "We let you hang out with a drug dealer for five minutes."

Daley said, "That was the biggest wedding I've ever been to," and he whistled. "How much money did that sucker cost? And the gorgeous babes…"

"And I got stuck in here," Mitchell said. "Thanks."

"Can you two grow up?" Sidra said, and they both started talking about the Silver Stud being an old man, and, "Hope you like making jello."

They arrived at the park and took a right down a little service road that led to a concession stand tucked away in the back. Mitchell parked the van with the nose close to a picnic table. Sidra and Daley sat on the table and Mitchell on the hood of the minivan.

"I go home smelling like weed, Renee's going to kill me," Mitchell said.

"We don't have that problem," Daley said.

Mitchell was already digging into the chips and cookies because he didn't get hors d'ourves, and he wasn't happy about that even though he already started laughing. "About this old man?"

"I have a date with him Monday." She tore open a Slim Jim with her teeth and then popped open a can of PBR. "What's sick is that he's fifty-two and he thinks I'm twenty-five."

Daley said, out of the blue, "How'd you make straight A's in school? Your fellow classmates would expect you to be the president of your own company by now, but no, you're cozying up to a drug dealer's brother and out here smoking weed like you're sixteen all over again."

"And what would your fellow classmates expect from you? At least I knew how to party and make good grades. You had your freshman sister doing your homework for you. Your secret missions don't count as a career when no one knows what you're doing."

"That's why they're secret."

"Man," Mitchell said, "do I feel old. Stop talking about high school, I hated it with a passion."

Sidra took another hit on the joint and passed it to Mitchell. She pulled her hair out of the bun because it was falling in her face, but now her long hair was a mess. She said, "Do y'all remember when Mom got attacked by that dog."

"Attacked?" Daley said. "It was trying to eat her boobs."

"What dog?" Mitchell said.

"Happened here at the park," Sidra said, cracking up laughing. "We were at one of my soccer games and this dog wouldn't stop mouthing Mom's boobs, come to find out—" Laughing so hard she couldn't get the story out.

Daley said, "She'd forgotten she'd put a half-eaten hot dog in her bra."

Mitchell nearly fell off the hood of the van, laughing because now he remembered. Tears in his eyes.

"It was a Great Dane," Sidra said, trying not to choke on the Slim Jim. "Tore her shirt and bra right off in the middle of my soccer game. All I heard was screaming and Mom standing there with her tits hanging out. I thought I was going to die."

They sat there laughing and reminiscing about growing up until Daley had to pee. When he walked back, he was dribbling a soccer ball. He kicked it so hard, Sidra didn't have time to react and it hit her in the face.

"Fucking asshole." She touched her mouth and tasted blood. Mitchell bent over and let out a roar of a laugh.

"How did you miss that?" Daley said. "You're losing your touch."

Sidra wasn't losing her touch. "What did you expect me to do? Catch it with my teeth?"

Mitchell rolled with laughter.

She kept up with soccer just fine, so what she did was kick off her flats and kick the ball with a slight curve to Daley's face. He caught it, and so began their game of trying to hit each other with a soccer ball. Daley had his boots on, Sidra's feet were bare. The game was not even. Eventually, she made her way closer, got the ball from him, and then kneed the back of his leg, swiping his legs out from under him, putting Daley flat on his back. Sidra put her foot on Daley's throat. He was just about to push her off when she stepped down a little harder. Looked him in the eyes and dared him to do it.

The unspoken conflict between them would never end. Not after the way Daley ruined her life.

\*\*\*

"Absolutely not," Casey Lincoln said the next day. "You are not going on a date with Lorenzo Marquez. No, it's not going to happen." She'd met him at his cabin back in Monticello, and when he'd heard what happened at the wedding, he started pacing. Not that he had far to go, the place was so small. And as he kept on, his voice got louder and louder. "These people kidnapped my son. I didn't ask for your help so you can

77

find a date. You didn't do so well with Benny Valentino. I don't think you can handle a Marquez."

"I didn't go on a date with Benny. I'm only trying to get more information. Think about it, Casey. He could open up about a lot of shit."

Casey stood there in the tiny living room between an old plaid sofa and the twin bed. He had his hands shoved in his pockets like he didn't know what to do with them. "I'm not paying for the date."

"Where's my money, anyway?"

He walked off to the back to get the rest of the money they'd agreed upon. As Casey dug around in that packed room, Sidra noticed a paper on the table. Not exactly a medical bill, but an explanation letter with the name Joanna Lincoln on it, and a list of charges for procedures done last year at a cardiologist's office in Atlanta. Total amount came to over three grand. There was a stack of them.

"Hey," Casey said.

"What's this?"

Casey grabbed the paper with one hand and shoved her away with the other, shoved her hard enough that she fell back into the table. "This is none of your business." He pushed a wad of cash to Sidra's chest. "Go." He nodded at the door.

"That's why you stole the money," Sidra said. "From the Marquezes. Who is she?"

"My wife," he said. "And she's dead, so don't worry about it." Casey took the papers and folded them up. He took the lid off of a shoe box and put them inside. When Sidra saw some photos in the box, she grabbed it.

"This is my personal stuff."

One photo showed a petite woman who stood next to a hulking Casey. She was holding a baby boy, maybe a year old. Sidra's heart ached. A few more family photos, and then one of Casey's son. The boy had blonde hair with curls around his ears and eyes that looked just like his dad's. The photo showed a smiling face, his nose a little button, with a splash of freckles across his cheeks. This photo had to be recent because Brandon looked to be at least three or four years old.

"What happened?" Sidra put the photos back in the box.

Casey sat down hard in the chair. He was silent for a minute, then he said, "You can only handle this lifestyle for so long but it's like a wonderland when you're at the top. The money's good and you think you're untouchable. Joanna and I lived like a king and queen, and the world was at our disposal. She tried to warn me after Brandon was born. She said, 'You need to settle down and stay home more,' but I didn't listen, I kept going at it. This money," he said, and looked at Sidra, his face so torn and angry. "It's endless. And once you start, you can't stop. They have access to everything," Casey said. "They give you a little bit at a time. Pay all your bills. Give you a nice house, but you don't own any of it. And then Joanna got sick and I got fucked. That's when I understood they didn't care about me or my family."

Sidra sat down and looked at the money in her hands. This life people lived? They had no idea what was really involved. She had no idea either.

Casey said, "They killed her right in front of me. Shot her in the head while my son was in the next room screaming his head off. I wanted out, and I stole money. After ten years of this, I didn't think they'd kill her. Me, yes, but not her. Nacho said I could continue my networking and pay off what I owe him with interest or die like my wife. I took option A, and then Diane Hutchinson took my son."

Sidra didn't know what pissed her off more. That this guy was part of a global drug problem and didn't give a shit about other people or that she actually felt sorry for him and wanted to get his son back. Then what? Was he going to move away and go back to his ways?

"What makes you think they haven't killed your son already?"

Casey gave her a hard stare. "I don't. But I learned last night from one of the guys I talked to that he overheard this other guy say they were going to move Brandon. He thinks Brandon is okay, and they're taking care of him. But from my experience, they could be keeping him in a dog kennel somewhere."

"Jesus."

"I need to get him back."

"So what now?"

"They're supposed to be rounding up some girls on Wednesday night for shipment. I'm going to go stake it out and see who I can talk to."

Sidra stood up fast. "Jesus, you really are a jerk. You say this like these women are nothing. Like these people are just property. None of this mattered to you until it was your own kid on the line."

Casey stood up too and came at her.

"Oh, I know," she said. "You can put a bullet in my head, burn me, and toss me in your bone garden, and no one would ever find out. Thank you for saving me from Benny Valentino, because now I know you could have just left me there for the pickings like a rat on the street." With her heart pounding in her chest, Sidra tossed the money on the table. While they'd agreed on an additional three grand, Sidra insisted on more money under the table, money that wasn't to be reported to Shackelford. "Doesn't feel right taking it knowing what I do now. I'm going to go on that date with Lorenzo Marquez and I'll call you if anything pops up."

"You do that," Casey said.

"You know what's sad? That I think your son is better off with drug dealers than you."

They stood there for a minute, Sidra letting Casey absorb what she'd said. He tossed the money back at her, said, "You should go."

Sidra didn't pick up the money, backed out of the cabin. She was too afraid of what he'd do if she took her eyes off of him.

\*\*\*

Sidra was on her way home when Dad called. He said, "You talk to Casey lately?"

"I just left his place."

"Did he tell you what he did?"

"I'm not sure."

Dad chuckled, but he wasn't laughing. "Three guys in a supply house in Macon are dead. Guys associated with the Vega family, who's associated with the Marquez family, that's run by who?"

"Nacho Marquez."

"Ding ding ding. And, this hit was just like the hit in Gwinnett County last month when a house full of drug dealers were shot in the head. So I hope he got whatever information he needed last night so we can forget this sonofabitch."

# Chapter 8

**Sidra sat in** the Shackelford kitchen, her elbows on the table, with her head in her hands. For the last hour, she'd been nursing a mason jar filled with vodka. That's not correct. It had sweet iced tea in it too, for a little flavor.

Outside, eight grandkids, ages ranging from thirteen to two, ran around the backyard playing tag while everyone else sat in the heat watching them. The kid's shrieks shook the windows like Sidra had been sitting in a birdhouse.

Her thoughts swam with Casey and his son, images of his wife getting shot in the head while these kids screaming outside mimicked what Brandon must have sounded like. Her own past came at her full force, the sound of a newborn baby, the amniotic fluid still in the lungs and a face covered in white vernix and blood. A dark cloud hung over her life like a bridge between what was good and what it was now. Whatever it is now, felt like a lonely place. A hole caused by past choices.

*Feel my warm embrace,* the alcohol said to her, and she looked down at the amber liquid in the glass.

What would she do if she were in Casey's position? Those kids outside? Her family would move heaven and earth and burn down everything in their way to protect them, even if their own choices had caused it. She'd made plans to see Lorenzo Marquez, and she was apprehensive about that.

When Sidra looked up, she batted a few tears away, then startled because Mom stood there at the table, hovering silently. Sidra took a sip from her glass.

"It's two o'clock, Sidra," Mom said, her voice accusing.

"And I'm only on my second. That's a record."

Mom had on a pastel pink top with a lace neckline and light gray Capri pants. Her jewelry matched the pink perfectly, her hair styled and her makeup still on.

"You haven't been to church in months."

"I was out late working."

"Your brothers made it to church."

"I guess I'm going to hell then, Mom."

"Sidra." Mom turned away from her. "Why do you hurt me like this?" And then she had the audacity to make a fucking margarita on the rocks. Mom took a sip. "I guess it's only fitting that's where you're going to end up. You look like hell, too."

Sidra's hair was a mess, and she had on jeans and a ratty t-shirt. Some of the mascara from last night left dark circles under her eyes like she hadn't slept in days. And this is how she went to see Casey Lincoln this morning.

"I'm sorry I'm not perfect."

"I don't expect you to be perfect but I expect you to take care of yourself."

Sidra drank the last of her tea and vodka and got up to make another one. Mom wasn't right because it was two o'clock in the afternoon. Mom was right because Sidra drank too much. With less vodka, she took a sip and looked at Mom. "When the doubt between what's right and wrong is so strong, I think about what you used to tell us when we were kids about feeling good about what we were doing. But that doesn't work anymore. It's not about sharing my candy with my sister or doing extra chores. People's lives are on the line. This world goes by and no one gives a damn about us. So it doesn't matter whether I feel good about what I'm doing or whether I make a difference. There's an illusion to power. And all that matters is who can keep up with the charade."

Mom looked at her for a moment. "What the hell are you talking about?" Like Sidra was drunk. "Is there a question in there?"

"No, Mom. No questions."

Sidra could see past Mom's head out the window into the backyard. Her younger brother Woolsey ran around chasing one of his twin daughters.

"There are repercussions for everything," Mom said. "Your dad didn't start this business for a new hobby. It was nearly a last resort when the ice cream deal failed."

85

Sidra laughed. Between the time Dad "retired" from APD and starting Shackelford Investigation, he opened an ice cream shop called Shackelford Scoops. It lasted one summer and then he decided private investigating would be best.

"That was a great summer," Sidra said.

"Not on my thighs." Mom set her margarita glass down and walked over to Sidra, took her by the shoulders. "We love all of y'all so much. Daddy couldn't be any happier with how things turned out, he just doesn't want y'all to mess it up. There's a future here. No matter what you do, you make a difference. One small difference can be a lot to someone else. It's not about the choices or what matters, or doing what's right, it's a commitment you make to yourself to fight for other people even when we get the short end of the stick." Mom squeezed Sidra into a hug, then pulled back. She said, "I didn't want to say anything but you smell a little funny, too."

***

Monday evening, just before five p.m., Sidra checked herself in the mirror. She had on gray slacks and matching jacket, and opted for a black silk blouse and plain jewelry. With her hair washed and pulled back into a twist, she stood back and looked at herself. On a good day, she admired her own beauty. Today was one of those days.

Business dress.

For a business meeting. Not a date.

She was nervous because of who Lorenzo Marquez was, and his illusion of being a wealthy businessman making his money through a legit business. With confidence, Sidra closed her eyes and let her mind relax.

Emily Smith. Twenty-five. Graduated from UGA with a business consultant degree. She just prayed Lorenzo Marquez didn't figure her out.

It did not surprise her when Lorenzo Marquez suggested the bar inside La Sombra's restaurant. She felt a little over dressed but that was the point. An over eager college grad who needed business advice.

"Emily, you look nice." Lorenzo kissed both of her cheeks, and the bartender handed them drinks.

"You look very different when you're not in a penguin suit."

"You should see me in my Mariachi suit."

"Oh, I bet you look fabulous," Sidra said. "Do you sing and play guitar?"

"Only after a bottle of tequila."

Sidra held up her drink. "Cheers to that."

"Salud," Lorenzo said.

"Salud," she repeated, and they touched glasses.

Lorenzo had on dark gray dress slacks, a black dress shirt with the first three buttons undone, revealing a small patch of silver hair that matched his head. For an older man, Lorenzo was handsome. His eyes were a light brown, almost caramel, with a touch of hazel. His voice deep and smooth enough for seduction. She could imagine him back in the day as a ladies' man and wondered if he was married. Wedding ring. Sure enough. Sidra hadn't noticed it before.

Lorenzo noticed her looking, and said, "Thirty-two years next month. My bride, Eva, she is on a cruise with her sister to the Bahamas. I don't know why she likes these cruises so much." Lorenzo waved his hand while talking, and seconds later, the bartender handed them each another drink.

This made them both laugh. They hadn't even finished the first.

"They fill my drink every time. I give them one look, one hand up, and I'm always with a drink."

"Salud," Sidra said, and held up her Paloma cocktail. "Sounds like a great problem to have."

The restaurant was busy for a Monday evening. The locals stopped by to eat because the food was great. Families traveled and rented cabins for the weekend or an entire week at a time. Tables covered the open restaurant, with the bar along the back. There was a set of stairs that led to a party room. Good luck going up and down those stairs drunk. The floor was smooth concrete with a shine to it, giving the restaurant a rustic feel.

"Let's go here." Lorenzo led her around the bar to the back of the restaurant, to a quiet corner that had a brick fireplace and comfortable chairs with a large coffee table. Of course, with it being summer, the fireplace was dead, but at least the chairs were more comfortable. They sat together on a wicker loveseat about a foot apart.

"So, Emma, tell me what you're looking for." That seductive smile. She didn't have the nerve to correct the name. A minute later, a server showed up with a plate of appetizers. "Thank you, Juanita," Lorenzo said to the server. "Help yourself." He grabbed what looked like a spring roll and Sidra did the same.

"Delicious," she said, and when she finished, they ate the pesto stuffed mushrooms. "Wow."

"We wanted something different here. Not just Mexican food or American, but good food that people will come back to eat." Lorenzo leaned forward as he spoke with excitement. "American people love to eat, no?"

"You're right about that." Sidra finished her second drink, feeling more comfortable than she should. "To make a profitable business, you have to provide what people are willing to buy. And work your ass off to make money."

"Nooo," Lorenzo said. "Do I look like I work hard?"

"Maybe not anymore, but I'm sure there was a lot of hard work that went into La Sombra. And there are probably ways to make more money from the inside. How do you handle pinching people for every penny you can?"

"Es not the money people spend. Es when they come back, and they tell friends and family, 'Oh, you know that place in the middle of nowhere, La Sombra in Forsyth. It's beauty, and they have horses and food and kayaking.' That's when you make the money. Keep them happy." Lorenzo spread his arms wide. "Fifteen hundred acres. Two lakes. Two miles of the river on the west of the land. So much room to grow. We just have to get the workers on board."

Get the workers on board. Sidra realized that whatever was going on in the Marquez family business, there were people they trusted and people who were just workers. Trustworthy workers who wanted more money and didn't care how they got it? Those were the ones the Marquez family wanted to hire. People like Casey Lincoln.

But it was the Bermuda triangle. No one got out.

"And your website," Sidra said. "I looked at it. It's hard to navigate. The whole thing needs some work."

"Yes, yes," he said, and leaned back. More drinks came. "But the websites, I don't handle that."

"I have a friend who can check it out if you'd like."

Lorenzo shrugged. He wasn't concerned about upgrading his website for business purposes. Sidra could tell the money would come in, no matter what. "I want to know more about you." Lorenzo put his hand on her knee.

"Well, I'm regretting my major, which I had changed twice. And since my dad passed away, it hadn't been easy."

"Oh, Emma, I'm so sorry."

"It's okay, happened a long time ago. But now, I have college debt that I can't seem to pay off, and my best friend who I want to kill because we started this consulting business together, she left me high and dry with more financial burden because she moved to California." Sidra pressed her hand to her chest. "I'm so sorry. I don't mean to unload all my problems on you."

"S'okay," Lorenzo said, and squeezed her knee. "I asked." He looked at her, and she felt herself drown in his caramel eyes. He said, "We have a large business here. And my brother in Atlanta he owns another restaurant. And—" Lorenzo shrugged. "A strip club and a nearby hotel?"

"That's got to be interesting," Sidra said. "So, would any of your family members be interested in hiring a business consultant?"

"Depends on what you have in mind."

"I'm good with books and money, and planning and organizing. I'm also discrete." That got his attention. "But," she said, and held up a finger. "I have some projects that I'm currently working on and have to finish those for a client. But then, we can talk some more?"

"I like you, Emma," he said, and seemed to like her leg a little more.

A young beefy guy saved her when he walked up. "*Lo siento, Señor, pero tenemos un problema.*"

"*Un Momento,*" Lorenzo said to the beefcake, then turned to Sidra. "I need to go. I enjoyed our time together." Lorenzo smiled, his face slightly disappointed, but he stood and shook Sidra's hand, then gently touched her shoulder. "I'll be out of town for the next few days, but you'll stay in touch, si?"

"Of course. Thank you so much for your time. I can't tell you how much I appreciate it."

Lorenzo nodded and let go of her hand, then walked off in a hurry. When Sidra got to the car, she climbed in and said into the concealed microphone, "Did you get all of that?" as she pretended to talk on her phone.

"Do you have any idea what you're doing?" Daley said.

"I'm winging it."

"Sounds like you're about to wingding it."

A mile down the road, Sidra stopped at a gas station that was attached to a small storage unit and a cheap sandwich shop. She unscrewed the license plate that she'd put on earlier, just in case, and got out of the parking lot. No, this place wasn't shady at all.

\*\*\*

The yellow kitchen table still sat under the carport, still needed a second coat of paint, and after the past couple of days, Sidra didn't feel like messing with it.

Inside, she just wanted another shower and to climb into bed. She stood under the hot water and rewashed her hair again, feeling a slight complex because of Mom. The hot water didn't seem to wash away the stress as much as she wanted, and her mind flooded with everything that had happened in the last few days. The tension of being so close to Lorenzo Marquez had evaporated, replaced now with an overwhelming feeling of the possibility of working with him under an illusion for information.

*You're not the CIA, Sidra, you're a dumbass.*

She got out of the shower and was drying off when her cell phone rang. It was almost ten p.m.

"Can you come over?"

"I'll be right there," Sidra said.

# Chapter 9

**Brady Ardeen lived** in the wealthiest neighborhood in Fayette County. Willow Point Estates was a gated community off of Highway 74 in north Peachtree City. Sidra punched in the code and the massive iron gates opened as she waved to the security guard in the station between the gates. The iron gate connected to a ten-foot brick wall that stretched out for over a half mile on each side. After that, there was a lake on one side of the large neighborhood and another type of fencing through dense woods on the other.

Bradford pear trees lined the main entrance and stretched out fifty yards before she actually entered the neighborhood. The night wasn't all that dark as the moon shined bright and night fog settled in over the streetlights. Not a single house in Willow Point was less than two million. Each house was on at least five acres, and the entire community measured out to nearly two-square miles. These houses looked like mini-mansions. When she was little, she dreamed of living in houses like these. Every single one of them looked different, and Sidra was in awe each time she drove through the streets.

Brady's house was a European luxury with large front windows and a beautiful gray and black stone front. A huge fountain sat in the middle of a circular driveway with a stone dragon looking down into the water, watching over the small stone people looking up at their fate.

Brady Ardeen's live in nurse, Beverly, opened the door looking more tired than Sidra had ever seen her. "Everything okay?" Sidra said.

Beverly offered a smile. "He's coughing a lot." She didn't wear nurse scrubs. Instead, she had on leggings and a baggy t-shirt for ease when she helped Brady with something.

Brady's pit bull came running through the foyer, sliding on the marble floor until she came to a stop as she collided into Sidra's legs. "Hey, Mrs. Peaches." Sidra squatted down so that she could let the dog lick her face. Her tail wagged so hard she could barely contain her butt. "I missed you too."

Peaches was really Sidra's dog. She'd found her four years ago chained to a light pole. Her ear was torn, and she had gouges on her side, and she was bleeding and starving. This was back when Sidra worked for the animal control. Even after whatever the dog had been through, she was the sweetest dog anyone could want. She had those mesmerizing honey-colored eyes that melted Sidra's heart the moment she looked at her. But after a few months of trying to hide the dog because she wasn't allowed to have pets where she lived, she couldn't take her back to the shelter. Not while the dog was recovering. So, she made a deal with Brady, that if he took Peaches for a little while, Sidra would come back for her. But Peaches had gotten attached to Brady and now he won't give her back.

They walked down the marble hallway to the large master bedroom, where Sidra found Brady sitting up in his adjustable queen-sized bed. Sidra took one look at him and the guilt washed over her.

"Hey," he said, a half-smile on his face. Peaches jumped up on the bed and made herself comfortable.

After his car accident thirteen years ago, a car accident Sidra felt Daley caused, Brady was left a C6 quadriplegic. They were two reckless teenagers racing down Highway 85 like idiots.

Beverly said, "I'll be down the hall if you need me."

"Why don't you try getting some sleep," Brady said.

"Please," Beverly said. "Like I can sleep with you and that smoker's cough."

Brady laughed, which sent him into a coughing fit. Beverly handed him a tissue, then carefully held him back while he coughed. While his biceps and shoulders were strong, he had weak wrists and limited ability in his fingers, a symptom of his condition known as "quad hands." Beverly raised the sidebar on the bed that had been custom made.

Beverly said to Sidra on her way out, "Don't let him get up. He keeps trying to work. I gave him a laptop, that's all he needs right now."

"I feel like I'm in prison," Brady said. He patted the bed near Peaches, gesturing for Sidra to sit with him. "I'm on a deadline and Nurse Ratched won't let me work."

Brady could get into his wheelchair using a motorized sling attached to the ceiling. He had good use of his arms and upper body, but he depended on his motorized wheelchair to get him around. His dark brown hair stuck to the side of his face, and it looked like Brady had lost some weight. His face looked gaunt, and that wasn't normal.

Peaches snored as she fell asleep, and Sidra got comfortable and rested her back against the raised mattress.

"So what's the prognosis?" Sidra said.

"I have about a month to live."

"Brady, stop."

He laughed and started coughing again. Peaches opened one eye but didn't move. "I have a kidney infection in both kidneys and I seemed to have developed swamp lake in my lungs. I'm so glad I spent the last ten years of my life making millions of dollars so I could live like a king." Brady opened his arms wide, his hands in limp fists, but he smiled through it all.

"But you should be fine once the infection's gone, right?"

Brady sighed, his voice serious. "Kidneys are functioning, but there's a lot of buildup and if they can't clear it with meds, I may have to have surgery. And, it may be the beginning stages of kidney failure. The doctors told my mom years ago that this was a possibility because of the damage from the accident. And here we are."

Sidra hated listening to this. Hated getting bad news every time Brady got sick.

"I needed to tell you," he said, and it made her feel important. "The good news is that I don't feel a thing."

He'd nearly died because of the car accident, spent years recovering, and didn't let any of that stop him. He created video games for a big developer and had several independent games on the market. He spoke at conferences and flew around the world, connecting with people in a business that had grown tremendously over the last decade. People saw his wheelchair, but it became invisible once someone got to know him. Brady ran with a dream, and nothing stopped him.

Except a kidney infection.

Thoughts of Casey Lincoln's wife came to mind. Her heart condition and then someone putting a bullet in her head.

Brady said. "I was wondering if we could finish our conversation from a few weeks ago?"

This was about high school. About whether she kissed Jesse Gallop that night Brady left her at the Christmas dance senior year. And why she ran away after his accident. The conversation he'd started caught her off guard and she'd dodged it.

"After all these years, you still can't let it go?"

"You broke my heart, Sidra."

"And you broke mine."

Brady looked at her with those sad puppy eyes.

"Why are you doing this to yourself?"

"I'm mad at myself, Sidra. I'm mad for driving a hundred miles an hour down a two-lane highway. I'm mad at myself because I thought I was invincible. We were supposed to have it all, me and you. And I'm mad because I have a kidney infection."

"Brady, what do you want?"

"I never meant it, okay? No matter what you did or didn't do, I didn't mean it." Brady started coughing again, a wet cough that had a lot of phlegm in it. When he was done coughing, he lowered the bed a bit. "I'm okay."

They'd been high school sweethearts. Both graduated top five of their graduating class, and boy, were they stupid. They drank and smoked weed, and had sex wherever and whenever. Sidra lost her virginity to Brady Ardeen sophomore year.

Then there was the accident a week after graduation that changed everything.

"I never kissed Jesse Gallop." And that was the truth. Brady winced at the sound of his name. "You just wanted to believe the rumors. You're the only person I've ever really loved."

Brady put his hand on top of hers, his soft fingers curled into themselves, and the warmth of his hand spread into her entire body. And as soon as Sidra touched his hand, he pulled away. This is what he did these days. Pull her close just so he could push her away.

*** 

After she stopped at a liquor store for Coke and Jack Daniels, she parked under the carport at home and nearly hit the kitchen table. She made herself a drink. Screw it. She brought the table back inside. The legs unscrewed underneath, the top a little heavy, but she got it inside and put it back together.

Talk about a half-assed paint job.

Flamingo yellow.

That's what she felt like right now. Something that didn't make sense.

Sidra drank down the Jack and Coke and made another one. It had been a long day. A long week, but it felt like yesterday she was inside the paintball warehouse.

She didn't even sit at the kitchen table. She stood in the middle of the kitchen and looked around at this shitty rental that she was going to need to vacate soon, and thought about how fucked up her life was. She was supposed to be a soccer player. She was supposed to go professional. She'd gotten accepted to Florida State on a full scholarship, for God's sake. The guilt of the bad decisions swam through her like muddy water that wouldn't move. In her mind, she started listing all the points in her life that had made a significant change. But it wasn't just one path here and one path there. Her life was like continual forks in the road that branched out into paths with no signs, and the road kept branching and branching. Going backwards wasn't an option. She could never go back once she put a foot on the tangled road.

Sidra poured Coke and stopped, went straight for the JD bottle. Took a long drink. Then another. Every nerve slowed down, her muscles light and numb as the warm liquid swam through her veins, and she saw clouds above the road open up and she could breathe. In her bedroom, she pulled off her jeans and opted for sweat pants so old she could see through them. And she remembered they weren't sweat pants. They were gray cotton pants, and they were Brady's from years ago.

All she needed to do was look at it. Hold it in her hand. It didn't take her long to find what she was looking for. In the top dresser drawer, tucked away in an envelope, were three photographs. Old, but the color so sharp the images took her breath away.

Back in the kitchen, she grabbed the bottle and slid to the floor. One look at the tiny baby—her baby—and she lost it. The tears began to spill as she wept. All those missing years. All those things she'd never know about a baby boy.

She ran away after the accident when Brady wouldn't talk to her. She couldn't blame him. He'd almost died. She was gone for seven months, and the baby came four weeks early. Sidra almost died herself, when somehow, she hemorrhaged. The memory of bright red blood and contractions made her cry even more. She had been so scared and lonely. The doctor performed an emergency cesarean, the whole thing still vivid in her mind.

Sidra wiped her eyes and ran her thumb over the tiny face in the photo. She remembered the way he smelled and his tiny body and sweet little mouth. She'd kissed his neck before she handed him over to the woman who he'd call Mommy. Sidra ended up with a hysterectomy at eighteen because she couldn't stop bleeding. And bleeding. And bleeding.

But she ended up with an empty hole in her heart.

"Just do it," she'd told the doctor.

"You'll never have kids again," he'd said, like she didn't understand what was going on.

Sidra drank more, letting the liquor take over and make the pain disappear. No one knew what she'd been through. No one knew about the baby. Not Mom. Not Dad.

Not Brady.

*Take the pain, you deserve it.*

Sidra needed to tell him. He deserved to know the truth. She thought she could handle this. That she'd forget the whole thing happened and move on, but it's always been there eating away at her, making her sick.

She'd drown herself in work and booze just to get some relief from the weight.

The weight.

"I need to tell you," she said, and closed her eyes, took a heavy breath.

# Chapter 10

**On Tuesday afternoon**, Sidra sat in the Shackelford office with a headache that put her in a bad mood. The whole front half of the old Victorian house was for business. The parlor was turned into a sitting room with a leather sofa, two winged-back chairs, and a coffee table. There was a picture window with Shackelford Investigations on it and a logo decal underneath. To the right was Dad's personal office, and the other side was a large room with four computer stations, a TV, a closet with their P.I. gear, and a locked gun cabinet.

On a whiteboard, their names were permanently stickered on and next to it were jobs each one was working on. Amy sat at one computer working on her usual upkeep of Shackelford social media and marketing. She kept up with a lot of networking contacts, because the P.I. world was always growing, and learning was a part of the field. Amy's two kids ran around the house, and Mom flitted from room to room, moving stuff around and talking about Aunt Doreen down at the newspaper who wrote garbage.

"That woman is death sucking a sponge." Mom picked up a dry erase marker. She had on a colorful top with salmon colored Capri pants. "She's trying to tell me Maisy Attwell stole land from Buddy Shackelford over on Creek Bridge Road. Asking me about something that happened a hundred years ago, like I'm that old. I told ol' Doreen she should know she was probably in grade school at the Fayetteville Academy back then." Mom laughed and started updating Dad's schedule. "Doreen can go to hell. Writes nothing but gossip about us at that damn paper."

Sidra tried to listen to the conversation Daley recorded for her when she'd gone on her "date" with Lorenzo Marquez.

Amy said, "Wasn't Maisy Attwell your great aunt?"

"Yes," Mom said. "That's why Doreen's stirring up trouble."

Amy said, "Could Uncle Jim lose his land if they proved your aunt stole his property?"

"Oh, just hush," Mom said. "The Attwells and the Shackelfords made a truce in 1905 when they agreed that Kelby Kornberger was no longer a good fit for mayor."

Amy's kids started shouting as they ran down the hall.

"Can you tell them to shut up?" Sidra asked Amy.

Amy looked up from her computer, her doe eyes wide. "If you didn't drink so much, the little things wouldn't bother you."

"Never mind." Out of the office, Sidra caught the kids. "Can you two knock it off? I'm trying to work in here."

"Aunt Sidra," Violet said, blue eyes wide like her mother's. "Can I braid your hair?"

"No. Don't touch me." Which prompted a game of poke Aunt Sidra. She sat back down at her desk, the kids like magnets. Phin plopped himself on Sidra's lap.

Violet said, "Please," and Sidra said, "Okay," and Violet ran off to grab a hairbrush.

"Okay, Phin. This is going to be your first P.I. assignment. When I play back this conversation, you need to type it into the computer."

At six years old, Phin was a computer expert. Sidra pressed play on the file on her phone, the part where Lorenzo talked about food, and Sidra repeated what Phin needed to type, slowly spelling out the word *salud*.

"Who's Emma?"

"Don't worry about that."

Violet returned with a hairbrush. Sidra said, "This is the life. I got one kid doing my work and one kid styling my hair." Except her head was killing her.

Amy said, "Mom, you have emails."

"Just flag the ones with potential clients. I'll check the rest later." Then Mom tapped the white board with her marker, said, "Did you do this?"

Sidra looked up. Mom was referring to a case that Sidra had been working on. "We got distracted with the Diane Hutchinson stuff. I can check him out today."

"Well, get on it. I have to turn in paperwork on Friday to the insurance company."

Sidra went back to her phone and Phin.

"Well, damn," Mom said, looking up at the TV. "Isn't that where you and the boys were?" Mom pressed her hand to her mouth. "Oh, God." She couldn't turn up the volume fast enough.

Sidra nearly shoved Phin out of her lap. A helicopter was flying over La Sombra and a voice over was talking about a missing young woman. Her name was Lydia Desmond. Twenty-three years old. She was from North Georgia.

It was always the missing women and children that got to Mom. She'd lived through this same kind of news break. Amy Shackelford. Missing 1995. Fourteen years old.

Amy looked at the TV, her lips pursed with a silent understanding of what it was like to be gone.

The news continued with coverage of the gas station/storage units in Forsyth, where Sidra had stopped to change the plates. The police were taking photos of a 2010 red Ford Flex, and the events that unfolded early this morning.

Lydia Desmond's parents said she'd gotten out of a drug rehab program almost three weeks ago and stole their vehicle, along with some cash. Her mother had spoken with Lydia a few times over the last few weeks, begging her to come home.

Early this morning, Monroe County deputies attempted to pull over a guy for speeding when they chased him down Forsyth Road and finally caught up to him at the gas station. His name was David Brown, and he worked at La Sombra, an illegal with a fake ID.

The police spoke with La Sombra owner, Lorenzo Marquez, who said on camera, "We will do everything we can to work with the police to find this missing woman." Lorenzo didn't smile, his silver hair shining in the morning sun and the restaurant right behind him, as he nodded and seemed genuinely concerned.

The records show that Lydia Desmond checked in to La Sombra a week ago, and that she checked out on Monday night. The police were investigating why an employee was driving the vehicle, and where was Lydia Desmond?

"Please," Lydia Desmond's mother pleaded. "If you know where our daughter is, if you've seen her, please just call the police."

The news reporter came back into view and said that while La Sombra was cooperating, the police had to issue a warrant to search the area.

"That's sad," Mom said, and turned her focus back to her whiteboard.

Something about a problem. That's why the Beefcake interrupted them. Sidra looked at her phone and found the place. "Lo siento, Señor, pero temenos un problema."

Sidra opened up Google translate.

*I'm sorry, sir, but we have a problem.*

Did that have anything to do with Lydia Desmond? It was a stretch, but something was off. The Marquez family was known for drugs and trafficking.

"They're going to move the girls tomorrow night," Sidra said to Mom.

"What?"

"I gotta go.

# Chapter 11

**She didn't think** he'd talk to her. In fact, when she called Casey Lincoln to find out if he was home, the way he said yes, she thought he was lying. She pulled to a stop in front of his cabin, as he stood on his front porch skinning a rabbit.

"I've got to eat," he said with the look on her face. "What do you want?"

"Did you hear about that missing woman?"

"Which one?" Casey had a table set up and a pot on one side of it where he was putting innards. Sidra told him about Lydia Desmond. He said, "If they had anything to do with her disappearing, they wouldn't have kept her car."

"Maybe they hadn't gotten around to getting rid of it yet?" Casey shrugged and continued skinning the rabbit. Sidra said, "You said they were moving girls tomorrow night. What if she's one of them?"

Casey shrugged.

"I want to go with you."

"That's a bad idea."

"Why?"

"You'll just get in my way."

"Maybe the police would like to know my suspicions and learn where you live."

Casey tossed down the rabbit. "You could do that. That's fine. But you think they care about my son? Maybe this Lydia, yeah, they care about her. But not me and my son. Then what? You'll feel better because I'm locked away. What does that do?"

"Tell me about Lorenzo Marquez."

"Out of all the family, he's probably the least threatening." Casey wiped his bloody hand on a towel. "But don't mistake that for being nice. He'd turn you over to someone like Benny Valentino in a heartbeat."

"Which means that something happened to Lydia Desmond at La Sombra."

"Aside from laundering cash through there, they keep that place clean and open for business. Lorenzo Marquez wouldn't want anything to jeopardize that."

"Someone got sloppy?"

Casey smiled and shook his head. "Like maybe this David-o Brown-o? Mark my words, he'll die in jail sometime today before he can talk about anything."

"Like Diane?" Another shrug. "What are they doing tomorrow night?"

"Tomorrow night already happened," Casey said. "After I spoke to my friends in Macon, they moved the girls first thing. They have a lot of houses. I have a couple of contacts I've reached out to, but no one's talking. If I hear anything about this new one, I'll let you know."

Sidra really had her hopes up for getting an eye on the girls they were moving. "Where do they take the girls? Various houses?"

"Yeah, and it's a big Buy, Sell, Trade Industry. They're always moving inventory."

Inventory.

"Who's specifically in charge of them?"

"On the south side? Dani Cameo. A snake that would eat her own offspring to survive."

\*\*\*

With the internet at her fingertips, Sidra did a ton of research on Diane Hutchinson and Lydia Desmond. Starting with Diane, she went back as far as she could because she wanted to know how the woman was involved with the Marquez family. She was a thirty-eight-year-old white American woman who worked at a property management company in Atlanta called GT Greater Atlanta Property Management. Also known as GTPM. The same company that owned the paintball warehouse in Griffin. GTPM was owned by a larger company called Omega Holdings.

This is how the Marquez family owned so much real estate. Diane Hutchinson was arrested because a tenant claimed that she'd assaulted her. Further allegations were made that she'd falsified documents for illegal aliens, and that she'd blackmailed a well-known attorney who she'd seen at the local strip club owned and operated by Hector Marquez.

Diane's get out of jail free card came when she'd told the police about the Marquez family, and one of their drug houses in Clayton County. The raid on the house seemed fruitful for the Clayton County Police Dept., where they'd confiscated drugs, money, guns, and stolen goods.

After all the media hype and bad publicity, the Marquez family wanted Diane Hutchinson dead. She'd spent three months in jail for the assault on the tenant. Then she agreed to be a witness in the case they were building against the Marquez family from the drug raid.

Somewhere in all of this, Diane kidnapped Casey Lincoln's son. Why she kidnapped a little boy for a family that she was going to testify against, Sidra didn't know.

For the most part, the four Marquez Brothers and the one sister keep their heads high and noses clean. It was the people who worked for them that stayed in trouble while they did their dirty work. The family had been living in the United States for over forty years. From past news reports, the Marquez family did business along I-75, throughout Georgia and down to Florida. They were associated with a few other Mexican families in the United States. Most of these drug gangs didn't get along and were constantly fighting for territory. Sidra didn't have access to any personal documents. Not yet. She'd need Woolsey for that.

After two hours of that, Sidra poured herself a vodka and sweet tea. These people were deep. They had connections to everyone and control over a lot of business. When a country's own government is so corrupt, it's no wonder these bad guys can take over. Then they move to the US where people want the drugs gone but keep supporting them through other outlets. It was a network of people that extended deep into a lucrative world.

Innocent people like Lydia Desmond got caught up in this mess and they die. That's the reality of what Sidra was dealing with. Lydia Desmond was either dead or had been relocated to another state via the human trafficking world. It was that simple.

Lydia Desmond didn't look like a bad person. Her social media had been full of daily activities spanning from middle school to last summer. She was a budding photographer with years and years of photos telling a story. Her sister, Megan, who was deaf, bought them personalized best friend bracelets. The two sisters looked nothing alike, and that seemed to make them unique to one another. While they both shared facial similarities, Megan had blonde curls and Lydia had thin red hair. Lydia had a small birthmark under her left eye, and Megan had a scar from a cleft palate. The photos showed adoring parents constantly loving on their two daughters.

But through posts, and the back-and-forth comments, Sidra learned that Lydia accidentally ran over Megan's service dog, an eighty-pound golden retriever. The family was devastated, and this began Lydia's downfall into drugs. For over a year, other family members made comments about the cost of the dog, details about what happened, and Lydia should have been more careful.

On so many levels, Sidra could relate to this young woman. And this type of private investigating proved why people shouldn't post so much family drama on the internet. Sidra printed out a photo of Lydia and spent the rest of the day showing it in every bar and restaurant in Griffin. No one had seen her.

# Chapter 12

**The Police searched** La Sombra for three days. The only place left was miles and miles of the Towaliga River. Employees were interviewed, the cabin Lydia stayed in dusted and searched. She'd gone off grid only using her cell phone to text her mother. Paid cash for everything. The Ford Flex the police found had no personal belongings. No backpack or purse. No clothes, food wrappers, receipts or paperwork. Apparently it had been wiped clean.

Lydia disappeared.

Sidra didn't think anything of it when she knocked on Daley's front door and then stepped inside, uninvited. Knowing Daley wasn't home, she called out loudly, "Hey, Jorie. You want to go horseback riding?" and Jorie came out of her bedroom still half asleep.

Daley lived in a gorgeous renovated barn, and that didn't seem fair when Sidra's rental was a piece of shit and she drowned in debt. The living room and kitchen were one huge room. A wide open staircase led to a balcony where Jorie stood.

"Really?" she said. Jorie had taken three years of horseback riding lessons. Technically, she was a pro.

"Yes. Get your leather chaps on, girlfriend."

Sidra rummaged through Daley's fridge until she gathered enough snacks to put in her backpack for both of them. Jorie came downstairs dressed like she was going to a party. Jean cut-offs, a hot pink tank top, a little crocheted vest thing on top of that, and topped off with a pair of deep purple boots.

"I'm going to let you in on a little secret," Sidra said. "We're going to scope out this ranch and I need you to look like you're thirteen, not a music video pop tart." Sidra walked over to Jorie and took the plaid fedora off her head. "Put your hair in pigtails and think little girl cute."

"Do you want me to suck my thumb while I ride my horse?"

Sidra paused a moment, opened her mouth, didn't know what to say. This girl was growing up too fast. She gave her niece a shove. "Think covert operation. Not Instagram party."

When they were in the car, Sidra tested her. "So what's in your backpack?"

Jorie unzipped the bag. "Binoculars. GoPro. A flashlight. Gum. A map of Georgia. Duct tape. A railroad spike. Some antihistamine. A notebook and different colored pens. I also brought my portable phone charger. Extra socks. I don't know why I brought socks."

Sidra put the van in drive. "Why the railroad spike?"

117

"I found it in my dad's room. You never know what you'll need on an investigating adventure."

Daley's barn house belonged to his friend who owned the property in Brooks. Bishop's own house was about a hundred yards to the left. What these two guys did together to earn money, Sidra didn't know. Bishop had a private helicopter that his company owned, which was gone, and Sidra assumed Bishop was, too.

The driveway curved through woods for over a mile and came out to a field that was in desperate need of cutting. An old house sat crumbling near the entrance, with a rusted out pickup truck under an aluminum car port that was falling over.

The last two times Sidra had been to La Sombra was in the evening and night. During the late morning, the place was even more mesmerizing than she remembered. The Outpost for the horse trails was down a two-lane road past the restaurant. The short ride had a view of the lake and a large rolling field. She saw the pavilion and the large area used as a stage during concerts.

"This is cool," Jorie said.

To ease her nerves about being here, Sidra had on a cowboy hat, boots and large sunglasses. Her hair was in a low ponytail with a braid down her back. Hopefully it was a good enough disguise.

Sidra checked in at the Outpost, paid the fee in cash to avoid the Shackelford name trail, but had to show her ID to the girl at the desk. This was only problematic if someone checked the logs.

Sidra had been standing there for five minutes when she heard a voice that made her go rigid. The way she froze caused alarm for Jorie. She touched Jorie's arm and shook her head.

Sidra breathed, and kept her head down, taking her sweet time reading over the injury liability waiver form, then looking Jorie in the eye.

Sidra said slowly, "You know that railroad spike?" hoping her niece understood. Jorie nodded. "Why don't you take some pictures for Grandma?"

Jorie skipped away, took out her cell phone and began snapping photos of the Outpost. Other families were in there doing the same. Sticking their heads in one of those comical board paintings with holes you stick your face in. Jorie snapped quick photos of miniature horse carvings with intricate details, then finally made her way to the counter where hand painted horseshoes hung on the front of the counter.

And while Bruce talked about a horse trailer, he'd put his hands on the counter right next to her. Missing his pinky and ring finger on his left hand. Sidra's heart slammed into her chest. She had a gun in the bottom of her backpack. A Glock subcompact .45. The only time she'd had used it was to get a racoon out of her trashcan.

Bruce laughed, that deep voice punching her brain like a freight train. He told the girl, "Radio in to Tommy to tell those boys I don't have all day, now."

"Yes sir, Mr. Zeller."

As Bruce walked off, Sidra handed the girl the paperwork. "Who was that?"

"Mr. Zeller?"

"I swear I've seen him before.

The girl said, "Mr. Zeller borrows our horse trailers sometimes. He's nice, he just wants stuff immediately like we don't have a job to do."

Sidra smiled. When they finished with paperwork, they were led to their horses. Past the stables, Bruce was giving a worker the trailer he'd borrowed. They were taking it off the truck hitch.

A guy named Cole walked them inside the stables, talked about the horses and how they were all pretty calm. He said, "This is Piñata," and handed Sidra the reins to a beautiful tan horse. Then he handed over a brown horse to Jorie and said his name was Cancun. They spent fifteen minutes going over a brief lesson on horseback riding.

"I need to use the restroom," Sidra said. "I'll be right back."

Sidra bypassed the restroom and when she saw no one was near the trailer, she moved over to it. The back was wide open, and Sidra stepped inside. Why would Bruce Zeller need to borrow a horse trailer? On the left side of the trailer near the floor, there was blood. Not a lot, but a patch about three-by-three inches.

"I rode for three years," Jorie said as Sidra approached. "I know what I'm doing." And then she mounted the horse like she was bored. Sidra kept looking over her shoulder, waiting for Bruce or Lorenzo to recognize her. This was the same stables she had been in with Lorenzo the night of the wedding.

Sidra asked Cole, "So what happened with that missing girl?"

The guy rolled his eyes. "I don't know and I'm not supposed to talk about it."

"Per your boss or the police?"

He said, "Trail begins that way. Stay on the blue trail." Had Cole been invited to the Bermuda Triangle?

The sun was already blazing hot. The only good thing were the overhanging trees branches that covered the path, and kept the sun from melting them.

Jorie let her horse trot off too far in front and Sidra said, "Hey, slow down," trying to keep a careful eye in the woods and trying to not fall off her horse. Last time she rode a horse was at a friend's ninth birthday and the horse was a pony going in circles.

Sidra noticed cameras every so often, mounted on trees and wondered why. The police had to have noticed them too.

Jorie turned her horse around, came back. She said, "Geez, Sidra, will you relax. You're white knuckling the reins like you're riding a shark. If you relax, Piñata will relax and she'll stop jerking her head back like that. You didn't listen to anything Cole said, did you?"

"I was busy. Maybe I need a different horse." Sidra and Jorie had stopped in the middle of the path, covered in mossy overgrowth.

"Your legs are too tight. I bet you could walk a mile with a watermelon between your legs. Watch me." The reins were loose and flat against her palms. "Loosen the reins and she'll settle down. They walk this path all day long, they know where they're going. Trust her. All you have to worry about is not falling off."

Easy for her to say. Piñata started following Cancun, and Jorie was right. Once Sidra relaxed, the horse did, too. They walked side by side for a while and even though Jorie didn't know where she was going; the horses did and Cancun stayed in lead whenever the path became narrow. When the path forked, a post marked blue to the right, Jorie gave a leg tap with a right tug on the reins, and Cancun followed the path.

"Aunt Sidra, do you wear tampons? Because Grandma says I'm too young for them, but this period thing is ruining my life. I got blood on my pants in the middle of class and had to back out like a deer in headlights. Thank God I had gym shorts in my locker. Everybody knew what happened. I have appearances I need to keep up. Stuff like that cannot happen to Jorie Shackelford."

"I've got news for you. Bleeding through a tampon is worse. But if that's what you want, I'll get them for you."

This girl would never know how she'd saved Sidra's life thirteen years ago. Sidra looked over at her niece, smiling and happy. Gave up one baby and came home to another. Spent nearly five years helping Mom raise Daley's kid while he was off fighting a war in Afghanistan. The obligation to be a mother to her was strong. She couldn't lie to her, no matter what. Tried to tell her stuff straight and not treat her like a kid.

Jorie said, "How old were you when you first kissed a boy?"

Sidra laughed. "Are you kissing boys, Jorie?"

"No," she said, nearly blushing. "But there is this boy that I like. His name's Parker and he's so cute. And Chloe said she heard him talking about me in science class. Also, Chloe said her dad thought you were pretty. Very pretty."

Jorie yammered on while they crossed a shallow creek and Sidra held on tight. The water came to the horse's ankles, but Piñata walked through it like a pro, and Sidra let out a breath she didn't know she was holding.

They walked a little ways, crossing a yellow path and came to a party of ten who were trying to make their way to the creek where Sidra and Jorie just came. This was where Sidra noticed a sign on a fence: DO NOT ENTER. RANCH VEHICLES ONLY.

"Hey, Jorie," Sidra called. "Let's go this way for a minute."

"Where?"

Sidra looked up to see if she could spot any cameras. While she didn't see any, she was sure there were some around here. "So listen, I'm going to walk down this way for about five minutes. Can you manage the two horses?"

"Sounds kinda difficult," Jorie said. "I'm coming with you."

"No," Sidra tried, but Jorie got off her horse. She walked up to the metal gate and unhooked the rope latch. She swung the gate forward, pushing it all the way open against the other part of the gate so that the sign wasn't visible. "We got lost."

"You are just as bad as I am."

Jorie mounted her horse. "Like two peas in a pod."

They walked along a road covered in pine straw and sweet gum balls, fallen branches and a few tree stumps to the side of the road, the horse's hooves clomping on the road. They walked for about five minutes when Sidra spotted a couple of cabins in the woods up ahead. The police had obviously been here because the path and grass was disturbed by tire tracks and footprints.

These must have been older cabins, before they built the luxury ones La Sombra was known for. They walked the horses further into the woods up close to the cabins. She wasn't going to find anything here, not after the police finished a three-day search. She wasn't going to find a sign that said Lydia Desmond disappeared here.

Sidra dismounted her horse and walked up to the little porch. Reminded her of Casey's place out in the middle of nowhere. She peeked through a window and saw the place was empty. The door was locked.

"Aunt Sidra," Jorie said, her voice with concern.

Sidra turned and spotted a young Hispanic guy walking towards them.

"Hey?" he said. He had on dirty jeans and even dirtier work gloves.

"Is this the outhouse?"

"Outhouse?"

"The bathroom. Baño?"

"No, no baño. No guests." The guy was waving his hands. "You get on horse. Go." The guy grabbed Piñata by the reins and started walking her to the road. Cancun automatically followed the guy.

Sidra walked on as well. "Do you know anything about the missing girl?"

"No baño aqui."

Sidra caught up to the guy. "Lydia Desmond?"

That stopped him. He said, "You no policia. Who you?"

They were back on the road now. "I was just curious. Did the police find anything?"

"No. Nothing." He handed Sidra the reins. "Go home." The guy shook his head. Not what he wanted to say. "Ride. You go."

"How many cameras are out here?"

"Cameras?" The guy stepped closer. "Ay, Chica. No hagas preguntas."

Sidra looked down at her belly. She had no idea what the hell he just said. "Pregnant?"

"Que?" The guy reached behind him and Sidra froze, but he pulled out a radio.

"Wait," Sidra said. "Wait. Un momento, please. Por favor?" She dropped her backpack, grabbed her wallet and pulled out two twenties for the guy. "No, blah blah." Pointed to the radio. "We adios."

"Mas." He nodded to her wallet.

"Fuck," she said. "I've got fifty dollars left to my name because this fucking La Sombra is a rip-off."

The guy held up the radio, clicked the button. "You money. Me no rich."

Sidra gave him the last of her cash and then mounted her horse. "Asshole," she said.

"Que, Chica?"

They rode off. Jorie tapped Cancun's sides with her heels to make him run down the road, and Piñata wasn't sure if she was supposed to catch up.

"Do you think he'll tell?" Jorie asked once they were back on the original path.

"If so, we play dumb." Sidra's heart finally slowed down enough for her to breathe. Thought that fucker was going to pull out a gun. The thought nearly made her laugh. And she brought Jorie along with her like an idiot. She couldn't tell Jorie not to mention this to her dad or Grandma.

Sidra said, "Were you okay back there? The guy and all that?"

"He looked like he really didn't want us snooping around. But I wasn't scared, if that's what you mean. Don't tell my dad, but me and Chloe skipped class one day and hung out underneath the stairwell, eating snacks and watching Netflix all day. Mr. Compton caught us, though. Thank God he didn't tell our parents. Now, that was scary."

"I'm not supposed to condone you skipping class, so consider this me yelling at you. Don't do it again."

"Oh, I won't, I swear." Then she giggled. "That's where Chloe got caught making out with Jared Hoffler."

They were halfway through their ride when Sidra asked Jorie about the pictures she'd taken inside the Outpost. Jorie whipped out her cell phone and started sending Sidra photos. She'd probably drive a car like this someday.

Sidra stopped the horse. The pictures were great. She got a good one of Bruce Zeller's face. He wasn't paying attention, had been looking over at the entrance.

Hours later, Sidra's phone chimed. Incoming group text message.

**Mom**: *I'm ordering pizza. Who's coming over.*

127

The phone started blowing up with yes, no, excuses, and memes.

**Daley:** *I'll pick up Jorie, then head over.*

**Sidra:** *Jorie's with me. I'll bring her.*

**Daley:** *What are y'all doing?*

**Sidra:** *Horseback riding.*

Then a minute later, Daley sent a screen shot of Jorie's location because he tracked her.

**Daley:** *WHAT THE FUCK!!*

**Sidra:** *We're fine. It's no big deal.*

**Daley:** *YOU BROUGHT HER TO A FUCKING DRUG DEALER'S HORSE RANCH!!*

**Sidra:** *Stop being so dramatic.*

**Daley:** *WHAT??*

# Chapter 13

**When they got** back to Shackelford, Sidra and Jorie stepped inside the kitchen through the back door. Jorie said, "Hi, Aunt Marquette," and gave her a hug.

"You two stink like soggy cheetos," Marquette said. Then to Sidra, "You in so much trouble, girl." Marquette let out a throaty laugh. Woolsey's wife had a soft spot for Sidra but didn't put up with anybody's shit. Dark cleavage spilled out of her shirt as she bent over the table, tearing apart bite sized pieces of pizza for her two-year-old twin girls.

Sidra walked into the silent dining room, moments ticking away before a bomb exploded. No one smiled or said anything. Sidra grabbed a plate and tossed a slice of pizza on it. This was normally what happened. They didn't know how to talk things out like a normal family. Mom looked out the window, chewing silently, contemplating the gossip, and barely able to contain herself because she'd call Amy as soon as she could. Dad looked down at the salad on his plate, eating the healthy stuff first. Woolsey sat at the other end with an entire box of pizza to himself, tossing the black olives in a little pile. And Daley chewed his food and didn't take his eyes off of Sidra, who was silently begging the world to be in her favor.

Then Jorie said, "The good news is that we had fun," and Daley lost it.

He tossed his pizza down hard enough it bounced off the plate and landed on Mom's good table cloth. He said, "How could you be so stupid? A woman just went missing there. What the hell were you thinking? She's thirteen years old. We don't bring the kids into the business, Sidra. It's understood. You don't get to make decisions for Jorie, you're not her mother."

Sidra let that sink in, then said, "If you think of it as two people who just went horseback riding at a horseback riding ranch, it's not a big deal."

"Daddy," Jorie said, all sweetness. "We were inconspicuous."

"Do you even know what that means?"

"Do you?"

Daley eyed his daughter with a stern expression that he started giving her lately.

"Don't you dare take this out on her," Sidra said.

"Let's calm down," Mom said.

Daley said to Sidra, "You don't get to take her anywhere ever again."

"That's not fair, Dad. Aunt Sidra didn't do anything wrong."

"You stay out of this."

"You know I want to be a private investigator. Aunt Sidra's the only one who lets me do things."

"You don't get to do things until I say so. You're too young."

"Fine then." Jorie grabbed her plate. "I'll go sit at the kids' table with the babies then."

"You're making a big deal out of nothing," Sidra said after Jorie left.

"I don't think he is," Dad said, his salad gone and motioning for a pizza box. He put a slice on his plate and looked down at it with the same disappointment he gave Sidra sometimes. "Maybe before this girl went missing, but not after."

"Maybe I need to find another job."

"Why don't you?" Daley said.

Sidra got up as well. "It'll never happen again."

"You're damn right it won't," Daley said, and Sidra wondered how her asshole brother was going to deal with tampons and Jorie kissing boys. God, Jorie really was just a baby. But Daley would need Sidra before she needed him.

*You're not her mother.*

Dad grabbed her arm. "Now wait a minute. Let's not think of this as wasted time."

Sidra sat back down and looked at Woolsey. "Can you research Bruce Zeller?"

"No," he said, his mouth full. "No business at the dinner table."

"I told you about Bruce, right? The guy Benny Valentino was going to sell me to for three thousand dollars? Well, he was returning a borrowed horse

131

trailer to La Sombra." Sidra showed Dad the photo of Bruce. He wasn't familiar. Daley barely looked, not wanting to help. "There was a little bit of blood in the trailer, but that could be anything. They have cameras along the trail paths. The police could have missed something."

"Like a body?" Daley said.

"Not with K-9s."

"Sounds to me like the police can handle it," Dad said. "You're working something without funds to do it. That's manpower we can use elsewhere. Other clients that need help. Paying clients."

"I get it," Sidra said. "I just thought I'd check the place out."

***

The normal life of a private investigator was fairly boring. Mostly paperwork, tracking and tracing, and the internet was their wonderland. Her skills with databases weren't as great as Woolsey, but if there was ever a brick wall, she'd text him something and he'd find it or point her in the right direction.

But every once in a while, Woolsey was stumped.

This Bruce Zeller didn't exist. Which was normal for criminals. They didn't take photos, didn't use social media for networking, they bought everything with cash, and never lived near where they worked.

Even after Dad told her explicitly not to, Sidra continued building her case. Research on Dani Cameo was added to the Diane Hutchinson and Lydia Desmond file. Casey and Joanna Lincoln had a file. She'd gotten the names of each sibling in the Marquez family. Found out that Lorenzo Marquez's eldest son died in Juarez, in a cartel shootout.

The information didn't go deep, but it was something to start with. Every year the statistics were the same, that drug use was at its all-time high. Makes the drug problems of the 80s and 90s seem like a candy problem compared to now. The world was overpopulated with scumbags who needed a constant fix, scumbags who couldn't deal with life. And the celebrities who gave millions to the drug trade, their pretty smiles and million-dollar houses. Who were they really?

A week after Lydia Desmond's car was found, the police still had nothing to go on. Casey Lincoln had been wrong about Davido Browno. He wasn't murdered in jail. Not like that. David Brown had tripped in the bathroom and fell on a pencil, damaging his vocal cords. What a clutz.

Sidra stopped at Clemmie's for a bite to eat. Val asked her, "Where the hell have you been?" like Sidra was supposed to report in. She ordered a patty melt and mac and cheese, when what she really wanted was a strong drink.

Petula Clark sang from the speakers and it reminded her of Mom. From the booth at Clemmie's, it was like she watched her own life pass. The food didn't seem to hit the spot. She had too much on her mind right now and nothing appeased her appetite. Mom gave her another insurance fraud case to work on. A guy who claimed he hurt his neck. God, these people.

By the time Sidra got home, she had photographs and video of the guy coaching a summer baseball team. Sure, he was injured all right. Showed a ten-year-old how to slide and everything.

Sidra got a Jack and Coke and walked out the back door to smoke a cigarette, something she hadn't done in months. On the little concrete slab, she spotted the Batman lunch box. Sidra didn't know how long it had been there. Inside was more money and a cell phone number.

She smoked her cigarette and finished her drink before she called.

Casey said, "Meet me at Bingos? You know where that's at?"

It was a bar, wasn't it? "Yeah," she said.

The name of the bar wasn't Bingo's, it was the Spotlight, but no one ever called it that. Bingo was the name of the owner, so that's what people called it. It was on the square, on Mulberry Street. Bingo's was a motorcycle hangout joint. Full of smoke and pool tables. The music was either old country or older country. Nothing else.

Sidra felt comfortable going there, the folks were friendly enough. She walked in and got a, "Hey, darlin'," from an old broad in a leather vest, her cleavage spilling out while she lined up a shot.

Even though it was a summer night, Sidra sported her blue leather jacket. She spotted Casey at a small table near the back. She said, "Why couldn't you come to me?"

"Fayette is a dry sack of shit county." Casey finished his beer. "What can I get you?"

"Anything's good with me."

"Easy, girl. Talk like that'll get you more than you bargain for."

Sidra smiled. "Surprise me then."

He came back with an amaretto sour. "My wife's favorite."

When the pool balls broke, laughter erupted from their left, and the old broad, Margie, was calling pockets. With the smoke going to her head, Sidra pulled out a pack from her purse and lit one up.

Three big guys sat on stools at the bar. A couple sat at a small table watching the pool game going on and chatted with a couple of women at the table nearby. A man and woman, pool sticks in hand, were dancing near the jukebox as they waited for their shots.

"What do you want?" she said.

"You met a guy named Luther Smith."

"Don't recall."

Casey pulled out a cell phone. Showed her a picture of the Hispanic guy from La Sombra who'd pushed her off from snooping around the cabins. "Doesn't look like a Luther Smith to me. Maybe a Luthero Smitho. Why are you asking me this?" Because how would Casey know she'd run into the guy?

"Old friend," Casey said. "I asked him about Lydia, said some chick and her kid were snooping around. Long braided hair." Casey leaned over, gave her hair a tug.

"Time for a haircut. Am I right?" Sidra sipped her drink. "So what did Luthero say? Does he have any information about anything?"

"The girls that were moved? There were four of them. Three of them were in Gwinnett, one at La Sombra." Casey held up a hand before she could interrupt. "Apparently they don't take guests from La Sombra. That's not part of the deal. But they hold people there sometimes. After I hit Macon, they moved these girls somewhere else. But they decided Lydia would be a good take, but she ran. Luther doesn't know what happened to her."

"Who's they? Is Lorenzo making all the decisions? What about Bruce Zeller?"

"A hotshot mover from Texas. Been on about six months, if that. He didn't like Benny Valentino, so you have that in common," Casey said. "They keep La Sombra pretty clean. If the police found anything suspicious, they're not talking about it."

Casey looked above her head, and his face changed. "I think my fan club just showed up."

Sidra turned and noticed one bald white dude and two Hispanics walk in. They looked like trouble. Not the usuals who showed up here. One guy went to the bar, got a round of beers, then they sat down at a table near the entrance. The group playing pool continued their game, not really ignoring the fellas who walked in.

"You friends with these guys?"

"Slick Head's Dani's," he said. "The other two, I don't know their names. People like them tag along for action, it's the other one that's a problem."

"You think you can take him?" This made Casey laugh. "I mean, you're like what, a lean, mean two-thirty? My bets are on you, so don't let me down."

"And you'll handle the skinny ones?"

"Puh-lease. I'll let the biker gang take care of them. I'm going to get my girly ass out of here before my dad yells at me."

"You're funny," he said. "We could forget this place and go back to mine and play Yahtzee."

"Yahtzee? Who the fuck plays Yahtzee?" Sidra stood, tapped her empty glass on the table, and Casey nodded. She went to the bar, got another amaretto sour, and a beer for Casey. While she waited, she watched the three jokers who'd walked in. Slick Head didn't take his eyes off of her. She leaned on the bar and watched him, too.

"Who are those guys?" Bingo asked. He was an older man, thin gray hair combed over the side, but he looked solid. He had a wad of chewing tobacco in his mouth even though he wasn't supposed to. Health code violation and all. But who was going to say something to a guy like Bingo?

"No idea," she said, "I think you worked with my grandpa. Clifford Shackelford? He worked at the fire department in Spalding County for forty years."

"Yeah," Bingo said. "I remember him. How's he doing these days?"

"Been dead about five years now. Old age. It was okay, he was happy."

Bingo passed Sidra the drinks. "I was young back then," he said, and some tobacco juice dribbled out of his mouth. He wiped it with the back of his hand. "I messed up one day, didn't get a hose in right, and boy, Clifford, let me have it. Nice guy, but he could be a mean sonofabitch."

Those Shackelfords, Sidra thought.

"Let me know if you need anything else."

"Yes, sir."

Sidra took the drinks back to the table and sat down. "I have a gun in my purse."

"Lot of good it does there. I keep mine in my pants."

"That's why you only play Yahtzee."

They took sips of their drinks. Casey said, "Do you know how to play pool?"

"That's the game that involves balls and a stick, right?"

Casey smiled, something slow and seductive. Sidra rolled her eyes. "Come on," he said, and Sidra followed him across the bar with Hank Williams Jr. singing an upbeat tune that had old Margie dancing with her pool stick.

"8 ball," he said when they reached the other pool table. Casey racked the balls. Sidra broke, and walked around the table looking for angles on a good shot, decided on the twelve and called stripes when it landed in the pocket.

The first game they played; Casey ran the table. The second game, he kept using his balls to bump hers to keep her from making a shot, and when he finished screwing with her, he ran that table too. Halfway through their third game, Slick Head and his friends walked over and watched them.

"Care to join?" Casey asked.

Slick Head's chest was twice the size of Casey's, but his lower half was nothing. The juiced up guy was on 'roids and cocaine, and the veins in his neck showed it. The other two looked like stick twins in matching flannel plaid shirts, one green, one red, like they were ready for their Christmas photos.

Slick Head said, "Yeah, I'm in," then pointed to his friends. Red played, Green sat out. Sidra joined Casey on a team and agreed to play a round of 8 ball.

They ordered another round of drinks, and Casey said, "Are you from around here?"

"Oh, we do business all over. We travel for our business partners." Slick Head laughed and looked at his two friends. He reminded Sidra of a bald Johnny Bravo. He had on a black t-shirt, his sunglasses tucked in the neckline.

"Where?" Casey asked and stared at the guy for a long minute before he answered.

"Florida," he said. "I live in Disney World. You heard of it?"

"That's the place with the little Dumbo ride?"

Slick Head looked at Red. "Dumbo ride. You hear that, Mikey? You ever been on the Dumbo ride?"

"No," he said, with a laugh. "I like roller coasters. Fast ones." Then he turned to Green, and they laughed.

For the second time in their game, Slick Head brushed up against Sidra a little too close. She let the first time slide, thinking he was a dick and didn't get the idea of personal space. The bikers at the other table were rowdy, and swapping places with the ones who'd been sitting down after they won their game. Three big guys still sat at the bar chatting with Bingo, who was telling a story about a car fire. While Sidra couldn't hear the whole of the story because of the loud music, her eyes caught his mouth, and she saw some of what he was saying.

And then Casey and Slick Head bantered on about Disney World, and through the context of the conversation, Sidra realized they were talking about the Drug World. Dumbo rides. Cotton candy. Princesses.

While they waited for Casey to take his next shot, Slick Head came up behind to pass, but he'd pushed his crotch too close. The guy put his hand on Sidra's waist as he did it, and before she could say anything, Casey said, "If you touch her again, I'm going to punch you in the throat."

Slick Head let out a laugh. Sidra touched his shirt with the tip of her pool stick, left a little blue mark on the black. She said, "He won't have to do that. Because if you touch me again, I'm going to kick you in the balls."

Maybe the guy had too much to drink. Maybe he was really jacked up on something. He took Sidra's words as a friendly challenge, stepped closer, and grabbed a handful of her ass. Sidra punched him in the nose so hard, and so fast, he blinked a couple of times in disbelief. Blood dripped from his nose. And before Slick Head could react, Sidra kicked him in the balls, waited for him to bend over, and kicked him in the throat. The guy had no bite, just grabby hands and a big bark.

For the first seventeen years of her life, not only did she try to keep up with her brothers, she'd jump into any fights when she had to, even if it was amongst each other.

Nose, throat, balls. The good places. It all happened really fast and then the bar seemed to have gone silent except for Charlie Daniels on the jukebox. When she looked up, one of the biker guys had Red by the shirt, and Green was pointing a gun at Sidra.

No one said anything. In two steps, Casey was at the guy with the gun. He grabbed it before Green could aim at him, then Casey punched him. Green fell on the chair he had been sitting in, knocked out like a limp noodle.

Casey waved Red over and the biker guy let him go. He said, "You tell Dani Cameo if she wants to talk to me, to come and find me herself."

"No, me go."

Casey slapped him upside the head. "And you tell her that if I find out she has my fucking son, I'm going to kill her." Casey gave Green a shove. As he dragged his friend out of the bar, the guy woke up confused.

Slick Head got up.

Bingo looked like he hadn't moved a muscle, and Sidra thought he probably had a shotgun handy. He said, "Lincoln, take that shit out of here."

Casey pulled his wallet out of his pocket and put a wad of cash on the bar. He said something that Sidra didn't hear; she was too busy watching Slick Head make his way to the door. Casey caught up to him, grabbed him by the shirt, and left.

Sidra started to follow.

"Hey, Shackelford," Bingo called out. Sidra turned. Bingo held up a bag of ice. Yeah, her hand was killing her. Sidra took the bag of ice. Bingo said, a smile on his face, "That made my day, kid," and picked up the cash on the bar.

Sidra smiled and turned, Margie saying, "Bye, darlin'," as she walked through the door.

She found Casey in a small alley past two store fronts. She heard them fighting. Casey said, "How long have you been following me?"

"Fuck you," Slick Head said. Blood dripped down the side of his face. "There's money on your head." The guy moved into a squat, bear hugged Casey's waist, and shoved him into the brick wall. It was a bad move. Casey put the guy in a headlock and managed to get him in a backbend.

"Okay, okay," he said. Casey let him go and punched him again. He stumbled back, and Casey hit him again like he was chump change.

Sidra stood there with the bag of ice on her hand, trying not to be nervous. "What are you gonna do?"

"Take care of him," Casey said. He put his arm around the guy's shoulders, said to him, "You want to go back to my place and make a fire? S'mores sound good?" Then to Sidra, "You okay?"

"Are you really going to—"

"Shhh. Don't ruin the surprise. And don't go straight home. Make sure no one is following you."

# Chapter 14

**Hand throbbing, Sidra** drove around Jackson for twenty minutes before she got on Highway 16, but she didn't go home. She drove to Brooks, down 85 Connector, and backed into a cutout of trees across the entrance from where Daley lived. From this point, she could see any headlights left and right for a half a mile each way. It was pitch-black out here.

Across the street, waist-high weeds covered the field. The rusted mailbox leaned over, tired of doing its job. For miles, it looked like no one lived around here. Thirty minutes after she'd been sitting out here in the dark, a black SUV pulled out of the gravel driveway.

The SUV turned right, then stopped, tapped the brake lights twice. Sidra flashed her lights. The SUV backed up and Sidra rolled down her window. Bishop. The guy who owned all the property.

"Whatchu doin' out like this?" Bishop, a black guy, about thirty-five, good looking, but definitely off limits, per Daley. Sidra couldn't see shit inside that vehicle. He had the interior lights low, sneaking out of his own yard like a bandit.

"Making sure no one's following me. Where are you going?"

"Oh, just out for a little ride." He let out a deep, throaty laugh. Bishop was a quiet guy for the most part. He tapped the side of the SUV four times, the sound on the metal echoing in the night. That's when Sidra noticed Bishop's dog. A massive rottweiler named Logan, trained in God knows what. Logan didn't like anyone. Didn't listen to a single command from anyone other than his owner. When did he let the dog out? Was he even in the vehicle or had he walked up the mile long driveway through the woods? One would never know. Bishop and his bad ass dog.

"See ya, Hotcakes," Bishop said, and she flipped him off.

Sidra started the van and made her way through the pitch-black woods and thought about how creepy the woods were at night. She could only see what the headlights illuminated, could only go about ten miles an hour because of the twists and turns. If a tree fell over the road, they would need a chainsaw to get out of here.

Bishop's house was to the left, and Daley's barn house to the right. She would have slept in the van to keep from waking her brother and niece, but Daley swung the front door open. "Bishop called."

Sidra went inside and found Jorie curled up on the sofa, an array of snacks on the coffee table. "Hey," Jorie said. "We're watching all the Fast & Furious movies."

"I'm going to use the bathroom."

"What happened to your hand?" Daley said.

"Smashed it in the car door."

"Pretty dumb," he said, and went back to the sofa, the argument they'd had completely forgotten about.

She used the bathroom, then came out and sat on a love seat. She took off her jacket and boots and put them on top of her purse. Picked up a blanket from the floor and got comfortable. Sidra had just dozed off when Daley burst out laughing, nearly causing Sidra to fall off the sofa.

"What are you jumpy about?" Daley said.

"Nothing."

***

When Sidra got home the next morning—technically it was nearly noon—but it was Monday and she'd slept late because her hand was bothering her. After a couple of naproxen, she thought she smelled coffee and donuts and remembered she was hungry. When Sidra looked up, Bruce Zeller sat on her sofa.

He said, "Good morning," and Sidra thought about the gun in her purse. If she'd have looked left when she came in, she'd have seen him first thing and ran out. But there was no need to look in the living room.

"How'd you get in here?"

"I killed your landlord and took a key." Bruce drank coffee from one of her mugs. A blue one with a wolf on it. He said, "You took so long that the coffee I got from

146

Dunkin' wasn't enough. Hope you don't mind. I'm kidding about your landlord, I didn't kill him. Your back door is terrible. You should get that fixed."

"There's nothing wrong with my back door."

"No?" he said. "You should look."

Sidra reached into her purse and pulled out her gun. She aimed it at Bruce. "What the fuck do you want?" She moved to check out the back door. Bruce had kicked it in. Broke the door frame from the wall. "I see picking locks is above your skill level."

Bruce smiled.

Sidra kept her back towards the kitchen and walked to the bedrooms, keeping the gun ready in case Bruce had a friend. She had a view of Bruce on the sofa, the two bedrooms and the bathroom. The house was small.

"I came alone," Bruce called out.

Back in the kitchen, she said again, "What do you want?"

Bruce sat there with the mug in his hand, his three fingers on his left hand wrapped around the handle. "Lorenzo Marquez would like to speak with you."

"About what?"

"Lorenzo doesn't talk to me about his personal business. I'm the errand boy. He tells me where to go and I oblige."

"Tell him to call me. I'm not going anywhere with you."

Bruce started to get up.

147

"Slow down," Sidra said.

"What happened to your hand?"

"Nothing that'll stop me from pulling this trigger. I'm five seconds away from calling the police."

"Not your daddy? What's his name? Harvey Shackelford?"

"Okay, so I lied. But it's not any worse than what you do. You were going to sell me to some top dollar Delores. I know y'all had something to do with Lydia Desmond disappearing even if the police haven't found any evidence."

"That's some mighty big allegations there. You sure you don't want to come with me to talk to Lorenzo Marquez? I'll even let you bring your gun."

"Get out."

"The way I see it, these things always go down the easy way, or the hard way. I'm trying to make it easy on you."

"I'm aware that bad things will happen to me if I shoot you, so this is my last warning. Get the fuck out of my house."

"I think now I could have gotten a lot more than three grand for you." Bruce stood there casually, completely underestimating her. When he took a step forward, Sidra fired a shot into the sofa. "The next one will hit you and I won't stop shooting until I run out of bullets."

"Suit yourself." Bruce left.

***

With the construction going on next door, no one heard a thing. Not even nosy Mrs. Applebaum across the street. Sidra walked next door and asked one of the guys, "Can you come look at my door?"

"Que?"

"My door? Can you look at it?" She made the motion of opening and closing a door, then used her fingers to point at her eyes. "Look at my door?"

The one guy looked at the other guy, said something.

"Fuck," Sidra said. She walked back to her house and grabbed a couple of hundred-dollar bills Casey had put in the lunch box. Within two hours, those two guys had not only reframed her door, she now had a heavy-duty metal one. If Bruce tried that shit again, he'd break his foot.

***

*Maybe I should have called*, Sidra thought as she rang Brady's doorbell. The sun was still blazing hot at three in the afternoon. Peaches barked on the other side of the door, but it still took a few minutes before Beverly opened it. She had a towel in her hand and was wrapping it around the wet shirt she had on.

"Hey," Beverly said, and stepped aside as Sidra walked in. Peaches was so happy to see her, she couldn't control her butt. "Brady's in the pool." Sidra

149

followed as Beverly said, "Don't slip," and pointed out water on the marble floor.

In an atrium at the back of the house, Brady had a custom-built therapy pool that he used multiple times a day. If it were up to him, he'd stay in there all day. The pool wasn't deep, but it was six by ten feet. He'd work his upper body, while a sling held his lower body for support. He could never do this by himself, which was a main reason he had a nurse.

Brady was doing a freestyle swim, his arms moving in circles but not going anywhere. "Nice day for a swim."

Sidra smiled. The room was bright and sunny, windows all around them, including the large skylight windows above. The room had various plants and a couple of chairs. Beverly sat at the edge of the pool, her legs dangling in. Peaches was right next to her.

"Must be feeling much better than last week."

Brady didn't hear her. Beverly said, "The antibiotics are working well. He has a doctor's appointment at the end of the week. And he's not so grumpy." Brady splashed her with some water. "Hey," she said. So he was listening.

Brady said, not really out of breath, "Peaches could use a walk. I'll be finished up here in about fifteen minutes. I'll meet you on the back deck?"

"Sure," Sidra said.

"Her leash is in her dresser in the foyer," Beverly said.

Peaches had perked up immediately with the word walk, and followed Sidra to the front of the house. She found a leash and clipped it to the dog's harness and set out for a walk in this million-degree weather. Peaches walked on the grass, smelling and marking everything she could. Five minutes later, Peaches barked, her ears on alert, tail erect.

Two huge German shepherds were in a driveway of a massive Palatial Colonial home. As Sidra tried to pull Peaches away, the two dogs approached them. Peaches barked and jerked Sidra around. Six months of working at Fayette Animal Control, and Sidra still wasn't good at reading dogs. The shepherds weren't coming in aggressively, but Peaches was going crazy, trying to drag her to them, the Pit bull way stronger than she looked.

"Peaches, stop," Sidra said. The two shepherds smelled Peaches, tails wagging in a friendly way. Peaches got frisky and wanted to play. "Your boyfriends, I take it?"

A minute later, a whistle came from the back of the house. The dogs didn't hesitate, they obediently ran in that direction.

"I thought you were going to get eaten," Sidra said to the dog, who proceeded to let out a bark. "I appreciate how well you can handle yourself." More barking. "Oh, you're a lover, not a fighter. That explains a lot."

Sidra returned to Brady's house. Around back she found him sitting in his wheelchair, on a concrete porch with three fans going. Sidra plopped down in a chair and let the air hit her. Brady moved the wheelchair to let Peaches inside. She was panting like she just ran up Stone Mountain.

"I'm glad you're feeling better," Sidra said.

"I'm not better, I don't think. I'm just not as tired as I had been."

Beverly opened the door and stepped outside. Now dry, she had on comfortable shorts and a t-shirt. "Let me see your elbow again."

"It's fine," Brady said.

Beverly stood in front of him, not taking "it's fine" for an answer. She moved his left arm, turning it in different directions, then inspected the elbow itself. "It's bruised. Are you sure it's not hurting?"

"Yes, it hurts," Brady said with a laugh. "But it's not broken." He looked at Sidra. "I fell out of my chair."

"It's not funny," Beverly said. "You scared the shit out of me."

Looking at Sidra, he said. "I almost fell in the pool."

"He thinks everything is so funny," Beverly said, a smile on her face. "I'll start dinner, but do you want something light for now?"

"He's making you cook?" Sidra said. "Jeez, what a hard-ass."

"Oh," Beverly said, "He makes me do everything," and gave Brady a smirk.

152

"Not everything."

Beverly pushed his shoulder. "I'll bring out some water and juice. Sidra, do you want anything?"

"Do you have anything better?"

"Oh, yeah."

"We have liquor?" Brady asked her.

To Sidra she said, "I have liquor. Don't tell my boss I think he's a hard-ass and I drink on the job sometimes."

Brady watched her go. When Beverly left, Sidra said, "You like her, don't you?"

Even though Brady was usually a happy guy, his smile was different. A smile she recognized too well, and hadn't seen in a long time. "I do," he said. "Sometimes I want to fire her and tell her to just move in with me for the company. She likes taking care of me, I can tell."

"That's good," Sidra said. "You deserve to have someone like her taking care of you. I hope you've taken into consideration that you have a lot of money and people know that."

"Don't even," he said, his tone changing.

"Other people offered to take care of you too and you declined."

"Other people ran off as soon as I became handicapped."

"That's not what happened." Sidra looked him in the eyes for a long minute, those eyes that swept her away. Eyes that could pull her in and have her at his

153

mercy. He was waiting for her to say more. Instead, she said, "I'm not going to argue with you, Brady."

They sat in silence until Beverly stepped back outside with a tray. She set it down on a glass table, pulled it over towards them, careful not to spill anything. Beverly handed Sidra a glass with some fruity concoction.

"Thank you so much."

"I have chicken salad and pimento cheese." Beverly checked a pouch hooked on to Brady's wheelchair. "Your cell phone's in there. I'll start dinner in a little while. You said you had some work to complete by tonight?"

"I may be up late."

"Okay. I'm selfishly trying to get a nap after dinner."

Brady smiled at her. "Why don't you take a nap now? Forget about dinner, there's some leftover pasta. Sleep as long as you need to."

Beverly bit her lip.

"Bev, you know I don't need constant supervision. I'm not a complete invalid. I can do a lot for myself."

"I know. Okay, call me if you need anything."

"I will," he said, and Beverly left.

She popped her head back out, said to Sidra, "In the cupboard, behind the Cheerios," and pointed to her glass.

"Thanks."

After Beverly shut the door, Sidra said, "Why do you have a live-in nurse?"

"Why do you drink so much?"

"You can do everything for yourself," she said, letting his question hang there. Because he pointed it out, she wouldn't be having another drink.

Brady could drive. Move from his good wheelchair to a smaller one made for the shower. Get in and out of bed. Have food delivered. Worked from home.

"Not everything, Sidra." He shoved a buttery cracker with chicken salad into his mouth. "When I need help, I need it immediately. Like a little while ago when I fell."

"There's always Life Alert," she said.

"Sounds like you're a bit jealous."

The words caught her by surprise but gave her something to think about. Life was like that, though. Sidra said, "I hate to ask, but I was wondering if I could hang out here for a few days."

"I don't really have the room."

# Chapter 15

**At nine p.m.**, they made French toast. The counters were lower than normal, but Sidra didn't have to bend over to make it work. Brady had been back and forth between his office and the kitchen, said things like, "Please don't burn down the house," and "I would have preferred steak but I guess this will do," and to top it off, "Beverly always puts extra cinnamon."

They sat at the kitchen table, Brady in his favorite spot, where his wheelchair fit perfectly.

"Do we need to check on Beverly?" she asked.

"She's fine. Did you know she was in school for her Masters?"

Sidra finished her French toast. "I don't know anything about Beverly."

"She wants to do nursing internationally. Go into specialized medicine." Brady took their plates, carefully balancing them on one curled fist and against his chest. He rinsed everything and loaded it into the dishwasher. Took him a few minutes, but he got it done. He said, "I have a lot of work to do. You can join me in the office if you can be quiet."

"I can be quiet."

Sidra poured herself a glass of water, and followed Brady into his office. A gamer's dream come true. While it looked like a mess, it was his sanctuary. He had shelves of video games, and little prototypes of monsters and robots he'd created. Shelves full of every kind of video game super hero. From Super Mario Bros. to Star Wars. Framed posters hung on the wall, one of which was his famed character Merge Weaver, a teenaged boy in a magical wheelchair. Brady's desk had two large monitors, a keyboard, a joystick and a touchpad mouse.

He nodded to the large TV mounted on the wall. "You can play video games if you want."

"I don't play video games, Brady."

"But you do play games," he said, not even looking at her.

"What's that supposed to mean?" Sidra set her glass down on a small table and moved to a bookcase behind the sofa. Fiction novels, graphic novels, stacks of comic books, nonfiction cultural books. He had a crap ton of books about art and drawing, animation, digital art.

When Brady didn't answer, Sidra looked over at him. "I didn't play games with you. What we had was the real thing."

"I guess."

"What do you mean, 'I guess'? That's bullshit and you know it." Sidra grabbed a large book about the Netherlands and flipped it open.

He looked over at her.

157

"Okay," she said. "So we were young and stupid and did a lot—and I mean *a lot*—of stupid stuff. But we're adults now. We can have honest, open communication, and talk about real life things now. I'm glad we're friends. I mean, I tell you stuff, right? And you tell me about your work, and about Peaches. Where is Peaches?"

"With Bev."

"Oh, right. Bev." Sidra plopped down on the sofa, swung her feet up to the arm. "Smart. Amazing. Funny. Wants-To-Be-A-Nurse-Hero Bev. I can be all those things too, except for the nurse part. Did I tell you I was kidnapped a few weeks ago? I got chained to a floor in my underwear. Some guy named Bruce, who broke into my house today, was going to sell me to a butch woman named Delores for three thousand dollars."

"You're making that up."

Sidra lowered the book to her chest. "Brady, I swear I was doing my job and this bad shit just happens to me. I'd leave the job, but I don't know what else to do."

"You're good at running away from things."

Sidra groaned loudly and went back to the book. Not really reading, just looking at the pictures because she couldn't focus right now. She let Brady take his jabs, believing she left him because of his accident. Sidra reached for her drink, sitting up to drink it. *Not strong enough*, she thought, then remembered it was water. Brady broke up with her. He's the one who pissed Daley off that day. But Brady's the one who ended up in the wheelchair.

\*\*\*

She only stayed at Brady's the one night. Slept next to him in his bed, and left around lunchtime the next day. Bruce and the Marquez family aren't what scared her. It was their surprises. Like Bruce showing up in her living room. Benny and his chloroform. She didn't want to live in fear. Sometimes in life, these things had to be done. Pissing off the wrong people, calling them out and waiting to see what they'd do. But dancing with the wrong people was indeed dangerous. She needed to stay vigilant.

It wasn't the vehicle that woke her up two nights later. It was Bruno the Jack Russell terrier. Four minutes of non-stop barking, then instant silence.

She'd been asleep in the house next door, the bare floor dusty from the construction. She climbed out of her sleeping bag, rolled it up, and put it in the closet. Staying low, she was careful not to trip over a roll of carpeting and tools in the living room. Through the blinds, she saw a van backing into this very driveway. Sidra ducked. Listened. Nothing happened for a few minutes. From the window in the second bedroom, she watched a guy get out. Not a big guy like Casey, but he was muscle for sure. A kidnapper? A hitman?

He slid open the van's side door, got out a small black bag as he looked around. He didn't notice her because he'd done his homework and thought the house was empty, and he was expecting Sidra to be in her own house.

The guy, dressed all in black, was alone. With a couple of choices in mind, she could catch him by surprise in her house, or wait him out and get him when he returned to his vehicle, or she could just stay hidden next door. When he made his move toward her house, Sidra noticed a mound of white across the street, not moving. Bruno.

That asshole.

Sidra waited a full five minutes, then made her way through the backyard to her own, kept her back against the wall of the house, until she came to her bedroom window. The guy was in there checking it out. She went to the back door, already unlocked, and slipped inside. The saying goes, "don't bring a knife to a gunfight." Sure, but you have to have a little strategy behind it if you do.

The guy had made his rounds through the house. Still quiet, still slow. Probably wondering where his target was. She crouched down near a half wall that separated the kitchen from the living room. He walked, and Sidra stuck a tire iron between his legs, lifted hard until he tripped. He had a gun with a silencer, trying to see where to shoot as he was going down, let off two shots. Sidra stayed low and swung the tire iron across his back, again at his gun hand, heard a crack in his hand as the gun hit the floor. On the third swing, the guy grabbed the tire iron with his good hand and lifted a leg to send Sidra flying over him. She landed on her back on the coffee table.

While the guy went for his gun, Sidra rolled off of the coffee table and grabbed her own. Her bullet caught him in the shoulder. "I have more," she said. She moved to the right a few steps, picked up the guy's gun, set it on the end table in the living room. Not taking an eye off of him for a second, she said, "You got another weapon on you?"

He didn't answer. Looked at her while his shoulder bled. He sat on the floor between the kitchen and living room, contemplating his next move.

Her hands steadied as she sized up the guy who came to take her. Or kill her. Feet spread apart, hands close to her chest with the gun, she was ready to shoot again if he came at her.

"Who sent you?"

The guy groaned, said something like, "fuck you." Sidra picked up his gun with her right hand, aimed it at his leg, and pulled the trigger. Wow, much quieter. The guy cried out as he lifted his leg.

"Let's try this again. Who sent you?"

"Nobody. I was in the neighborhood." Sidra aimed his gun at his crotch. "Okay, okay. Jesus. This was supposed to be an easy job."

"I'd say this is going pretty easy." Sidra felt confident with a gun in each hand. "Are you here to take me or kill me?"

The guy had blood all over him. She could smell the sharp metallic of the rich scent. "Either way, you're dead," he said.

Sidra flipped on the light, got a good look at him as he squinted against the brightness. His face had a hard edge to it, dark eyebrows that gave him a serious look. He leaned up on his good arm, the one that didn't have a bullet in the shoulder.

"This kind of stuff gets you off?"

"Money does."

"Always." She thought about Casey and wondered what happened to Slick Head. Had Green and Red given Dani Cameo Casey's message. "How much time you think you've got?"

"My leg is bleeding pretty bad." He tried reaching for his black bag. Sidra kicked it out of the way. "You just going to let me die here? Then what are you going to do? Better think it through."

"Hope you got your money up front." She realized he was trying to stand up. But he couldn't. Sidra put down her own gun because she liked his better, then called Lorenzo Marquez on her burner phone, too pumped up and pissed off to think about anything else. He didn't answer until the tenth ring, the phone never going to voicemail.

"Emma," he said, his voice above a whisper.

"Tell Bruce to come get his guy."

"What?"

162

"The guy you two sent to kill me? He's bleeding all over my carpet."

"I know nothing about a guy."

Sidra snapped a photo of him, sent it to Lorenzo. "He's no my guy." A pause. "Ask his name."

"What's your name?"

"Whoever's on the phone, tell them I work for the Vega family."

"He works for the Vega family."

Lorenzo laughed. Sidra said, "Why is that funny?"

Lorenzo said, "Maybe you lie to too many people, Miss, uh? What you say your name?"

"You already know."

"This Vega family works for my family, but now there is a problem, eh? You live in Fayetteville, no? Tulip Street?"

Why ask if he already knew? "Yes."

"I come get him."

"No. How about I bring him to you. La Sombra, in an hour." She didn't even know if the guy would make it that long.

"No. I come get him. Everything will be okay."

*** 

She should call the police, that's what she should do. No, instead she was going to let drug dealers come and pick up their guy she'd shot. This Vega family wants Casey Lincoln. The Marquez family wants Casey

Lincoln. She'd been seen with him at Bingo's. What the hell had she gotten herself mixed up with?

They arrived in a black Lexus sedan; the windows tinted black. Lorenzo and Bruce were in the back. They were the only two who got out. They walked in, and Sidra stood in the living room, two guns drawn on them. Bruce came in first, put his hands up, said, "Put the fucking guns down before you hurt someone."

Lorenzo stood to the side and stared at her. Something had changed in those eyes. He had on jeans and a navy polo shirt, a huge buckle on his belt showed a bull. His silver hair combed, not a strand out of place.

Sidra put the guns away because they hadn't pulled anything on her. Bruce bent down, looked at the guy who'd lost a lot of blood.

"No ID," Bruce said to Lorenzo, Lorenzo still looking at her, not saying a damn thing.

"He killed my neighbor's dog."

"Looks like you got pay back," Bruce said. "What happened?"

"I thought you sent him for me when I wouldn't go with you." And then she told him about what happened. "His van is next door."

Bruce slapped the guy's face. "What's your name?"

"Fuck you."

"Nice to meet you." Bruce pulled the guy to a sitting position, not even caring about the blood. The guy moaned in pain. "I understand if you didn't hear me with the two bullet holes in you." Bruce pulled the guy closer. "What's your name?"

"Edgar Burke. I work for the Vega family."

"That's good to know, Burke. We'll make sure you get back to them in one piece." Bruce let the guy drop to the floor.

A minute later, another car showed up, this one had a few more people in it, and they didn't look like good people. Four at least. All dressed in black. Hard faces. Taking orders and not giving a shit. Two of them put Burke in a body bag and he wasn't even dead. A cold chill ran down her spine, the suffocation reminding her of the time Mitchell wrapped her in a heavy blanket like a roll of carpet. She couldn't move or breathe and Mitchell had laughed. Good God, why had she called these people?

"What are you doing?" she said. "Why are you putting him in there?"

Now Lorenzo spoke. "Seedra," he said. "You come with me, we can talk."

"Fuck no." They zipped up the blue bag as Edgar Burke struggled. She could hear him yelling inside.

"S'okay," Lorenzo said. "Bring your gun. I promise, no harm will come to you."

"No," Sidra said again, and when she turned away, a guy was there. What did she think was going to happen when she decided to call Lorenzo?

# Chapter 16

**Sidra sat on** a soft comfortable sofa that seemed to swallow her, along with her emotions as she stared at a guy to her right who was watching TV. She was in a large room with the living room and kitchen connected, a large table near the front door. She was in a cabin at La Sombra. No one had guns on her, no one seemed hostile.

A few minutes later, Lorenzo and Bruce walked in, and before they sat down at the table, a dog barked outside. While most dog barks seemed the same, they weren't. She'd heard this one too many times. It was Bruno. He ran inside and looked up at Lorenzo.

No one said anything. Lorenzo and Bruce sat down, as quiet as the night, not focused on anything in particular, not saying a damn thing. The one guy focused his attention back on the TV. She carefully stood up, walked to the kitchen and poured a glass of water. Gulped it down and looked at Bruno.

"What happened to the dog?"

Bruce said, "We tried to bury him and the damnedest thing happened. Dog woke up." Bruce laughed. Sidra thought about throwing the glass at him.

Wishing she could hit him in the head and knock him out.

She walked to the table, slammed the glass down hard, and spoke to Lorenzo. "Why did you bring me here? I don't know what you want with me, but if someone from my family gets to looking for me and they see all that blood in my house, they're going to call the police."

Lorenzo reached into his shirt pocket and pulled out her cell phone. Slid it across the table. "Call them. Tell them you okay, you be home soon."

Sidra looked at her phone. It was 2:45 in the morning. She pocketed the phone and said, "Which gives you plenty enough time to kill me and hide my body."

"Sit," Lorenzo said.

"How about I go?" Sidra pointed to the door.

No one said anything. Lorenzo with his cold eyes. She could tell she wasn't getting out of there anytime soon. He looked at her, unmoving, his hands resting on the table. Cooperating with them would probably be best, but damn it, she said she didn't want to come here with them, and they took her.

"What happened to the guy? Burke? And what's going to happen when this Vega family can't get in touch with him?"

Bruce looked at his watch. "We'll be taking care of that problem soon."

Lorenzo said, "Sit."

Sidra pulled out a chair. Before she sat down, she took a long look at the guy sitting in the living room.

Lorenzo said, "He no problem."

"No problem?" Sidra said. "He's the fucker that got me in a choke hold. Tell him to get out from behind me."

Lorenzo told the guy to leave, and he did. Sidra had a view of the hall and the front door, just in case.

Lorenzo said, "You are in no harm here."

"Really? Because you're holding me here against my will. This is kidnapping. Is this what happened to Lydia Desmond?"

Lorenzo leaned back in his chair, and Bruno took the opportunity to jump in his lap. The two of them best friends now. He rubbed the dog's ears until he closed his eyes.

"You tougher than I thought when you wore that little dress, eh?"

"I was never going to sleep with you, okay?"

Lorenzo laughed.

Sidra said, "What about Lydia?"

Bruce said, "We think Lydia got kidnapped."

"You think?"

"Your family," Lorenzo said. "How many kids?"

"Don't you know all about me?"

Lorenzo shrugged. "I make conversation." Lorenzo pet Bruno. "Parents think they do the right things for their kids. And the kids grow up and they want more, and they become smarter, and sometimes the kids have to take from their parents the power so that they can live and learn. You understand?"

She didn't, so she shrugged.

"In this life," Lorenzo said, "people work for us. And sometimes they want what they cannot have. So they take it. And when they take it, we have problems. We don't know what happen to Lydia. No camera, no nothing. But the people we think cause us problems? They gone."

"What do you mean, gone?"

"Eliminated," Bruce said.

Sidra thought about David Brown and wondered how many other people had something to do with Lydia. "What do you think happened to Lydia?"

Lorenzo said, "We don't know," real slow, like she was stupid. "This missing girl is no longer my concern. The police find nothing."

"What about your brother, Nacho? Would he know what happened to her?"

Lorenzo sighed something long and heavy, tired of talking about a girl who was no longer his concern. Whatever happened to Lydia, no one was talking about it.

"I guess I can go now," Sidra said.

"Where is Casey Lincoln?" Lorenzo said, his voice going up. Bruno sensed something and his head popped up. "Someone say you with him."

She was going to make this easy on Lorenzo and said, "Casey saved me from Benny Valentino, and this

169

guy" —Sidra looked at Bruce— "who was going to sell me to Delores—"

"What are you talking about, this guy?" Lorenzo said, looking between Sidra and Bruce.

Bruce said, "It was a misunderstanding."

The way Bruce looked at Sidra and said this, she knew Bruce worked behind Lorenzo's back for money. "A misunderstanding," Sidra said, and nodded, and thought it out. If she pissed Bruce off, he'd come after her. If she didn't say anything about it at all, Lorenzo wouldn't feel the need to keep Sidra quiet if she went to the police about what his guy had done. Especially now after La Sombra's been in the spotlight. At least Sidra had leverage if she needed it.

"I don't know where Casey is," she said. "He called me that one time but the phone number doesn't work anymore. Probably a burner."

"I want you to give him a message," Lorenzo said.

"I don't know how to get in—"

"You tell Casey I need him to do something for me."

"I don't think he wants to do that."

"You tell Casey Lincoln that I can get him his son."

"But he has to do you a favor." Sidra stood up. "This goes round and round, and somebody fucks any of you over and they get a bullet. I don't care what happens to Casey Lincoln, but I care about a four-year-old little boy. And I care about Lydia Desmond." Sidra pushed her chair in. "I won't be your go between person. If you have to tell Casey something, then find him yourself."

"Maybe," Lorenzo said, "you prefer to talk to someone in the Vega family. About Burke? Maybe we go put his body back in you house. Or the Shackelford front porch."

Sidra shook her head. "I didn't call you because I needed you to get rid of a body for me. I called because I thought you sent him and I wanted you to know I got him before he got me."

"We understand." Lorenzo looked at her. "Do you understand?"

"Yeah," she said. "I understand. Somebody needs to take me home now. Bruno, let's go."

The dog didn't move.

"Bruno," she said, her tone sharper this time.

Lorenzo said, "The dog. He stay with me. I take care of him."

Bruno eyed Sidra carefully. She said, "Is he going to end up as dog bait?"

"No." The look on his face was pure disgust. "Why would I do that?" Because he saw a huge difference between dog fighting and human trafficking. What a gem.

"Who's taking me home?"

***

The wet bloodstain on the carpet spread, and the blood on the linoleum had dried. Should have called the police. Guy comes in to kill her and she calls

171

Lorenzo Marquez. Burke's gun was nowhere to be found, which meant they took that too.

Sidra leaned her head back. "Fuck."

There was a four-year-old boy out there who needed help. And whatever happened to Lydia Desmond needed to come to light. The problem was that everything had to do with the Marquez family. The key wasn't just going in and kicking ass.

The key was finding an opening and keep moving in.

Lorenzo wants Casey to do a favor for him. Would he really give his son back? No. No favor would equal the exchange of the boy.

Sidra looked at the bloodstain like it was going to disappear. The first thing she did was clean up the blood on the laminate floor, seemed to make a bigger mess than necessary. Here's a job she's never had. Crime scene clean up. She pulled the floor threshold up, bleached that in the bathtub. Cut the bloody carpet and padding out. It had soaked through to the subfloor. The house was so old, the carpet must have been the original beige crap from a hundred years ago.

The construction guys from next door usually showed up around eight. She had a few hours to borrow an electric saw, cut the subfloor out and return everything. When she thought, *How the hell am I going to dispose of all of this?* She remembered the dumpster on the other side of the house.

Don't be stupid.

Think.

The little fire pit in the backyard came in handy. She burned everything until it was dust. By the time the construction guys showed up, she had a hundred-dollars ready so they could cut out a new piece of subfloor she was sure they had handy.

\*\*\*

While she needed to deliver the message to Casey Lincoln, she didn't want to go to his cabin. With a deep feeling, she knew they were watching her, waiting for her to do something like that. So she'd have to wait, and like she'd told Lorenzo, Casey may or may not contact her. She'd been antsy all day, nearly biting a hole in her fist.

Last night when they took her, Sidra had her cell phone in her pocket. Then Lorenzo gave it to her. The cheap burner phone wasn't anything expensive. Although it was passcode protected, could they have gotten in? Sidra slid the back cover off and took the battery out. Underneath that was a tiny metal square that she recognized as a tracking chip.

Across the street, Mrs. Applebaum had been calling for Bruno all day. She stood in her front doorway, ringing a little bell this time, not making an effort to come outside. Sidra walked over. "Have you seen Bruno?" Mrs. Applebaum said. She wore a floral house coat that reached her knees and a pair of white slip on sneakers.

"There was a dog hit by a car over on South Glynn," Sidra said, trying to ease Mrs. Applebaum's worry with a lie.

"Did you get a good look at it?"

"No, but I didn't see a collar."

"Bruno won't wear a collar. I can never get one on him. The little bastard keeps running off so much, the animal control knows him by name. I was hoping they'd call if they picked him up."

"He might not be coming back."

"How do you know?"

"Well, if a car hit him…"

"But you don't know for sure?"

Sidra shook her head. Why'd she even bother?

\*\*\*

The next day, Mom and Dad called a Shackelford meeting. A work meeting, in its official form, meant come prepared to listen to budgeting, new data platforms, technology changes, and what's been working and not working with handling assignments.

The only thing on Sidra's mind was trying to figure out how to get in touch with Casey. She walked into Shackelford, made herself a drink, and went into the dining room to top it off with something strong. When the Victorian house had been renovated, a wall had been taken out to make the room bigger. They did a lot of business around this table.

Everyone was there waiting for her. Sidra sat down next to Amy, then got up to go to the bathroom. Casey didn't even have a mailbox, from what Sidra noticed. She'd only found the gap in the trees to the gravel drive because of a sheet of metal leaning against a tree.

Back in the dining room, Mom started about the assignments over the last three weeks and how the Diane Hutchinson case put them behind.

Sidra said to Dad, "Have you talked to anyone else about Diane?" Everyone stared at her. "Tanner Wells? Arthur Walburn?"

Before Dad could answer, Mom said, "Where's your laptop and notebook?" Like a fucking class. "Write down what you have to say and we'll discuss it when I'm done."

Sidra turned her phone over in her hands. She'd put the tracking chip back inside. If they were tracking her, she needed it to look like she didn't know about it. She hadn't used the phone for anything other than the text message about the meeting. After this, she'd go get a new phone.

She got another drink and then looked out the window. Would they have followed her here? No, there was no point. But Violet and Phin were playing in the backyard, climbing on the swing. Sidra said, "What are the kids doing here? No kids at the meetings."

She'd interrupted Woolsey this time, who'd been talking about a new app they needed to download.

Amy said, "I couldn't find a babysitter. What's the big deal?"

"Nothing." Sidra walked out of the dining room, and checked the front of the house. Didn't see anything there. Dad's office had a view of the shared parking lot. A black truck and a blue sedan were parked closer to the realty office.

Back in the dining room, Sidra sat down, tapped her foot.

Dad said, "You got a humming bird stuck up your rear end?"

"What?"

"You're flittin' around like you've got something on your mind," Dad said. He put his pencil down and steepled his fingers together on his notepad. "Why don't you go ahead and tell us what's bothering you."

"Can I talk to you alone?"

"Is it business or personal?"

"Business, I guess."

"Then, no. Talk here."

Sidra looked around at her siblings. They were pissed because she was holding things up. She said, "It's personal, then."

Mitchell and Daley laughed like it was an inside joke.

"Forget about it," Sidra said, and swallowed down her drink, which did nothing to calm her down. She found a stray string on the tablecloth and began picking at it.

Woolsey was talking about the app again, when Mom snapped, "Sidra, stop."

"Why do you even still have this old thing? Look at it." The table cloth was a vintage needlepoint with colorful flowers all over. Full of stains from over the years.

"My grandmother made it and I'd appreciate it if you'd stop picking at it."

"What's your problem?" Mitchell said.

Sidra rubbed her face, looked at Mom. "May I be excused, please? I have some things to do."

Her brothers laughed again. Amy said, "I have stuff to do too. Violet has soccer and Phin has karate, but here I am."

Dad slammed his hand on the table. Everyone shut up. His voice quiet, he said, "What's the problem?"

Sidra looked at him for a minute. "I shot someone. Then I covered it up."

Dad leaned in close. She wished she wasn't sitting next to him. "You're not serious, are you?" His eyes had narrowed. "What do you mean you shot someone?"

"You know, when you have a gun and you shoot someone."

"Thank you for explaining that to me, Sidra. I had no idea."

"He broke into my house to kill me. I shot him."

"Did you kill him?" Daley said.

"Well. I shot him, but they put him in a body bag."

"Who's they?" Dad said.

177

"I called Lorenzo Marquez."

"Jesus," Dad said. "Sidra, are you serious?" She nodded. "You're going to go to jail for murder." Dad got up, walked out of the dining room.

Mom leaned over. "He was in a good mood this morning."

"Sorry."

"Is this about the horseback riding?" Daley said, scrolling through his phone, probably to check on his daughter.

"No."

Dad came back in the dining room after he'd composed himself. "We still have to follow the law, you know that?" He sat down. "You break the law and you go to jail."

"Unless you don't get caught," Daley said, and Dad gave him a look.

"Why didn't you call me?" Mitchell said.

"Or me?" Daley said.

Woolsey held up his hands. "Don't call me unless you have an IT problem."

"I can handle this."

"Doesn't look like it," Dad said.

Amy got up. "I'm going to check on my kids."

"Lorenzo Marquez wants me to get in touch with Casey Lincoln. To do him a favor and in return, he's going to get him his son back. He said that if I don't help him he's going to put the dead guy on the front porch."

"Uh huh," Mitchell said. "I'd like to see him try that."

178

Dad said, "Tell me everything."

Sidra told him the God's honest truth and her opinion about what was going on. Woolsey looked at the chip, said she was correct, it was a tracking chip. He looked through her phone, didn't see any hidden apps. He hooked up her phone to his laptop, ran a diagnostics but he told her to back up what she could and do a factory reset. "Should be fine," he said.

"Why didn't you call the police, Sidra?" Mom said. "It was self-defense. That's how they would have seen it. Now what are you going to do?"

"I'm going to get in touch with Casey and help him get his kid back. I know this puts us in danger, but Jesus, he's four years old. The three of you sit here acting like you've never had to make these kinds of decisions." She pointed to Woolsey. "And you're the information machine feeding them so you know the business." Looked at Daley. "Two years ago, Claus Tempelton?" Daley had gotten the guy with a sniper rifle, but he'd deserved it. "That guy from the Soloman Gang. Come on. Stop acting like I haven't been watching y'all."

"You could have been a soccer star," Dad said. "Now you're covering up murder."

"I guess if I hang around a little more I'll know how to work in all the departments in Shackelford Investigations."

# Chapter 17

**Her brothers thought** they were funny and drove around with the tracking chip until they finally tossed it in a trash can at Southern Regional Hospital in Riverdale. Meanwhile, that night, Sidra drove back to Bingo's dressed in black jeans, a Garth Brooks t-shirt, and a leather vest she'd made by cutting the sleeves off of a leather jacket she'd found at the Goodwill. With her hair down and flowing, she put on one of those skull caps with an American flag design, and felt ready for Halloween.

For forty minutes she sat at the bar, drinking a Monday Night Han Brolo and watching the Braves lose a game to the Red Sox. Not a single player could drive the ball out tonight. This was the second loss in two days.

"Baseball's overrated," Sidra said to no one in particular.

The guy next to her said, "Can't even get a fucking run tonight," and shook his head.

Bingo came over, looked at her, shook his head. "You auditioning for Hell's Belles?"

"You the director?"

Bingo smiled. While she'd been there, she didn't think he recognized her. He said, "What you need?"

A motorcycle?

"To get in touch with him."

Bingo nodded, reached beneath the bar and came out with an old, red push button phone like her grandma used to have. Not the rotary dial, the newer push button kind. He dialed, punched in a few more numbers, then hung up. "When it rings," Bingo said, "answer it."

Sidra had another beer. Five minutes later, the phone rang. "Hello."

"Hello." Sounded like Casey.

"It's me."

"I know."

"That guy I went on a date with? He wants to talk to you. He wants you to do him a favor and he can get your kid."

Casey didn't say anything.

"Are you there?"

"Yes."

"What do you want me to do?"

"Nothing."

"A lot has happened." She took a drink of beer. She hadn't talked to him since the last time she was here when Slick Head showed up. Sidra stepped to the side of the bar for some privacy, had to take the clunker phone with her. Didn't Bingo know what year it was? "A guy came after me. I thought Lorenzo sent him so I

181

called him." Sidra sat down at a small table by the far wall.

"Why didn't you call me? I would have kicked his ass."

"I shot him. And I would have called you but I don't have your number."

"Right," he said, because he'd given her a burner number that he killed.

"Right. So I called Lorenzo to come pick up his guy, and he took me. And the guy worked for the Vega family. Edgar Burke?"

"Never heard of him."

Sidra looked at the phone. "You trust Bingo?"

"Yes. Why?"

"Some people are just too nice."

"Don't underestimate Bingo for a clown. He called me the minute you walked in. Said you're all dressed up tonight. Look up, Sidra." She looked up. "To your right."

She spotted Casey sitting at a table next to the jukebox, sort of hidden by the pool tables. "What kind of detective are you?" He hung up the phone.

Sidra put the phone back in the cradle, walked to the bar for her beer, and said, "Thanks, Bingo."

"Got your business squared away?"

"Yeah."

Sidra walked over to Casey. "You got me."

"You look really nice in your Garth Brooks shirt and leather vest." He looked at the thing on her head. "What are you, a hog ridin' pirate?"

She drank beer to keep from blushing. "What are you going to do?"

Casey shrugged. "Talk to Lorenzo, I guess."

"How do you know he won't just kill you?"

"I don't."

\*\*\*

Casey Lincoln couldn't just walk into La Sombra. Too many eyes and chatty lips. Sidra called Lorenzo the same way she'd gotten in touch with him before. The plan was to meet at a neutral place in the warehouse district near College Park. Far enough for both parties to drive, and dangerous enough to be elusive. While the Marquez family owned a lot of people and knew a lot of places, Sidra had a friend who owned a little hole-in-the wall walk-in wings place off of Park Street. Hartsfield Jackson International was one of the busiest airports in the United States, and located in College Park, and was one of Georgia's most crime dense cities.

The trick Casey taught her was to hold out on the location until the last minute, keep Lorenzo and his entourage going in circles so they couldn't get too comfortable. Meanwhile, Casey paid Teacup five-hundred dollars to borrow his Wings joint for a few hours. Teacup was a skinny black man who'd put a bullet in someone for bad talking his homemade wing sauce. But he didn't want any trouble, said he was leaving, and thanked Sidra again for helping him out of trouble that one time. "Lock this door before you leave, you hear? Go out the back." And then Teacup left.

Sidra's phone rang.

"There's only one black sedan at the dummy location," Mitchell said. "Do you want to send him to a third?"

"No, I'm sure they know what we're doing. We're going to call him now."

The Wing joint was in a strip between a cell phone place and a CBD store. All the businesses in the strip were closed except for the CBD store that wasn't busy at all. It was nearly midnight when the black sedan pulled up in front of Teacup's Wings.

Casey stood in front of the counter with his arms folded. Sidra sat in a chair to the right. Lorenzo and Bruce were the only two who walked in. Then there was Bruno, prancing around with his new attitude, and walking between them. He gave a low growl to Sidra and Casey, sniffed the front of the restaurant, then walked back to his new owner. If anyone else was in the car, they weren't getting out.

The lights were low, and Lorenzo didn't seem at all worried about his safety. Bruce had a gun on his hip. They kept their distance as Lorenzo said, "Señor Casey," and nodded, and pulled up a chair. He sat down under some black and white photos of Atlanta, Bruno, right next to him.

Lorenzo said, "This is Bruce. This is Casey," by way of introducing each other. "I think we all know you two will shoot each other if so much a mouse squeaks. So let's be civil and we talk, eh?"

"And be civil," Casey said. "Can you define civil? Do you mean civil in the same way my wife was murdered or a different kind of civil?"

Lorenzo sighed. "I no kill your wife. I have nothing to do with that. You work for Nacho, you take your problems to Nacho. You want out, he say no, that's no my problem."

"You're all family," Casey said. "I hurt him, it hurts you."

"Yes, yes. But—"

"What do you want?" Casey hadn't moved from his position, kept his arms folded across his chest, his tone sharp.

Bruce hadn't moved either except to lean against the wall, his hand with all five fingers ready in case he needed his gun.

Teacup's Wings was quiet for a long minute, the only sound was the refrigerator with all the beverages in it humming along like a blind old man without a clue.

Lorenzo said, "Dani Cameo is a problem and Nacho won't see it. She play two sides, and just keep moving up." Lorenzo used his fingers, like they were walking up stairs. "My son, Romulo, he supposed to be in charge of Macon and Valdosta, but no, Nacho say Cameo. And my son, he go back to Mexico. Like he no family. And who is Dani Cameo?"

"Not family," Casey said.

"Exactamente. Nacho no see that. I work hard. I run twenty-eight million out of La Sombra last year. The south is mine too, but no."

"What do you want?"

Lorenzo shrugged. "You tell me."

"What I want," Casey said, stepping away from the counter and Bruno barked at him, "is to find my kid without all this go between favor bullshit. I'm in your family's crosshair as we speak, so don't lead me to believe the target can be removed."

"There is no out, Casey Lincoln. There is no out of this business. Find your son, no find your son." Lorenzo touched his fist to his chest. "You here. Is better for you say goodbye to Brandon and move far away. I tell you, Romulo come back to the States, you have my word, I give you my protection. Tu comprende, Cabron?"

*** 

When they were gone, Sidra locked the front door. Teacup's Wings had bars across the windows and front door, and when the tail lights stopped at the traffic light, Sidra turned away from the window. Mitchell called to tell her the black sedan had passed him and drove towards Camp Creek Parkway.

"This is how they operate?" Sidra said. "Going behind each other's backs and taking out their people?"

Casey opened the fridge with all the drinks, pulled out a Dr. Pepper and replaced it with a ten-dollar bill. "You know the difference between the Mafia and the Cartel?"

"Pizza versus tacos?"

"Wow," he said.

They left out the back door of Teacup's Wings where she'd parked the van earlier, and drove down Park Street.

"Both of those countries have very interesting histories," Sidra said. "Their wars for independence aren't even parallel, yet the countries have the Mafia and Cartel criminal organizations that turn out to thrive over all these years and are still the most dangerous organizations in United States history."

"And with the Russians and the Serbians... we're just a cesspool for corruption."

"Started with the people on our own Capitol Hill."

Sidra drove north, hopped on Virginia Avenue until she found North Loop Road. She circled around the entire airport twice. The lights and the runways were impressive in the middle of the night, an airport that never slowed down with people hustling about trying to catch their flights. The sound of the planes ripped through the air.

When they were on the back roads, Casey said, "There are two things the cartels don't want you messing with. The business. And the family. Everything else is fair game."

"But Nacho put Dani Cameo in front of his nephew."

"Romulo has a history of scraping off the cake frosting, if you know what I mean."

"Stealing?"

"And raping. Whatever he likes to do. And Cameo is a ruthless bitch in charge of organizing and moving the women. The cartel has no code. And when that person is gone, someone else takes their place. They are constantly at war with each other and the smaller drug gangs."

"Do you trust him? Lorenzo Marquez?"

"Hell no. He thinks he's about to play me like a guitar."

Sidra passed Bethsaida Road and paid attention to the car behind her. At nearly two a.m., there weren't a lot of cars on the road and the driver spent a hot minute trying to not lose her in the traffic near the interstate. Now it pulled back. Not bothering with a blinker, she slowed down and took a right into a neighborhood.

"Tail?" Casey said.

The car followed. "Yep."

The neighborhood was one of those one way in, one way out deals, but it had multiple side streets.

"Black Mustang," Casey said.

"Do you recognize it?"

"No."

The Mustang pulled over, but Sidra kept going, looped back around, and exited the neighborhood. She'd tailed so many people, got burned multiple times, and knew that the Mustang would most likely back off.

But no, she spotted the Mustang coming out of the neighborhood too fast in order to pull out in front of another car. "Mario Andretti back there."

"Turn on Highway 138."

"I've done this before," Sidra said, and stopped at the traffic light. A minute later, she took a left. There was a lot more traffic now moving into Riverdale.

Casey said, "Drive faster or we're never going to lose them."

"We're perfectly fine ten miles over the speed limit. I don't want to get pulled over."

Casey pulled out his gun. "Then slow down, I'll get them when they pass."

"Are you fucking crazy?" Sidra said. "Put that away. That's how you got in this situation as it is. You don't go around playing in car chases and shooting out cars, especially not in Riverdale."

The Mustang stayed two cars behind. A complete amateur, zipping in and out of lanes every time Sidra did, like the driver was afraid of losing her. Just to be sure the Mustang was following, Sidra took a left going north on Highway 314, then a right on Bethsaida, which was a poorly lit residential road that continued on for miles.

The Mustang sped up. The Mustang dropped back. There were two people in the vehicle. Her only concern was someone shooting at them, but they'd have done that by now. As the road opened up, the blue lights of multiple police cars illuminated the intersection on Highway 85 like a holiday party.

"This'll be fun," Sidra said, and pulled into the Dunkin' Donuts parking lot where three Riverdale police cars had a black SUV boxed in.

"What are you doing?"

"Getting a donut."

Sidra looped around the Dunkin' while the Mustang took a right on the highway.

"Passenger tail light is out," Casey said, and ducked his head when they got closer to the cops.

She made her way through the shopping center's large parking lot, and waited five minutes before getting back on the highway.

Low and behold, ten minutes later, Casey said, "Shit, they're at the McDonalds," and nearly broke his neck to get a better look. She made a U-turn and pulled into an empty parking lot across the street.

"Were they tailing me or you?" Sidra reached for her binoculars.

"Definitely you." Casey took a drink of his Dr. Pepper. "We're in your vehicle and these guys are idiots."

"So you think someone would only send idiots to tail me?"

"I'm saying that I'm more on a professional status considering they haven't been able to find me."

"Maybe they think I'm an idiot and I'll make a mistake which will lead them to you?"

"You can't go home," Casey said. They sat in the semi-dark, watching the driver of the Mustang pick up food from the window all the way from across a highway at a gas station. Definitely two guys in the car. One was Hispanic, the other she couldn't tell.

"Can you hand me the flip phone out of the glove box?"

The mustang continued south on Highway 85, and a minute later Sidra pulled out of the parking lot and had to do another U-turn. It wasn't hard to stay behind a mustang with a taillight out.

Sidra called 911 on an old burner flip phone. She kept the phone away from her mouth and said, "This asshole driving down the highway nearly ran me off the road. All he's doing is playing around, zipping between cars."

"Ma'am, can you repeat that?"

So Sidra did. "I'm really about to—Hey, asshole," Sidra yelled as she pulled the phone back. "Learn how to drive. I think he's drunk."

"Can you tell me where you're located?"

"Just past the roller coasters going toward the Pavilion. He's flying down the road in a black Mustang with a busted right taillight." Sidra rolled down the window and pulled the phone further away, the wind making it difficult to hear. "I can't hear you," Sidra said, then flipped the phone shut and tossed it in Casey's lap. "I can be a professional too," she said, as she rolled up the window.

Three miles down the road, the cops had the Mustang pulled over. They were on the highway in front of a fast-food chicken place. Sidra didn't pass them. She looped around another shopping center, made her way through the parking lot and had the perfect view of what was going on.

"Nice play," Casey said.

"I learned a lot from my dad."

They didn't even need binoculars as they watched two more backup police arrive. The two guys from the mustang were already in handcuffs. One of them was in the back of the police cruiser, while the other one sat on the ground between the Mustang and a police car. An officer helped the guy up and put him in a different vehicle.

"Must have found drugs or something," Sidra said. "Wow." They brought out a K-9 dog who was sniffing around the Mustang.

"All that for two little thugs?" Casey said.

"I'm sorry you disagree with the law."

"My tax dollars could go to better things."

"Do you even pay taxes?"

Forty-five minutes later, the Mustang was impounded, and the scene was clear. Sidra said, "You might as well stay at my place and then we can find out who these guys are in the morning."

"Your place?" he said. "You just want me to protect you."

Sidra let it go. She was sure she was the one protecting Casey.

# Chapter 18

**The next morning**, Sidra woke up and found Casey standing in the middle of her driveway smoking a cigarette. He looked like a strong and powerful keeper of the gate, watching the street and waiting for disaster to screw up the day. Sidra couldn't live her life looking over her shoulder the way Casey did. When he finished the cigarette, he brought it inside and flushed it down the toilet.

Neither one of them slept well, and Sidra was sure Casey had a broken back from the sofa. He walked out of the bathroom, stretched and said, "What's the plan?"

Sidra drove down to the police station around 10 a.m. and spoke to a friend named Larissa Hurst, who was a clerk with the Fayetteville Police Department. She was in her mid-forties and played on the adult rec soccer team in the fall and spring when the weather was cool. Larissa didn't run fast, but she'd put a player on the ground if she had to.

Sidra said, "I need something."

"You always need something." Larissa had on jeans and a black FPD polo. "I done told you this needs to be a give and take relationship. Now, where's that cute brother of yours? I want his phone number." She let out a deep laugh. "I can't wait to get back out on the field with him."

And it was a sight watching Larissa chase Daley around on the soccer field. "You can have him. I'll knock him over the head and bring him to you."

"Oh, no baby. He gonna come willingly to Larissa." She laughed again. "What you need now?"

Sidra leaned against the tall counter. "Last night a couple of guys were brought in. Drove a Mustang. Pulled over by the Popeyes?"

"Uh huh," Larissa said, looking at a computer and typing on a keyboard. When she looked up, she said, "I don't have that public yet."

"I need names and addresses."

Larissa rolled her eyes. "Trying to get me fired. Oh," she said, her eyes getting big. "These two yo-yos had two unregistered handguns, a grand in cash, hundred-fifteen oxy, and three stolen credit cards. You got your form?"

She was asking about a request form from Shackelford Investigations for the information. "Not today, but I can bring it by later."

Larissa looked at her. "Girl, you gonna get me fired. I can't print anything off."

"But you can talk to yourself while you work."

Larissa said, "I better have a ring on my finger by the end of this year."

***

Sidra was already on the phone with Woolsey when she got in. "Can you run all that for less than twenty bucks?"

"I can do it for less than that," he said, and then yelled, "stop jumping on your sister's head," then she heard one of the twins crying. "Give me twenty minutes."

Sidra drove away from the police station, said to Casey who was in the back behind the curtain, "You're clear." He walked up to the passenger seat and climbed over the console.

"Antonio Guzman," Sidra said, "was the driver. He's wanted in Fulton County for car theft. Arrested twice for possession and selling drugs. Darriel Finley was the passenger. They had guns, drugs, and stolen credit cards on them last night. I'm sure they're looking at a hefty jail sentence. Fayette County thanks us for the easy arrest."

"Antonio Guzman hangs out with the black gangs in Atlanta," Casey said. "He's not a big player but he'll do anything for money."

"I have their addresses. We can check them out and see where it leads."

They started with Antonio Guzman because Casey knew of him. His address was in Stockbridge. Like a lot of suburbs in Atlanta, Stockbridge had its good areas and its bad. Mostly during the day, any place nearby was safe. People, even drug dealers, weren't hanging around outside of their homes during the day waiting for trouble unless it was a drug house that needed to be protected.

For the most part, Stockbridge was a safe enough area, compared to Fulton County. Everything was compared to Fulton County. The county came with a warning.

Antonio Guzman was twenty-nine years old. The house he lived in looked like every other house in the neighborhood. It was a gray split-level ranch with a broken-down car parked in the driveway. One of the garage doors was busted, like someone couldn't get in and lifted the corner with the jaws of life.

Sidra and Casey parked down the street and waited. What were they going to find? Probably nothing. She played the private investigator waiting game. In the back, Sidra lifted the lid off of a tote bucket and pulled out a bag of Doritos. "If you have to pee," she said, "I have a toilet."

"I noticed." Casey dug into the bag of Doritos. "You wouldn't have a beer, would you?"

"I do." Sidra reached into the bucket and came back with a warm bottle of water. "Pretend it's a Bud Light. You won't even know the difference."

The house had a chain-link fence around the backyard. Grass throughout the yard was calf high, and a child's plastic playground was in the middle. Along the fence, grass and weeds had grown nearly halfway up the sides. The entire neighborhood was rundown, with people trying to do their best to make ends meet, but it was never enough.

Antonio may have lived here, but Sidra had no idea whether he was the homeowner. It had been well beyond the twenty minutes Woolsey needed. and she was about to call him when her email chimed. As she read the report, she said, "So how does one get into this type of business?"

"You fill out an application," he said, his tone loaded with sarcasm. "My sister Lexie and I didn't have a good childhood. She doesn't want anything to do with me anymore. We started stealing stuff pretty young."

"What's pretty young?"

"I was twelve the first time. Small stuff, easy money. When Lexie got involved, I think she was thirteen. I felt real bad about using her, but she was good at it." Casey licked Dorito crumbs off his fingers. "You need money so you do something for someone and before you know it, you're doing illegal shit. Except no one feels like they're doing illegal shit. We just do what we have to do to get by and try not to get caught. It's a life. A terrible life that sounds great when you're making money, but then shit happens."

"It's a multi-billion-dollar industry. But it's not just the drugs. Antonio Guzman did time for stealing cars five years ago. Got out of jail but he loved it so much, he went back for two years for a parole violation because he got caught breaking into a home." Sidra pulled up another report. "Criminal activity shows he's associated with Jimmy John Jackson?"

"JJ is part of the Wax gang in Atlanta. They operate under a gang out of Chicago. Wax is no joke. They shot up some Latinos about a year ago, caused a shit storm with the Marquez family. Nacho flew all the way to Chicago to have a sit down with some people up there."

"And now this Wax gang is under control?"

"No such thing."

The house belonged to Omar and Renata Guzman, not Antonio. "I'll be right back." Sidra grabbed her gun from the console.

"What am I going to do?" Casey said.

"If it looks like I'm in trouble, then you have my permission to protect me. Otherwise, stay here and eat your Doritos."

Sidra walked to the house and knocked on the front door, not really expecting anyone to answer, but an older Hispanic woman did. She had on a large floral shirt with matching bottoms and looked like she was ready for the beach. No, Sidra realized, the woman was still in her pajamas.

"Hi," Sidra said with a big smile.

"Who you?" the woman said.

Sidra had to go with honesty. "I'm an investigator."

"No." The woman waved her off and tried to close the door.

"I need to talk to you."

"Mi English is no bueno."

"S'okay," Sidra said, repeating the word the way Lorenzo Marquez said it. "Antonio was arrested last night."

"Que?"

"Antonio with policia."

The woman gasped and spoke rapidly. "Chinga tu madre."

"My mother?" Fuck, she really needed to learn Spanish. She tried hard not to speak louder. "Do you know who Antonio was friends with?"

"What?" the woman said.

"His friends? Amigos? Or where he, ah... trabajo?"

The woman stared at her for a minute. Then a hulking shadow passed over Sidra and Casey stood there. He held out his hand to the woman, said, "Hola, Señora. Mi nombre es Casey," and then he sniffed the air, and spoke in fluent Spanish. The woman smiled like she knew him, and Casey said, gracias, and delicioso, and, si, si mucho, as he patted his belly. The woman turned, kept talking, and Casey looked at Sidra.

"When did you learn Spanish?" she whispered, as she followed him into the house.

"Sometime in the last ten years while I worked for the Mexican cartel."

They followed the woman as she hobbled to the kitchen. Jesus, whatever she was cooking smelled like her favorite restaurant. In the kitchen, Casey and Sidra sat at a small table and Casey introduced them. Sidra smiled and waved. The woman's name was Petra.

*What the fuck?* she mouthed to Casey when Petra had her back turned. He shrugged. Virgin of Guadalupe candles sat on the table, and Sidra spotted a little altar just off the kitchen, with more burning candles and statues of Jesus and more saints on the top. Four crucifixes hung on the wall. At least she would have something to pray to if she died in here.

Petra set down a loaded plate of food in front of each of them. Swear to God, no offence to the altar, it looked like she was dining at a Mexican restaurant. Corn tortilla tacos stuffed with pork, topped with crumbled queso and cilantro. Holy shit, homemade salsa. Sidra took a bite and could hardly contain herself.

Casey said, "We would have never gotten tacos your way," took a bite and half a taco was gone. "These are homemade tortillas." He closed his eyes as he chewed.

Petra set down two glasses of a white, milky drink, said, "*Horchata*," and smiled. She sat down, talked to Casey in Spanish, while Sidra only caught a handful of words.

Petra's eyes were wide with concern, gasped, shook her head. "No, mi hijo," she said. She looked at Sidra. "No, my son. He a good boy. Take care of me. Bring money." She held her hands out.

"Do you know how he gets that money?" Sidra said. Casey translated, and then Petra just waved her hands like it wasn't true. But then she had tears in her eyes

201

and she wiped them with a tissue she pulled from her pocket. When the tacos were gone, Sidra said, "May I use your bathroom?"

Petra spoke in Spanish, but used her hands, and Sidra figured it out. She moved down a hallway, passed the bathroom, and opened a couple of bedroom doors until she found one that looked like it belonged to Antonio. Must have been his. There were several pictures of a guy and a girl, so in love. She spotted some bills on the dresser with his name on them. A check stub from a mechanic shop in Stockbridge. The room was dark, the bed unmade, and clothes tossed all over the room. The closet was a mess, like everything he owned was thrown in there. A swivel chair had clothes piled on the seat. Nothing in the pockets. Antonio had three laptops stacked on top of one another. A drawer near the bed had gold watches, more stolen credit cards, a pile of cell phones. He had a small box of weed and pills and powder separated into tiny bags, then put into bigger bags. Under the mattress, tucked into the box spring, was a metal box that contained more cash than she made in six months. So tempted to take the box, but she put it back.

Sidra returned to the kitchen and sat down. Casey leaned forward at the kitchen table, listening to what Petra said. His voice was gentle and calm, and he gave Sidra a couple of strange looks that she didn't understand. Whatever information he got, seemed to make him happy.

Dad would always tell her to never let her guard down. Maybe she did because Casey was there, all relaxed as he spoke with Petra. But this is what Dad meant. Anything bad that could happen was going to happen really fast.

The back door swung open, and a chick walked in. Casey stood up fast and pulled his gun, as the chick pulled hers. Then they both began shouting at each other in Spanish. She was waving the gun around, Petra said something about that, and then the chick bent over, hands on her knees to look Petra in the eyes. Her back fully exposed to Casey, and he did nothing except lower his gun.

She had on black jeans and a black t-shirt. One side of her head was shaved to the scalp, and the other side had black hair down to her shoulder. She had skin as light as Sidra's, but those dark brown eyes could have been the devil's.

Sidra said, "Can we speak English here?"

The chick turned to her. "You've dodged two of my people."

"Who the fuck are you?"

The chick looked at Casey. "Who the fuck am I?" and then she took two steps toward Sidra, leaned closer, said, "I'm the one you should be worried about."

Sidra stood up, which put them face to face. "You can kick my ass and I guarantee I can kick yours, so how about you use your gun or back the fuck up." For a minute, she puffed out her chest and licked her bottom lip as she looked Sidra up and down.

A minute passed, then Casey tried to grab her by the arm. He ended up taking her gun, which pissed her off even more, then he shoved her down into the chair he'd been sitting in.

Petra made the sign of the cross and left the kitchen.

"Where the fuck have you been hiding?" the chick said. She looked white, but had a Latino accent. A huge spider tattoo was on the back of her head, with little spiders crawling behind it. The name Cameo was written across the side of her neck in a swirly script. Her fingernails were black with the tips red, like she'd dipped them in blood.

Casey dropped the magazine out of the gun he'd taken off of her and set it down on the table. He sat down, took the bullet out of the chamber and held it between his fingers. Then, for a long minute, he tapped the bullet on the table. Tap tap tap. Didn't take his eyes off her. Lorenzo Marquez wanted Cameo dead. Said he'd give Casey his son for that. With one hand he held his gun on Cameo. With the other, her own bullet.

"You send Antonio Guzman to follow me?"

Cameo tilted her head and looked concerned. "Don't tell me you killed him."

"Police picked him up in Fayetteville. I take it you sent him?"

"I have a couple of people missing right now that I've sent to find you in one way or another."

"People have been following me."

"People have been looking for you. I don't appreciate what you did to Juanito. Did you kill Steven?"

"I don't know who that is."

"Edgar?"

When Casey didn't answer, Cameo lifted her foot and kicked him in the knee. Casey didn't move, looked right at her and kept on tapping the bullet on the table. Sidra didn't say anything, tried to make herself disappear back into the chair.

"Did you kill him?" Cameo asked again.

Casey didn't answer the question. He said, "I'm only going to ask you this once. Where is my son?"

"Fuck, Casey." Cameo attempted to stand up. Casey looped his foot through the chair's foot hold and pulled it, causing her to stumble back.

The look in his eyes was like something died inside of him. He said, "I don't care where you work or who you piss off. Who you fuck or who you take. I don't care who you kill or how you make your money. Somebody needs to get me my son."

"You took two hundred grand from Nacho. He's pissed off."

"He killed my wife."

"Wasn't much of a wife the way she used to fuck everybody."

205

With that, Casey slapped her out of the chair. Slapped her hard enough that she fell to the floor and blood dripped down her nose. Cameo put her hand up, either to block the next blow or hit him when he came for her.

Sidra said, "Can we stop this?" and stood up.

Casey said, "Stop what? This is it. This is me getting my son back. You can't handle that, go the fuck home." For a brief moment, Casey closed his eyes when he realized he'd snapped at her. He gave her an apologetic look, but it was too late.

Cameo stood up. "Why don't you both go the fuck home." She grabbed a dishrag to wipe her bloody nose.

"Where's my son, Cameo?"

Cameo gave Casey a cold hard stare. "Me and you. Let's go talk to Nacho and he can tell you."

Casey said, "Watch your back. Lorenzo Marquez wants you dead."

"Yeah, well, we ain't partners no more," Cameo said. "I guess you need to pick your side."

They were walking down the steps when Casey said, "Do I need to walk home?"

Sidra didn't answer him.

# Chapter 19

**Domestic cases were** always hard to deal with, and for the next few days Sidra kept her head down because Shackelford Investigations was a business and money needed to come in. The need to keep looking for Lydia pulled at her, and while she thought of Brandon, she had to leave it up to Casey to find his own son.

Sure, she could go gallivanting around Georgia and knocking on doors, but there were other assignments that needed to get closed. The whole family was in and out of Shackelford all day long. Sidra helped Mitchell with surveillance of a dog-napping case, which was great, when they found the dog in six hours. Then a Granny contacted them because her son stole her daddy's 1920 victrola record player right out of her house the other day when she went to the doctor, and she needed Shackelford to find it. Mitchell was still working on that one. Daley needed help with digging up information on a child custody case, and Sidra drove all the way to Athens to talk to the child's grandmother and get a stack of phone records she'd printed out. Woolsey was knee-deep in going through emails from a company about digital theft, and he was pissed off because they didn't have any policies in place. How does a company that has fifty plus employees not have a policy explaining that they are not allowed to sell digital information to a competitor? "Stupid people make us money," Woolsey had said.

Amy had her hands in so many pots, no one could keep up with her. She helped her husband Ian with his website business, kept up with her two children, worked with a nonprofit organization to help get young girls off the streets, and then, her most elusive work was with a company that used the dark web to help catch pedophiles. Amy was good at getting into the mind of a pedophile, and that was something Sidra couldn't understand.

Mom was the Ops manager of the business, strict about organization and communication. She babysat when she needed to, had lunch with Aunt Daphne once a week, kept up with the local gossip, found time to bring lunch to the fire department down the street, and most importantly she brought in a lot of work through word of mouth. Still, Mom hadn't stopped fussing about toilet paper for five minutes because no one told her they were out.

"It's like everyone wants to come here and take a crap," she said.

Daley and Sidra sat in the office and caught the brunt of Mom's ranting, because no one else was there. He sat across from her, his cap backwards on his head.

He yelled to Mom, "You can tear up some old bed sheets and use those."

"You're an idiot," Mom said, walking down the hall, then stood in the doorway. "That's how I ended up dropping you so many times as a baby."

"Not enough," Sidra said. The whiskey and sweet tea she'd been drinking was nearly gone. She didn't mind warm drinks, even on a hot summer day. She found the liquor refreshing. Mind-blowing, in fact. The jar had been sitting there long enough that the condensation on the outside dried up.

When Mom left, she was in the kitchen. They could hear her all the way down the hall. Something about someone left one bite of ice cream in the container, and whoever this take out belongs to, it's molded.

Daley held up his fingers to his head like a gun. Pulled the trigger. "I wouldn't have to listen to this if I had a real job."

"Stuff like this doesn't happen in a real office."

Mom walked back into the office, said to Daley, "When you're done, you go clean that mud off the back steps from your muddy boots."

"I thought I was your favorite."

"You are," Mom said, her voice full of sarcasm. "And you—" she pointed to Sidra. "Go get some toilet paper before you go home today." Then the phone rang. Mom took it out of her back pocket, said, "Shackelford Investigations. How may I help you?" in a voice that didn't sound like the devil.

Daley stood up. "How funny would it be if I wrote a handbook, specifically mentioning non-verbal abuse in the workplace?"

Sidra smiled. "Pretend Woolsey wrote it, and Mom'll sign it."

"I'll go get toilet paper if you hose off the back steps."

"Sure."

"You're still on for tonight, right?"

"Yeah," she said. He was talking about tonight's surveillance. She hadn't stopped for four days straight, had been running on five hours of sleep from last night.

"I talked to Brady this morning," Daley said.

Sidra popped her head up, hid the fury as she picked up the Mason jar. "Stay away from him," she said. "I think you caused enough problems in his life."

Daley grabbed a backpack, put an iPad in there, and started shoving a few files behind that. "He and I were both at fault. Stop blaming me for something that happened thirteen years ago. Maybe if you would have stuck around instead of running away, he would feel a little more support from you."

"You left too, asshole."

"I joined the Army."

"Oh, big macho guy puts a guy in a wheelchair, then joins the army. If that's how you deal with your guilt, so be it."

"What is your problem? You're just as bitchy as Mom."

"Don't let her hear you say that." Sidra leaned back in her chair and sighed. "You ever feel like you want to do something and can't?"

"Yeah. Is this about the drug dealer's missing boy?"

"He's not a drug dealer. Not anymore. It's not just him. Lydia Desmond is still missing. The police haven't gotten any more information. It's like she just disappeared."

"Don't make yourself miserable with things that are out of your control. You've got to learn to desensitize yourself, otherwise it will bring you down faster than an elephant snowballing down a mountain in Alaska."

She looked at him. "Elephants don't live in Alaska."

"It's an analogy."

"An analogy?"

"Yeah."

"Mom's right, you're an idiot."

After Daley left, Sidra hit the dining room for more whiskey then topped it off with sweet tea. She closed her eyes and let the whiskey go down. At ten this morning, she'd told herself it wasn't too early to drink. Now it was one o'clock, and she was on her third. At least her brain slowed down, and she didn't feel as pissed off as she had been when she woke up.

She stepped outside and unwrapped the hose and began spraying off the mud from *Mitchell's* boots, not Daley's. Mom had already mopped the kitchen this morning. That's what started it.

Mom stuck her head outside. "I told Daley to do that."

"Mom, what's wrong?"

"Nothing," she said. "It's just that y'all come in here and make yourselves so comfortable that you forget this is my home."

"Well, I'm not the one who decided to put Shackelford Investigations in your home." Sidra sprayed the walkway from the steps to the driveway. "If you need more help, just ask. You don't have to yell at us."

"I'm not yelling, Sidra." She folded her arms across her chest. "And don't miss the mud that's on the other side." When Sidra turned, she caught Mom with some water, not a full spray, just enough to splash her with a few drops. "You're as bad as your brothers," Mom said, a laugh in her voice.

Back in the office, Sidra continued with her computer work, but couldn't focus on a damn thing. She found herself running a criminal background report on Casey Lincoln. This is when things became obsessive. One check led to another, then another, and before Sidra realized it, three hours had passed and she'd gathered pages and pages of information on Casey Lincoln and his wife Joanna. At twenty-seven, she was ten years younger than Casey.

Sidra didn't know where Casey was born, but she found an elementary school record in Arizona. She'd have to do criminal checks in every state if she wanted the information, but she wasn't spending that kind of money. He'd also lived in Texas for four years prior to moving to Georgia. He had no prior arrests in Georgia. His name only popped up as being in association with the Marquez family and multiple drug dealers. While he didn't have any warrants out in his name, his name popped up multiple times in Gwinnett County, Fulton County, and Clayton County. Major counties in Georgia's drug trafficking.

Not being able to stop herself, Sidra moved on to Dani Cameo, who had been part of the Georgia foster care system, from which she ran away when she was fifteen. While the records were sealed because Dani was a minor, Sidra found out her name was Danielle Cameo Roberts. She was thirty-five, but damn, she didn't show it. Sidra would have guessed her younger the way she carried herself and the way she dressed, the half shaved head and tattoos. Cameo studied at Georgia College of Law in Atlanta. Which was surprising.

How'd she pay for law school? And how did she end up dealing drugs?

Sidra searched more sites, paid for another criminal background check, and found that Dani Cameo spent a year in jail in Savannah awaiting a trial for a murder that she was later found not guilty. She was arrested in connection with the sale of drugs that she was later found not guilty. In Spalding county she had three arrests for drugs, one arrest for attempted kidnapping, one arrest for misconduct in public, whatever that was. All charges were dropped.

When Dad got home, she showed him the records. "What's this mean?"

Dad looked at the multiple charges, going between the four pages, put on his reading glasses. "Either they found she didn't commit the crimes, or she turned someone else in and they let her go." Dad shrugged. "Hard to say without the details. This is a rabbit hole, you know?"

"Like an elephant snowballing down a mountain in Alaska," she said.

"You get that one from Daley?"

"Yep." They laughed. Then she told him about getting followed and meeting Dani Cameo.

"These people," Dad said, and shook his head. "They don't think what they're doing is wrong. And if she works for Nacho Marquez, he probably paid to get her out of charges if he knows the right people."

"And Lydia Desmond?"

Dad put his hand on hers. "Trust me when I tell you I know what it feels like for a daughter to go missing. And you need to trust me when I say you need to let the police handle this."

Ignoring him, she said, "Can I talk to Tanner Wells about it?"

"Then what?"

"I don't know, Dad. I guess I'll ask Amy about organizations that help deal with human trafficking or see if Lydia's photo pops up in the dark. Benny Valentino mentioned Tanner Wells's name when I was in the paintball warehouse. That's why I went to talk to him that day. I'm just trying to figure this all out."

"You're not going to let this go, are you?"

"Would you?"

***

Tanner Wells was busy, and this time she needed an appointment to speak with him. Sidra met with him in the morning and oddly enough, he didn't want to meet in his office. Rudolf's was a little restaurant in Peachtree City that had a fantastic brunch. The atmosphere was quiet and casual, but the menu was expensive. $15.99 for eggs benedict. She could go down to Clemmie's, get the same thing for half the price.

Sidra met Tanner at a table at the back of the restaurant. Sunlight poured in from the windows along the front and traffic was still terrible at this time. She had on her nice suit with a rose pink blouse under the jacket.

"Hi," she said, and Tanner stood to shake her hand. A nice gentleman, he helped her out of the suit jacket, draped it over the back of her chair which he'd already pulled out. Tanner looked nice in his navy suit, the blue shirt he'd chosen matched his eyes. His hair was meticulously combed, his smile perfect, showing just the right amount of perfectly white teeth. Tanner Wells was such a pretty man. But Tanner Wells liked the way he looked and used that to his advantage.

"Thanks for agreeing to meet me here," Tanner said. "I knew I'd have a late day today and sometimes I just can't seem to get started because my office walls are closing in on me."

"I'm the one who's thankful that you took time out of your schedule. Do you mind my asking why Peachtree City?"

"Oh," Tanner said, smiling at her confusion. "I live here. I work in Spalding but I grew up here. Mama and Daddy retired over near West Point Lake, but I'm still here. Do you remember my daddy?"

"Mayor of Peachtree City for six years. He and your grandfather had a lot to do with the planning of the city."

A waitress came over to take their order. Tanner got a coffee, Sidra a mimosa. When drinks arrived, they ordered food. Tanner a coconut mango muffin and a side of scrambled egg whites. Sidra a stack of blueberry pancakes and a side of bacon.

"Tell me," he said, adding a packet of sweetener into his coffee. "How did you end up being a private investigator?"

"I suppose I was destined for it. I didn't always work for Shackelford, though. It took me a little while to get my footing."

Tanner smiled that pretty boy smile. "Weren't you the big soccer star around here?"

Sidra nodded. "I forget that a hundred thousand plus citizens in a county is still considered small town living. You can't throw a rock without hitting someone that knows somebody."

"I'm amazed at the very idea," Tanner said. "I meet people in other counties that have cousins I went to school with in Peachtree City. The other day, I met a man in Atlanta who was the brother of one of my schoolteachers. Isn't that something?"

Their brunch arrived, Tanner smiling ever so politely at the young waitress.

"What about you? Did you always want to follow in your dad's footsteps?"

"I think so," Tanner said. "He always made it seem so easy. By the time I graduated high school, it was just a given I'd end up in law school. Is that why you wanted to meet with me to talk about my charming life experiences?"

"As interesting as you are, not really." Sidra poured syrup on her pancakes. "I don't know how well your memory serves you, but I was wondering if you can tell me anything about a Danielle Cameo Roberts? Goes by Dani Cameo?"

Sidra wasn't looking for it, had barely noticed it, and would have missed it had she been looking down. But Tanner flinched. For a moment his eyes fluttered, almost playing it off as confusion to the question.

Tanner shrugged, then cut into his muffin with a fork. "The name doesn't sound familiar. I don't forget

217

faces, though," he said with a smile. "But the name's not familiar."

"She works with the Marquez family." She knew he was familiar with them. He's the one that did the paperwork and helped prosecute the gang members.

Tanner chewed, took a sip of coffee, and chewed some more.

"I ask because she's had multiple charges filed against her that were dropped."

"I'd be more than happy to look into it for you if you'd like. But I can assure you we have a solid team out there. If charges were dropped, there wasn't enough to prosecute her."

When he said that, Sidra remembered their last conversation. He'd told her he would look into Bruce Zeller and then told Harvey she'd made accusations about no one doing anything about missing people.

"I'm sorry if we got off on the wrong foot last time. I'm not trying to make you or anyone feel defensive, it's just that I've got to ask questions in order to get answers."

"I understand," he said, his voice slow and charming. "No harm done."

"Can I assume that when I leave here, you won't be calling Harvey?"

"Then I'll assume you can handle your own business. How are the pancakes?"

"Delicious," she said, which wasn't a lie. For the price, the pancakes better do more than digest in her stomach. "What else can you tell me about the Marquez family?"

"From the outside, they appear to be clean business owners. Upstanding citizens. They donate a lot of money to various charities. Ignacio Marquez is on a building committee in Atlanta. They're working with some organizations to help with public housing, cleaning up the streets, things like that."

"And from the inside, they're drug dealers and human traffickers."

Tanner sipped his coffee. "In a nutshell. We aren't always aware of what they're doing because they change strategy so much. A lot of times the smaller gangs take the fall for what the bigger players actually put into action."

"Well, I heard from a bird that Dani Cameo is in charge of the Spalding County area all the way down south to Lowndes. And I just find it odd that she's been arrested and let go." Sidra shrugged. "Sounds to me like she's in someone's pocket."

Tanner tilted his head, narrowed his eyes at her. "In my experience, everyone who's worked any of these cases is very passionate about getting the crime off the streets. You should know that," he said. "These criminals get smarter and we have to change gears fast just to keep up with prosecuting them all. Seems like we're always two steps behind."

What she didn't want to do was ask the next question. "What can you tell me about Casey Lincoln?"

219

Tanner stared at her for a long moment. "Where are you getting all of this?"

"Come on, Tanner, I'm an investigator. My family is excellent at what we do."

"I guess what I mean is why? Because the last time we spoke, you said Diane Hutchinson was dead. What are you trying to dig up?"

"That depends?"

"On what?"

"Whatever people are trying to hide."

Tanner gave her that pretty boy smile. "You are something else. I bet you give your daddy hell."

"Uh huh," she said. "And I bet you make your mama proud."

Tanner laughed like it was the funniest thing he'd heard all year. They finished their food, and Tanner paid the bill. In the parking lot, he said, "I sure hope we can do this again."

"I'd love to," she said, and meant it.

# Chapter 20

**Investigating was looking** at the surface of multiple things, digging deeper and deeper until you find something that connects the pieces, like getting lost in a dark cave with a hundred ways to go, and suddenly walking out into sunlight.

All she needed was a way in to expose where the Marquezes had Brandon and Lydia Desmond.

Sidra hadn't looked into Benny Valentino or Bruce Zeller deep enough. She'd have to get on the ground and go talk to people. Yet, she'd probably end up with someone else coming to her house in the middle of the night.

Take out Cameo and Casey gets his son back.

Sounds so easy.

Sidra had more questions than answers. Like, where did Cameo live? And all the Marquezes? Where did Benny live? How did Casey find Diane Hutchinson? She thought about the map Casey had hanging on the wall in his cabin with all the push pins. He was taking people out. One drug house at a time. There were so many street gang wars going on that no one had figured Casey hit the houses.

Casey had answers to her questions, but the two of them weren't on the same page.

Before she left Rudolf's parking lot, she took out a notebook and started making more notes. Checked some boxes. Drew a big circle around Tanner Wells's name. She could get more inside information from him if she wanted to, she could tell by the way he looked at her.

\*\*\*

Sidra stood on Casey's front porch and watched a spider roll an insect into a nice little ball, then crawl up the web to wait for more unsuspecting victims. When he answered, she walked right in and went straight to his map. "What are all the pins?"

"I thought you weren't talking to me." He slammed the door shut and walked over, took up all the space. "The red pins are houses that I know of. We used them to hold product. Those houses are pretty solid places in the business. The blue ones we used to make deals. You don't make exchanges where you keep product. Deals, meetings, offices... shit like that."

Sidra looked at the map. Atlanta was the most concentrated, but he'd also put pins in areas down major highways. "Forsyth's green. La Sombra is in Forsyth. Is the green legit businesses?" There were eight green pins.

"Aren't you the smart one."

Sidra looked at him, her arms folded across her chest. "What are their businesses again?"

"Two Restaurants. Two strip clubs. A laundromat. Two shitty hotels, one in Atlanta and one in Macon. Plus, they own a property management company in Atlanta called GTPM."

Sidra nodded. "And what are the yellow pins?"

"Where I think they live. I worked for Nacho for eight years and I've never been to his house, but I think it's in Atlanta. Lorenzo lives here. Angel here. His sister, Teresa, lives here. I don't know where Hector lives, but I think he and Angel share a home. The black pins are the places I took out."

There were four black pins on the map.

"How'd you get Diane Hutchinson?"

"Lucky break."

Sidra threw her hands up. "That's what the fucking problem is. You lie to me and I can't help you." Her hair had been down, and she pulled it all to the front and braided it, the end going nearly to her waist. "Still no answer?" She flung the braid over her shoulder and walked away. "We need to try this again. In my honest opinion, you can't keep going to these places and shooting them out. You're either going to get yourself killed or end up in prison. Where does that leave Brandon?"

Casey worked his jaw. She could tell that all of this was getting to him. He took a deep breath, still didn't say anything.

"And honestly. What's your plan when you get him back? Hide out here for the rest of your life? Stay on the run with a kid? What's the plan?"

"I haven't thought that far." Casey looked down at his bare feet, so conflicted he looked like he wanted to punch something which didn't surprise her considering his history. He met her eyes. "Diane lived in Fulton County. I followed her home one day after she met with her lawyer."

"I just had a meeting with Tanner Wells."

"Is that why you look so pretty?"

The question threw her off. Still dressed in slacks and a pink silk blouse, she didn't feel pretty. She tried for the professional look, but not pretty. "Tanner said he didn't know you or Cameo." Actually, he'd deflected the question when she asked about Casey.

"Why were you asking Tanner Wells about us?"

"For information. Cameo specifically because she'd been arrested multiple times, and the charges were dropped. He said he didn't recognize the name."

"Really?"

"Why's that surprise you?"

"Because she got money from his family right after high school."

"And you couldn't tell me this before?"

\*\*\*

224

Sidra drove straight to the Spalding District Attorney's office, asked Jolene Pike if Tanner Wells was in his office.

"Um," Ms. Pike started, then Sidra walked down the hall. "I think he's on a phone call," Ms. Pike called from behind her.

Tanner Wells's office door was open, and he wasn't on the phone. He stood at a wall of bookcases and had a file open in his hand.

She walked over to him, and Tanner looked up.

He smiled, surprised to see her. "Didn't think I'd see you so soon."

"I have a bone to pick with you." Sidra closed the space between them. "You said you didn't know Dani Cameo? Now, I can go digging, but I can get answers a lot faster from you. Did your family give her money years ago?"

Tanner didn't look mad or caught in a lie. But his smile faded, and he tilted his head at the question as if he was trying to figure out how to answer it. He nodded, closed the file in his hands. "If you have to dig up information, that means you're unaware of the details. Which means someone told you this. Where'd you hear it?"

"Does it matter?"

"No," he said, and sighed heavily. "It's an embarrassment, honestly. Every year my daddy awards a student a full scholarship to a school of their choice, give or take some stipulations, of course. And

Danielle Roberts received a scholarship from the Calvin Wells Organization. She went to law school, my daddy got her a job. And then she decided to work for the Marquez family. Just goes to show what type of person she truly is."

"Why didn't you just tell me?"

"Like I said, it's an embarrassment. A scholarship that's been redacted out of the books. She went to law school and gets away on a lot of technicalities. She's not stupid."

"Sorry to barge in on you like I did."

"No trouble." Tanner leaned against the bookshelf, stretched his legs out and crossed one over the other. "Maybe you'd like to have dinner with me and we can discuss it further. I'd love it if you joined me."

"I'm not really interested in talking about politics."

"Neither am I," he said, and gave her that smile again. "But you didn't say no to dinner, did you?"

Sidra smiled, looked down at her scuffed dress shoes. Tanner reached over and lifted her chin, the touch sending a shock down her spine. "Nothing serious," he said, his voice soft. "La Paz has fantastic margaritas."

"And a patio and good salsa."

His thumb rubbed her chin before he dropped his hand. "Can I pick you up at six?"

"Casual," Sidra said. "I'll meet you there."

When Sidra walked back down the hallway, Jolene Pike stood there. She said, "Keep your eye on that one."

Oh, she would. Like a hawk.

***

Halfway through dinner, they were laughing about things their parents told them as kids, and Tanner said, "For nearly a year my daddy had me convinced we had a pet tiger that only came out at night. And I would put out food and every morning the food would disappear. Here I was, five years old, trying to catch a tiger with cat food."

They were sitting on the patio, this Georgia summer weather was like breathing in a sauna. But after multiple drinks, she seemed to forget the heat because they were alone on the patio and getting loud with laughter.

"My parents told us," Sidra said, "that the only way we could get a dog was to get rid of one of the kids. Like someone had to go. So we spent an entire summer fighting over who we'd get rid of so we could get a dog. I think it was my parent's way of trying to figure out who really liked one another."

"So who got voted out?"

"Me! I've never forgiven those assholes for trying to get rid of me for a dog. Then we were so mad because we never got the dog. Then after that, my brother found this mangy dog and my dad made us find him a new home, but we kept him in the garage for like two weeks before he found out. You should have seen us

227

sneaking the dog around so Mom and Dad wouldn't find out."

They drank some more.

"I can't imagine," Tanner said, "growing up in a house with so many brothers and sisters."

"It was something. The biggest fights were over stolen goods. I buried my sister's hairbrush in the backyard just so I wouldn't get in trouble for stealing it."

They'd shared fajitas, and eaten the entire dish, except for a few grilled onions on the skillet. Tanner said, "Me and a buddy of mine were on our way through Florida. This was right out of college. We'd both just graduated from law school. And I'm flying down the interstate, and he yells for me to watch out. Well, I run over this alligator and I swear I thought we were going to flip over. And when I look in the rearview mirror, that damn alligator gives me a big 'fuck you' and kept on walking."

"Jesus. How big was the alligator?"

"From here to the street," he said, and they laughed. Tanner leaned back in his chair casually, his outstretched legs touched Sidra's and she leaned in a little closer to him at the corner of the table. They each ordered another margarita, and she was enjoying herself with Tanner, something she hadn't done in a really long time. There was this comfortableness that he gave off, and maybe that was because he could communicate with people, but so did she. She was attracted to him in a way that seemed okay. Safe. Not nearly the same way she thought she was attracted to Casey Lincoln. Casey was bad news. He killed people and slapped women out of their chairs.

Tanner gave off a different kind of magnetism. His confidence was sexy and powerful, and the way he looked at her now, his smile had changed. From friendly to flirty. As he drank, his southern drawl seemed more prominent. A good ol' southern boy.

He touched her arm, said, "You okay there?"

"I'm great."

"You kinda zoned out."

"Nope. Just staring," she said, and blushed.

"You want to go to the movies?" Tanner said.

"The movies?"

Tanner looked at his phone. "We have time. I've been dying to see the new Marvel movie."

"Let's go." Movies were the worst dates. No, this wasn't a date. This was something casual. Dinner and now movies. She was flexible.

They sat in the dark theater, Tanner holding her hand the whole time and Sidra felt like she was sixteen all over again. Thoughts of Brady swirled through her head.

This was nice. And it was comfortable, and she let the frustrations escape her as she watched the movie with Tanner. He squeezed her hand when he thought the hero was going to die.

229

And then he drove back to La Paz so Sidra could get her van. Before she got out, he touched her arm. He said, "I had a great time tonight."

"Me too."

"I can call out sick tomorrow," he said, and Sidra laughed. "I'm going to give you my address and if you want to come over, I'll still be up."

"Okay," Sidra said. Tanner leaned over, his face so close his body heat radiated off of him. She closed the space and pressed her lips to his. Nothing too intense, just testing the water.

He said, "I'll leave the front door unlocked."

"How about you be a gentleman and drive me to your place?" He kissed her again, this time with a little more oomph to it. Sidra took a deep breath, said, "Or we can sit in your car and be obscene here."

Tanner laughed. "That would not be good for either of us."

Tanner's house was in a nice neighborhood in Peachtree City. He put the car in the garage, and Sidra followed him inside. The place was clean, everything white, black, or brown. Nice art hung on the walls.

Tanner lifted a remote control and blues music began to play, something light and sexy and it made her smile. She would have definitely pegged Tanner for a blues guy. He was sharp.

"Can I get you something to drink? Then I'll give you a tour of the place."

He made her a strong drink, and she followed him around as he held her hand and walked her through the house. There were three floors. The basement had beautiful exposed beams and tiled floor, with its own large workout area and a bar. There were a few closed doors that Tanner didn't open. An in-ground pool outside and a hot tub built into a brick patio with a fireplace was in the middle of the yard with lights bright enough to see the entire backyard.

"This is nice," Sidra said, and thought about money she didn't have.

Back upstairs, he walked her through the living room, his large office, which contained a lot of pieces from overseas. "I got this in Africa." He showed her a gorgeous wood carving of a giraffe. He had pottery and art. Hand-blown glass. A basket filled with huge, painted eggs. Sidra sipped her drink as he pointed out more of his collection. She loved this stuff. Parts of history that told its own story.

Sidra pointed out a turquoise mask with gold teeth and jade eyes. "This is from Mexico, is it not?"

"It is," he said, surprised she knew. "It's not a replica piece, and it's worth a lot of money."

Tanner had a lot of books, too. Old books. She could sit in here and read for hours. Tanner turned her around and kissed her, her breath slightly knocked out of her as it took her by surprise. She closed her eyes and pulled him closer, thought about ripping his clothes off right there in his office. But then Tanner pulled away, and smiled, said, "One more," and held up his glass.

In the living room, Tanner said, "Come here," and he pulled her closer, the two of them swaying back and forth with the music, the sound soothing. He wrapped his hand around her back, and kissed her neck, her cheek, and finally finding her mouth. As they danced, he pulled her close, and kissed her again. When they came up for air, she didn't know how much longer she could take.

Sidra thought about all the alcohol she'd had today. First with the mimosa at brunch. She declined the beer Casey offered. Did she drink anything between that and dinner? She'd thought about a drink at home, but knew she'd have a margarita with Tanner and told herself no. Then she had two mango margaritas. Both 12 oz. Maybe they were strong as fuck, she didn't know. And even if Tanner gave her straight liquor, Sidra had been drinking pretty heavily for the last thirteen years.

"Right after the baby," she said to Tanner, who wouldn't keep still.

"What?" he said, that smile. That beautiful smile and his pretty boy face.

"Kiss me," she said, and he did.

One drink. Two drinks.

"This one," she said, and held up her glass. That wasn't enough to make her feel like this. "Like this."

Why the fuck did she feel like she'd been under anesthesia, that good, happy, I-feel-like-I-could-fly feeling, and then finished it off with a bottle of vodka? The last thing she remembered was telling Tanner she felt good and sliding her hand under his shirt.

# Chapter 21

**Sidra woke up** naked in an unfamiliar place. An enormous bed with fluffy white sheets swallowed her. Sunlight poured in from the large sliding glass door. She smelled vanilla and something cooking. Her head hurt, so she closed her eyes and tried to remember. But what? She couldn't sit up just yet and let a wave of nausea roll over her. She wanted to go back to sleep, but she was so bothered by a gut-wrenching ache, like she'd been punched in the soul.

The clock on the bedside table read 9:45 a.m.

She sat up and rolled her neck. Her body ached in ways she hadn't felt since last year's soccer match. The ache of being constantly bumped against while running for a ball. Sidra pulled the sheets, noticed a bruise on her inner thigh. Another smaller one on her calf.

*What the fuck happened?*

She got out of the bed, stood up on wobbly legs. Reached down to touch between her legs, something she'd done enough times that she'd notice anything unusual. Nothing hurt. She wasn't bleeding or in pain.

Her breathing came in short takes because she couldn't remember.

*She couldn't remember.*

Her clothes were folded neatly in a chair on the other side of the bed. She didn't know why seeing her folded clothes pissed her off. Why was she pissed off? Because she'd gotten so drunk so fast that she couldn't remember anything?

She stopped the tears from welling in her eyes as she put on her clothes. Her body felt sore, like she'd been working out with cold muscles, like they were refusing to cooperate.

In the kitchen she found Tanner, dressed in suit pants and a nice shirt, his tie draped around his neck. "Good morning," he said, and flashed her a smile. A smile that didn't seem so attractive right now. "I made pancakes. Are you hungry?" He poured her a glass of orange juice and set it on the bar.

"What happened?" she said.

He walked around the counter with two plates of pancakes. Pulled out a chair for her to sit in, and brought her juice over. Sidra sat down and asked again, "What happened last night?"

Why was he so cheery? He forked up a bite of pancake and shoved it into his mouth. "I don't think I've ever met anyone like you. You were fun."

Sidra opened her mouth to say something, but then shut it.

235

He said, "You ever think about moving to the beach and out of the city? I think about it sometimes. Waking up with the sound of the ocean, and the birds, and lounging around all day in the sand."

"Sounds nice." She cut a piece of pancake, but could barely focus on the food.

"My family owns a beach house in Savannah. It's beautiful out there in the morning. I'd love to have you sometime."

She couldn't look at him, and when he reached over to touch her hand, she nearly flinched and wasn't sure why. "You a little quiet in the mornings? I can make coffee. Would you like some?"

She put her hands in her lap, swallowed the lump in her throat. "No, thanks." She finally looked at him. Something had changed. His eyes seemed brighter, his voice a little louder. "It's been a while," she said.

Tanner let out a light laugh. "Could have fooled me."

An embarrassment crept over her, a white-hot electric charge that had the hair on her neck stand up.

"I have to leave soon." Tanner patted her hand. "Will you be ready for me to drop you off?"

Sidra nodded, tried to eat some of the pancake, but she couldn't. The juice didn't look good either. She was going to throw up. "I'm going to use the bathroom." She got up and bolted to the bathroom down the hall, where she threw up.

Tanner walked in. "Are you okay?" He leaned over her.

"I'm fine."

"You drank a lot last night."

*No, I didn't.* "I'm sorry. Can you give me a minute, please?"

"Of course." Tanner walked out, shutting the door behind him. Sidra got up and locked it. Took in deep breaths, but wanted to get out of the small space for fear she'd have a panic attack. What the fuck happened last night?

Sidra wiped her mouth with toilet paper. Opened the cabinet under the sink. One side was stocked with white, fluffy towels. The other side had extra toilet paper, mouthwash, a few extra toothbrushes. She pulled out one of the hand towels, wet it, and cleaned her face. Looked at herself in the mirror.

*You've got to stop drinking. Today, you have got to stop drinking.*

"Sidra, honey, are you okay in there?"

*Honey?*

"Yeah. I'll be out in a second."

She unlatched the window and slid it open to look for the magnet piece for the alarm. This bathroom was on the ground floor, so of course it would have one. Sidra used her fingernails to pry the little button sensor out of the frame. Thinking as fast as she could, she lay a folded hand towel on the windowsill and closed the window so that the magnet button piece she pulled out was held in place with the towel.

237

With shaking hands, Sidra flushed the toilet and looked around. She had to get out of there. Act normal. But what was that? She told herself to play the part. The part where she had to act like she didn't know that Tanner Wells drugged her last night.

***

Playing it off as a rough night of too much drinking, Sidra let Tanner kiss her goodbye with a promise they'd be in touch. She wanted to scream. Punch him. Run him over with her van. After he left, Sidra sat in La Paz's parking lot, trying to catch her breath.

This had never happened to her before.

She'd drank in high school, just like all the other kids. The cold hard truth was that after she'd returned from her time away—that's what she thought of it as, her time away when she had the baby—drinking was an everyday affair.

But this?

Not remembering a damn thing?

Sidra drove back to Tanner's house. When they left, he didn't set an alarm, but that didn't mean he couldn't do so using his phone. She parked on the street just past his driveway and made her way around the house. All the houses were large brick three story monstrosities in a very rich neighborhood.

Around the back of Tanner's house, she was able to get past a black iron fence that secured the place. The pool was off to the left, with the hot tub and fireplace.

Trees lined the back that obscured the neighbor's backyard. It was nearly eleven, and everything seemed quiet.

Her heart pounded in her chest as she pulled the screen off the window. She'd stopped at a pharmacy for super glue, took it out of her pocket and popped the lid off. Next, she slid the window up, and kept the magnet sensor connected to its other part, then carefully super glued it in place.

With free hands, she climbed in through the bathroom window. All she had to worry about now was the inside motion detectors that would trip a silent alarm, and the possibility of an inside camera. Working for an alarm company for six months, she saw that the alarm wasn't set, and it was also a crappy older model. Ah, the city where everyone believes they're safe.

All she wanted to do was look for the drugs he'd given her.

She'd never broken into anyone's house before, and Tanner, being in the position he was in, she could say goodbye to her life and hello to Mrs. Kitty in prison. With her heart pounding, she calmed herself down because what she really wanted to do was ransack the place. At the bar, she found nothing but liquor. Tanner had the good stuff. Knob Creek bourbon. Don Julio. Belvenie. He was stocked from the back to front with every kind of liquor available. And her family thought she was bad. One decanter bottle caught her eye. Nothing special about the bottle, it was just that it was the only one not in its original bottle. She sniffed it and smelled whiskey. She looked in drawers and cabinets, through the entire kitchen, even rummaged through the trash.

Tanner was a tidy guy, didn't have shelves stocked with a lot of food or dishes. Ate out a lot, she supposed. Single life led to loneliness, but it came with the freedom of not having to worry about anyone else. Come and go as you pleased. Drug someone if the mood struck.

And that's what bothered her. She was willing to have sex with Tanner all night long. The connection she'd felt with him, he could have talked her into anything.

Maybe he did.

His room was clean, everything folded in nice little stacks. The bathroom organized and wiped down like no one had touched a thing, like walking into a hotel room after the maid came along.

Tanner Wells didn't have any pills or medication except for a handful of over-the-counter stuff. Still, she looked inside the bottles until she was confident he had nothing hidden in there. She paid special attention to his bedroom, looking for hidden cameras. Not an expert at all in hidden cameras, but she didn't think there were any.

Then she remembered the downstairs. The third floor living area that led to the pool. The stairs led to an open living room with a sofa and a big screen TV.

She remembered, with vivid memory, Tanner bringing her down here. He'd been talking about hosting parties. To the right was a large room with various workout equipment. A small kitchenette with a bar. A spacious bathroom decorated nicely. A small guest bedroom. Then a locked room. With a metal door.

Why the metal door?

Last night, she didn't pay any attention to it at all. Did it lead to storage? This part of the house was a basement. It was all underground. The room with the metal door wouldn't lead to outside.

So what was behind the door?

She tried the knob. Pushed her body against it. A knife wouldn't jimmy the door open. She searched endlessly for keys throughout the house. Her pick locks were in the van.

Fuck it. She went for the pick locks, determined that what Tanner had drugged her with was behind this door. Feeling out of place, just knowing someone's front door camera was watching her, she moved quickly, grabbed her kit and her purse, careful of any eyes that may be watching.

In her mind, she thought about how she was going to explain to Dad why she'd been arrested as she worked the lock. *Oh, I broke into Tanner Wells's house, no big deal.* The lock didn't seem to want to budge. Took her nearly five minutes to get the lock tumblers to fall into place. Hesitated before she turned the knob.

Just a crack. Then slowly she pushed the door open. Nothing jumped out at her. She felt quickly for the light switch, flipped it on, confusion and curiosity hitting her at the same time. She wasn't sure what she was expecting, but this wasn't it. An antique, gold tufted headboard attached to a king-sized bed was against the far wall. To the left was a wooden desk with a large computer monitor, the hard drive on the floor. The walls were bare. To the right stood a tripod with a Canon DSLR attached, not much different from the one Sidra used for surveillance.

With her head tilted sideways, she tried to figure it out. The camera pointing at the bed told her it was used to photograph or video subjects in bed. The desk was bare other than the computer monitor, keyboard and mouse, and a hard drive. No camera hooked up to that. Just beyond the desk was another door. She concluded by the way the two rooms conjoined it was a closet, but she opened it up just as slowly.

Turned on the light. Now, this was interesting. Racks and racks of women's lingerie hung from hangers. This closet looked like a Victoria's Secret stock room.

The room didn't have that dark BDSM to it. In fact, everything was organized and in place. The lingerie hung from fancy hangers by style, not color. Although the room didn't have windows, it was bright with white walls. The bed had a white duvet thrown over it, but the sheets were missing.

The room was so bare.

The computer on the desk was an old HP, took a few minutes for it to boot up. And it wasn't password protected. Why would it be? It was behind a locked door.

The computer was full of files, and files named with two letters only, some included numbers. Inside the file folders were photos and videos of women who looked to be asleep on the bed, wearing bras and panties in various colors. There were no props other than a rumpled bed. But these women weren't asleep, Tanner drugged them. And they looked dead. Each file contained as many as a hundred photos.

Tanner, you fucking asshole.

In some of the photos, but not with each woman, Tanner posed himself, some naked, some wearing matching silk boxers or tight underwear, almost like a magazine spread. Her hands shook as she became enraged. She couldn't search through the files fast enough. She scrolled through, looking for something with her name, with SS, anything from last night.

Maybe he didn't have time to download the photos?

She stood in front of the camera, turned it on, and wanted to throw up. He'd dressed her in sunshine yellow lingerie with white knee boots. A hot pink lace teddy with black fishnet stockings. A red corset with thongs. And then, after these photos, there were some of Tanner himself. In some of these, he'd also dressed in women's lingerie.

Flooded with emotions, Sidra took the memory card out of the camera and put it in her pocket. In her purse, she had a flash drive and plugged that into the main hard drive, but she didn't have enough space to save everything and remembered her laptop was in the surveillance van in her backpack, so she had to go get it.

*Jesus, I'm so sorry I don't pray enough, and I promise I'll quit drinking, but please don't let Tanner come home.*

Without the proper cords, it would take her forever to download from PC to laptop via USB, but she didn't have any other choice. The first thing she did was put the memory card into her laptop, download her own photos, then she erased the memory card, even reformatted the damn thing to be sure they were erased.

Then she timed herself. Get as much as she could in thirty minutes and get out of there. Who were these women? There were at least thirty-six different women Sidra noticed so far.

Tanner Wells was going to pay for this.

# Chapter 22

**Sidra had been** weighing her options since the moment she broke into the house. Sure, she could go to the clinic and get a rape kit done. That would turn into a case of he said, she said. She could go to the police and file a report... he said, she said.

It all came down to that. She was on a so called "date" with him last night. He was a Senior Assistant with the DA's office. What were they going to do? Nothing.

He said it was consensual.

She said she was drugged.

At home, she took a long hot shower. She washed her hair and inspected her body thoroughly, examining every inch in such a protective way, yet feeling like her mind betrayed her body somehow.

Sidra got dressed, combed out her hair, and then took the picture of the baby out of the envelope. An ache crept into her chest as she looked at his tiny mouth, little eyes just slits, as she was the first thing this little guy saw after he was born. She was a comfort, if only for a short time. She'd held him and snuggled

245

him and made a promise to him she'd never forget him. *I love you*, she'd told him, and she forever would.

She tucked the picture into her back pocket and finished combing out her long hair, pulled the wet locks to the front and put it in a braid.

*You got a humming bird stuck up your rear end?* Dad had said to her. That's exactly how she felt again. She sat in the dining room at Shackelford Investigations because she'd called them into an emergency meeting.

Dad sat at the table looking over files. Daley ate leftovers he'd found in Mom's refrigerator. And when Mitchell finally walked in, he said, "Don't worry, I wasn't busy at all."

"Oh, good." Sidra bounced her foot. Touched her face. Rubbed her fingers over the tail end of her braid. A drink would calm her nerves faster than the way her life was going down the toilet.

Sidra looked over at the hutch. She took a deep breath, something catching in her throat. They were staring at her like... like she was the elephant snowballing down the mountain in Alaska.

She said, "I broke into Tanner Wells's house," then quickly held up her hand. "Let me back up." She needed to explain to them exactly what happened, in the context of what led to the break in. She needed them to understand the choices she'd made, and that she wasn't being naive when she made them. The words caught in her throat as she tried again, thinking about the lingerie in the closet, and how much she didn't remember.

"Sidra," Dad said.

"Give me a minute." She took a deep breath, cleared her throat until the tears that were about to spill disappeared. She told them about the conversation at brunch, the questions she asked, and what she thought about Tanner. She told them about what Casey had said. About the Wells's family giving Cameo money, and how Sidra visited him at his office to question him about this.

"And then he asked me to dinner, and I went. You know I can drink a lot, right?"

"How bad did you fuck things up?"

"Really, Dad? It's always me screwing up?"

"You just said, and I'll quote you, 'I broke into Tanner Wells's house', which leads me to believe you fucked up somewhere."

"Listen to me," she said. "I went to Tanner's office to talk to him. And he was so nice and he's so good looking, and he's accomplished and I felt comfortable with him. He asked me to dinner, so I met him at La Paz. We had a couple of margaritas. No big deal, right?"

"Fish bowls?" Daley said, shoveling in mashed potatoes.

"No. Mom size," Sidra said, referring to the smaller ones. "Then we went to the movies. Do you know the last time I went to the movies?" Sidra looked at Mitchell. "When we took the kids to see that robot thing three years ago. Being with Tanner was nice. And everything was so normal. Tanner Wells was the most charming, romantic guy I've been with in a long time."

"What are you getting at Sidra?"

"I know damned well that I can drink the three of you under a bus."

"Not me," Mitchell said.

"Yes, I can."

"No, you can't. Do you want to bet on it?" Mitchell said. "Let's get wingdinged now." Mitchell got up and poured whiskey into two highball glasses. He set one down in front of her. She stared at it for a minute, not touching it, but wanting it desperately. "Come on, lightweight." Mitchell downed the whiskey. Poured another. He said, "I got Granny's victrola back, by the way."

"Knock it off, you two," Dad said. "Get to your point."

"Tanner invited me over to his house and I had two drinks." Sidra held up two fingers. "Two. Do you understand two? So two margaritas, then two drinks." Sidra picked up the glass of whiskey Mitchell had poured for emphasis. "Two of these. Then I was out. Like a fucking light. He put something in my drink."

Dad leaned forward with such force, the table moved. "Did he hurt you?"

"I'm getting to that. This morning I woke up foggy, a few bruises on my thighs, but I don't know. He made me breakfast, we talked about the beach and if I didn't know better, I'd want to marry this guy."

Mitchell said, "Before you explode with my question, I believe you. But are—"

"I'm sure. I don't want to go into details about my sex life—"

"Thank you," Dad said.

"—but Tanner would have gotten laid, I swear. Why would he drug me? Something wasn't right."

"You need to file a report with the police," Dad said.

"And disappear like Diane Hutchinson? Some things don't add up. I accuse him of anything and guess what? Nothing happens. I went to dinner with him. The movies. Left my car at La Paz, probably seen on camera kissing him in his little sports car. This is the shit that happens to women and we're helpless."

Dad rubbed his face. "So you broke into his house?"

"To find the drugs he gave me."

"Like it's no big deal," Dad said. "I'm trying to keep a good business here, so the lot of you will have something of a future. You go breaking into peoples' houses—" He looked directly at Sidra. "Shooting people and calling drug dealers to cover it up. No one's going to want to do business with you. Is that the kind of business you want to run?"

"Not the kind of business I want to run," Mitchell said.

Daley turned to him. "Can you let Dad take his pants off before you kiss his ass?"

"I got something you can kiss," Mitchell said. "Tanner Wells is an all right guy."

"*Tanner Wells is an all right guy*?" Sidra repeated. "He didn't drug you and make you forget your entire night."

Mitchell thought this was funny. Pointed to her glass. "You're two behind."

"This is serious." Sidra tossed the drink back, no longer able to fight what was sitting in front of her. Her family was nuts. "You want to know what I found in a locked room in Tanner Well's house? Here, I'll show you."

She opened up her laptop and showed the photos. Not of her, of course not. Their eyes got big, a few smiles. "These women were drugged. Just like me." Dad sat back, a little uncomfortable. "And yes, I have proof of that too."

"What can I do?" Dad said.

"I don't know yet," Sidra said. She needed to figure this out. "I think he's in cahoots with the Marquez family."

"You should have joined the FBI," Dad said.

\*\*\*

Sidra brought the laptop to Amy because she'd know what to do. She stood out on the front porch as she waited. When Amy finally answered the door, Sidra walked in past her sister. "Can you look at something for me?"

250

Amy said, "Well, come right on in," and adjusted her knit top and bra strap.

"Where are the kids?"

Amy, finally done with her bra strap, said, "Summer camp. I have to pick them up at five."

The dining room was off the living room, and Sidra stuck her head in said, "Ian O'Brien. Top o' the mornin' to ya." Ian looked at her with a slanted gaze, stood there tucking his shirt into his pants with one hand and putting his glasses on with the other. "Oh, God. Did I interrupt something?"

"At least you knocked," Ian said, and Amy gave her husband a half-smirk, then moved into the kitchen.

Sidra followed her, said, "I'm sorry," and opened up the laptop.

Amy poured herself a cup of coffee. "I'll forgive you this time, but next time call. You want coffee or tea? I've got apple juice."

"No thanks. Just scroll through these and tell me what you think."

Amy fixed her coffee and when she sat down she said, "Looks like a fairytale come true."

"Have you seen any photos like these anywhere?"

"You know what I do, right?"

Amy worked with a nonprofit organization who did work in the dark web to bring home exploited women and children. "Yes."

"If you're talking about the style and the bed. No, it's not familiar." Amy didn't even flinch while looking at the photos. People became so desensitized to this sort of thing, but that didn't mean they didn't care. Not even when she saw the photos of her own sister. Amy paused, scrunched her brows, blinked, and then kept scrolling.

"What happened?" Amy said.

It made her feel good that her sister could look at these photos and tell something was wrong.

Sidra explained everything. And when Amy got to the pictures of Tanner in the lingerie, she said, "Whoa," and shook her head.

Sidra had to think. Had to come up with a plan. She felt violated in so many ways, even though she was certain Tanner hadn't raped her. Normally when two consenting people go to dinner and they drink and get flirty, they have consensual sex. It's mutual. But when one of those people unknowingly falls victim to something like this, it violates the trust.

On the legal side of things, Sidra had nothing.

She knew it would take her forever to figure out who any of these women were, if she could do that at all. They could be anyone. Runaways. Prostitutes. Normal young ladies who had no clue. Just like Sidra.

*Tanner Wells is an all right guy.*

Smart. Rich. Funny. Gorgeous.

Sidra turned the laptop so she could look through them with Amy. Seeing herself in that bed, she looked like a discarded toy. A play thing tossed aside. And she was. Would Tanner even bother to call her?

252

"Every time I see stuff like this," Amy said, "it's a glimpse into the mind of a monster. You don't unsee these things. You don't unknow them."

"I'm sorry," Sidra said. "I didn't mean to upset you." She knew Amy dealt with her emotional issues every day, getting swallowed up in a fictitious, passionate love affair with pedophiles and murderers, just to catch them on line.

And whatever happened to Amy when she was fourteen years old, she didn't talk about it. Sidra often wondered what it would have been like if Amy had never returned. There was the time and space before Amy disappeared, and the time and space after. When Amy returned, it had seemed to change them so much as a family. Changed Dad forever.

"Does it ever let you go?" Sidra said.

"No." Amy pointed at the screen. "Your pictures are different."

"I noticed that," Sidra said, "but I wasn't positive." They hadn't even looked through all of them yet.

They were sharper. More focused on specific areas of her body. Closeups of her parted lips. Fingertips on her cheek. The gold headboard with its tufted backing was blurred while the image of her in the corset was sharp and detailed. A hand resting near her belly button, just over the cesarean scar that Sidra hoped Amy wouldn't pay attention to.

Sidra scrolled through the photos of the other women again. The photos were taken without a real focal point. When someone was taking a picture of something, a face, for example, it became the center of the photograph. These, the lighting was dull, which made the photos dull.

But the ones of Sidra were different.

The photos of Sidra weren't just photos. These were photography. Focused and sharp.

Maybe Tanner had just learned how to use his camera? Or maybe he'd just bought a new camera. They hadn't even gotten through half the photos and were at number 250/872 when a selfie popped up.

"Who's that?" Amy said.

What the hell?

It was like a selfie of some sort that popped up in the middle of all the photos of Sidra. It was another female. Her eyes dark with black circles, red hair stringy and dirty. The photo seemed to be by mistake, as she wasn't exactly looking into the camera. As if set on a timer and she'd caught the wrong image. Whoever this woman was, she'd been there while Sidra was there. She could see her own hair splayed out on the bed.

"Do you remember someone else being in there?"

"I don't remember anything."

Sidra picked up her cell phone, scrolled through Facebook, and held the phone up next to the computer image. She thought about the photography, La Sombra, drugs.

"That's the same girl," Amy said.

254

"Lydia Desmond. What the hell is a missing girl doing taking photos for Tanner Wells?"

Due to the illegal way she'd obtained the photographs—breaking into Tanner's house—she'd have to do everything else right. Make sure her ass was covered.

"Lydia's been missing, what, a couple of weeks?" Amy said. "How did she get to Tanner's house? Or was she locked in the room already?"

"I don't believe the room's soundproof. If she was held in there, she wasn't desperate to get out. There wasn't anything there that looked like he would have had her tied up. Because if she was held completely against her will, she wouldn't have taken the photos. They wouldn't look like this."

"Unless she didn't have a choice." Amy sipped her coffee. "When this comes out. It's going to be a really big deal."

***

Of course Tanner Wells had no clue why she stood in his office the next day, gave her a surprised expression, and said, "What brings you by?" Sidra dressed in her suit again because she was trying to be professional, even though Tanner had taken a very unprofessional route. She wanted to claw his eyes out. Destroy him like he was a house, and she was the tornado.

Tanner came around his desk, leaned on the front, and crossed one foot over the other. Sidra stood there with her arms crossed, tried to remain calm, the flirtatious looks they'd shared completely gone. They were quiet for a minute, stared at each other, and Tanner's smile disappeared. He reached over to touch her arm, and she stepped back.

Refusing to play the part of a victim, she didn't question what he did. The facts were in front of her. "I know you drugged me and I know what you did to me in your secret room."

Tanner's face went serious. He stood a little straighter, then came to his full height to tower over her. He was used to questioning people and calling their bullshit, not the other way around. "I don't know what you're talking about."

"Why was Lydia Desmond at your house?"

Tanner flinched. "I don't know where you're getting these convoluted questions, but they're a little out of line."

"You know what I find a little out of line? You're a smooth-talking pervert."

"You didn't think I was a pervert when you were all over me."

"No, you're right. But that was before I knew your intentions and how sick you are."

"I'm sure we had the same consensual intentions. Call it sick if you want, but you were pretty damn kinky yourself." Sidra didn't say anything. Tanner said, "I think this is the part where you say you're going to the police."

"Call the police?" Sidra said. "But you didn't do anything wrong. You and I both know the police aren't going to touch you. But there are other people that will."

"Sounds like a threat."

"Where is Lydia Desmond?"

A long minute passed before he said, "You need to think about what you're saying, and I mean really think about it. You should probably go."

"No," she said, surprised she was calm. "You're going to be responsible for your actions. I have a lot of questions and you have the answers."

Tanner put on a forced smile. "Security can be here in ten seconds." He reached over and grabbed his phone.

Sidra dug into her bag. Tanner's face was full of alarm, like she was about to pull out a gun. But it was a photo. "I think the AJC may be interested in this. Fox 5. Atlanta Alive. Facebook."

Into the receiver, Tanner said, "Wrong extension. I'm sorry." He stepped forward, said through his teeth. "Where the fuck did you get that."

"There he is." Sidra pointed at him. "There he is. The real Tanner Wells. The guy who likes to drug women and take pictures of them."

He was thinking, those wheels turning every which way to try and remember his mistake. "I will have you arrested."

"On what charges?"

"I'm sure there's something." Tanner shrugged. "Why don't you get the fuck out of here."

"You fixed Dani Cameo's problems. Is that how you're in with the Marquezes? You fix their problems and you get the girls? That's a beautiful love affair. I get it. I went to your house, got drunk, *consensually* had sex with you and let you take pictures of me. Did you rape me, Tanner?" The heavy question weighed her down as Tanner choked on his misconduct.

"You were too drunk for anything."

"Drugged, you mean?"

Tanner would have had to carry her down the stairs, change her clothes, have his fun, then return her upstairs to his bed. That's a lot of premeditation to do what he did.

"Aren't you forgetting something?" Sidra said.

"Don't believe I am."

"How do I know about Lydia Desmond?"

"You're delusional."

Sidra handed him a copy of Lydia's photo. The one she'd taken of herself by mistake.

"This proves nothing."

"There're more photos," Sidra said. "I especially like this one."

"Jesus," he said, snatched the photo as he looked at his office door and crumpled the photo into a ball.

"You look fantastic in pink lace. I want Lydia Desmond safe or those photos go to the newspaper. And it doesn't matter how I got the photos; I was in your house *consensually*."

"Did you break into my house?"

"No, you let me in."

"You bitch," he said, and moved back around his desk, and Sidra was thankful to be further away from him.

"If I don't have Lydia within twenty-four hours, these photos go to Ziggy Gessler at the newspaper. If my family is threatened, photos go to Ziggy. If I so much as smell a squirrel fart wrong in my direction, photos go to Ziggy. You better make the right decision."

\*\*\*

They were forced into high alert, which wasn't much fun. It was like having a five-hundred-pound gorilla lurking over your shoulder. They'd all put in some efforts for safety. They didn't know what to expect. When people were under pressure, they did a lot of crazy things. Threatened people. Family disappeared. Sometimes they took the more quiet approach with a call from the IRS flagging the business for an audit. Assets frozen. A sudden plethora of bad reviews on social media.

But that's not what happened.

The sun had just set when Sidra walked across Clemmie's parking lot and a black Pontic Grand Prix hit her from behind. She flew up on the hood, hit the windshield, and rolled off when the guy hit the brakes. Hurting like hell, she jumped up ready to kick the driver's ass, but he drove out of the parking lot, tires squealing, and in his haste, hit another car going eastbound on Highway 54.

Hot electric pain shot down her back as she took a step toward the wrecked cars. The guy driving the Pontiac threw his door open and began running. It was Red from Bingo's. She thought about shooting him.

"Stop!" she shouted, but Red ran across the highway. "You asshole, stop!" Sidra followed, nearly getting hit again as she ran across the traffic. She chased him down Shannon Drive and he was disappearing quickly. Then a flash went past her, almost like a blur. Out of uniform, she recognized Officer Aubrey, a middle-aged black cop who looked too out of shape to be running as fast as he did.

Red dodged him, turned between some houses, and a couple of dogs began barking. Sirens got closer. Aubrey yelled for the guy to stop. She found him trying to pull Red off of a wooden fence, his hands gripped tight because he didn't want to let go. When he pulled him down, Red bolted again, back the way he came in the other yard, shoving Sidra hard into the side of the house as he ran. Aubrey took off after him again.

When she rounded the front of the house, Red had crossed the street, but Aubrey was right behind him, tackled him to the ground. For a moment, he struggled to grab the guy's hands, pat him down for a weapon.

"Stay back," Officer Aubrey told Sidra. Barely able to breathe, he said, "Thought you were gonna get away, huh motherfucker?" Red was on his stomach, both of his hands held behind his back real high on his shoulder blades. Aubrey had one knee in the grass, half his foot on Red's back. Ready if he tried anything. "I was eating my smothered pork chops, minding my own business." He looked at Sidra. "You okay? Your elbow's bleeding."

It happened when she hit the parking lot pavement. "He hit me with his car."

"No shit," he said. "Jesus, I can't breathe."

Two police cars arrived, cops jumped out and took over to handcuff Red. The cops talked for a second into their radios, and Sidra saw Aubrey walk over to some bushes and puke. A couple of cops laughed at him.

Aubrey said, "We ain't gonna talk about that, okay?"

"You can't handle a little run?" one officer said.

"Shit. I gotta do y'alls job on my day off."

Sidra rode back to Clemmie's in the back of one of the police cars and finally seemed to get her breath back. Aubrey up front said, "I hope you press charges."

Sidra sat at the back of an ambulance while an EMT cleaned her arm and asked again if she needed to go to the hospital. Her elbow was scraped and bruised, but

261

nothing she couldn't deal with. An officer had already taken her statement of what happened. She thought she was done and wanted to get out of there. Of course she'd seen Red before, and one question would lead to another, but she hadn't said that to the cop.

Police took more witness statements, including Officer Aubrey's. Sidra took some of her own photos of the wreck. All the police cars blocked traffic. She was ready to send them to Tanner Wells when a detective named George Merrick showed up. Sidra groaned. He and Harvey Shackelford weren't the best of friends.

His dark hair had thinned out over the years, and he had his tie tucked in his shirt through an unbuttoned space, the sleeves rolled up to his elbows. He walked over, said, "I heard you hip-checked a car."

"I tried to play Superman, and I lost."

"I heard you ran out into traffic like Ray Charles."

"I did."

"A woman named Mary Beth James died less than a month ago doing that same shit."

"I know."

"And you chased after this guy. That was pretty dumb, he could have had a gun."

She looked Detective George Merrick in the eye. He'd worked with Dad in Atlanta back when they were detectives there.

"It's not random," Sidra said. "It's a case we're working on."

"What case?"

Sidra sighed. "Can I talk to him for a minute before he goes in?"

Detective Merrick looked over at the police cruiser where Red sat. "You know him?"

"I've seen him once."

"His name's Mikey Alverez. Hangs out with some folks who don't play nice. The Pontiac had been reported stolen a couple of days ago. Jackass left his gun and wallet in the car when he ran. Guess he never finished Hit-and-Run 101."

"Five minutes," she said. "You can stand there the whole time and listen to the conversation." It was the only way he'd let her talk to him. They walked over to the car, and Merrick opened the back door. Red kept his head forward, grass and dirt still on his shirt. He had a little goatee with maybe twenty hairs growing. "Did you take money for this or do it for kicks?" Nothing. "You must not know how to shoot a gun if you decided to use your car. Come on, Mikey, they're going to find out you messed up."

He looked over at her. Angry, dark eyes staring at her. A depressed person could get lost in eyes like that. That's what the world of drug dealing was, a pitch-black hole where no one could escape. He said, "Post my bail, bitch. I tell you what you want to know."

"Give me a name and I might not press charges."

"You and your little friend run around in circles like rats in a maze. All they do is keep moving the pieces." He shrugged.

263

"Who paid you?"

Mikey faced the front. His way of remaining quiet. Sidra stepped away from the car and Merrick shut the door, gave the Officer a nod and he drove off.

"What was that about?"

"Lydia Desmond," Sidra said, only half lying.

"Does Monroe County know you're working on this? Did her family hire you?"

"I haven't found anything yet, but as soon as I do, I'll notify whomever I need to. He hit me with a car because someone paid him."

"Mikey Alverez and his brother Tito are wanted for an armed robbery in North Fayetteville. This just saved me the trouble of finding him."

Sidra nodded. "Glad I could be of assistance."

Three thugs she'd helped get off the streets now. Did it even make a difference?

# Chapter 23

**Antonio Guzman and** Darriel Finley were still in lockup, bail denied as they waited for an arraignment. She could talk to both of them and get the runaround. She'd told Tanner to make his move, and if this was it, she had to do something. But Tanner wouldn't send an amateur to run her down with a car. This wasn't him. This was something else.

She called Casey later that night, and it was nice to hear his voice. She told him about what was going on and getting hit by the car. He said, "You can come here if you're scared."

"I'm not scared, I'm cautious."

"Really? I bet you have a gun under your pillow."

She laughed. She was at Shackelford, sitting on the leather sofa looking out of the picture window, watching what few cars passed along Highway 85. It was night; the house was quiet, Mom and Dad in their bed.

She said, "I'm not at home. A guy's sitting on Shackelford across the street in the hardware store parking lot. I'm tempted to walk over there but I've had a lot happen to me in the last few weeks."

"I know I got you involved in this. I thought it would be a simple job for you to watch Nacho at the wedding, but didn't think you'd get so caught up."

"Yeah, well, if you knew me, you'd know I can get a little obsessive about my work."

"Is that bad or good?" Casey sounded a hundred miles away, not really able to make out the background noise.

"What are you doing?"

"Roasting marshmallows."

"I don't know what to say to that."

"I really am just roasting marshmallows and drinking a beer."

"A beer sounds good right now." It was nice to know that Casey wasn't burning a body.

"What's the guy doing?"

"Sitting there. Mikey Alverez said, and I quote, 'You and your friend run around in circles like rats in a maze and they keep moving the pieces'. What's that mean?"

"What I think it means," Casey said, "is that everything is in a bubble and keeps getting moved before I can get to it. That's how we moved drugs and money. Don't keep it in one place too long."

Sidra picked up her gun from the sofa seat next to her and stood up. "He can see me through the window." She walked out of the sitting room and up the stairs.

Sidra flipped on the light in the spare bedroom. Stood there in the doorway, waited a minute, then turned off the light, and went back downstairs. "Give me a second, okay?"

Out the back door, took a right to the big parking lot. When she got to her van, she grabbed a pair of binoculars, then walked across the backyard. Sticking to the trees, she headed to the hair salon next door and crouched down.

"I'm outside in the wooded area next door."

"I was wondering why you were breathing so hard."

"Shut up and eat your marshmallows."

She could see the guy's face clearly as he watched Shackelford, turned his head left and right to check the street, then looked down at his lap. Familiar. Bald head. Angry face. Upper body taking up a lot of space.

"Casey, I think I'm seeing a ghost."

"Who is it?"

"Slick Head, Steven. You didn't kill him?"

"You sound surprised."

"I am."

"I'm more of a warm-blooded killer," he said, and she could tell Casey was walking. "I have some morals about what I do. I let him go and told him to get out of town, and I thought he had when Cameo asked about him."

"He didn't listen. I kicked his ass once, I'll do it again."

"I'll come over there. Don't do anything. I mean it, Sidra. If you ever listen to anyone, let it be me right now. Just wait for me. I'll stay on the phone with you the whole time."

Casey did. And Slick Head Steven didn't seem to be doing anything other than watching the house. When Casey arrived, he parked on a street at the back of the house where they quietly stood talking.

"He thinks I'm in bed."

"Why don't you get in your car and go home."

It had been a long day. She wanted to go to sleep, but they were dealing with everything as it came up. She stood there in front of Casey, feeling so small, and she really wanted him to get his son back. To help her find Lydia Desmond. She wanted him to burn Tanner Wells to a crisp. She felt so angry about it, but she couldn't bring herself to even tell him about what Tanner had done. It was none of Casey's business.

Casey said, "I want out of this shit. Out of this life. I don't expect you to put yourself in danger for me. I'll walk across the street and knock on the window. But I can't get away from this until I find my son."

And as long as Casey Lincoln was in her life, she and her family were in danger. The cycle continued. She could walk away, but she'd never stop wondering what she could have done to help him. How close they would have been to finding Brandon?

"I've got some skin in this too," she said, and ran inside for her keys.

***

268

She took a right out of Shackelford, then another right onto Highway 54. Casey said from the phone, "He's not following."

She pulled over into a church parking lot, turned around, and stopped in another parking lot across the street. That's the thing about the south. A church and Waffle House on every corner. "No one else is on my tail."

"Hold up. He's getting out of the vehicle and crossing the street."

"Crap, my parents are in there."

"Don't worry."

Sidra left the church and heard Casey running. She should call her parents. She reached for the burner phone, ran through a red light at the intersection, and heard scuffling from the phone. Her mind in high gear, she pulled back into Shackelford parking lot and took off.

In the backyard, Casey and Slick Head were wrestling each other for the win. Casey had the size, but Slick Head had the upper body and arm strength. Sidra walked to the porch and grabbed Phin's t-ball bat. A short, stubby thing meant for a six-year-old.

Slick Head had Casey in a bear hug, both of them grunting, and Sidra swung the bat and hit Slick upside the head, nearly hitting Casey too. Slick let go of Casey reflexively to reach for his head. Sidra sidestepped and swung again, catching him in the back. This gave Casey enough time to tackle him to the ground.

And then the back porch light came on, and Dad stepped out, the sound of a shotgun racking making her freeze like a mime on the street. "It's me," Sidra said, and stood there, one hand up, the other still holding the bat. Dad, in his pajama pants and t-shirt narrowed his gaze, and lowered the shotgun.

"What are you doing?"

"Taking care of a problem. You can go back to bed."

"Who's with you?"

"Casey. And his friend."

"Sidra—"

"Dad, everything's fine. Go back to bed."

"You better not get blood on my grass." Dad stepped back inside and shut the door.

Sidra turned to Casey, still laying on top of the guy. He got up, punched Slick Head a couple of times, then pulled him up.

"Do you know how hot a fire has to get for a body to burn?" Casey said.

Slick Head spit in his face. Casey grabbed the bat out of Sidra's hand and hit him with it one time. Slick Head hit the ground like a bear who'd fallen out of a tree.

\*\*\*

His name was Steven Mollett. And he looked like one of those guys who'd do anything to stay in the good graces of his employer. Do anything they asked, and stay so focused on his job he couldn't think straight. Or maybe it was because of the reputation Casey made for himself. Steven wasn't talking, so Casey threw him in the back of his Explorer, duct taped like a hog.

"Keep an eye on him," Casey said, and walked away.

Sidra looked at Steven, his head bleeding, face swollen from the punches. Casey wasn't going to let him go this time. Should have gotten out of town.

The night was hot and mosquitos buzzed around as she stood in the cover of the trees from the back street. Steven was stupid to park across the street. If he wanted to watch the place, why not do it from back here?

Casey came back with a small plastic bag, which he shoved under the driver's seat. "I'll come back for his car tomorrow. You should stay here, nothing pretty is going to happen after this."

Sidra said, "I'm coming with you."

They'd made it all the way to Highway 92 without a word when a car came up behind them, bright lights on. The driver hit them from behind, a bump really. Enough for Casey to focus on what was behind him. The car in front of them suddenly made a U-turn.

"Watch out," Sidra yelled, just as Casey saw it and swerved. They ended up driving through a ditch. Casey corrected the Explorer, got back on the highway, the two cars right behind him.

One of the cars drove past Casey, got beside him and ran him off the road. Back in another ditch, this time, they hit a tree.

Sidra jerked forward so hard she thought her neck snapped. Casey started shooting at them.

"Run!" Casey said. "Get out now."

Sidra unbuckled her seatbelt, threw the car door open, and took off into the woods as low as she could get. Bullets were flying. She pulled out her own gun and ran. She hated leaving him, but what else was she supposed to do?

Sidra didn't have enough time to think about that. From the right came an arm, caught her around the neck. She fired off one round in that direction, then fell down with the clothesline hit to her throat.

\*\*\*

Sidra was back in the paintball warehouse. Her head throbbing and her throat felt like someone had choked her. She heard arguing in Spanish. She wasn't chained or locked up, but she was afraid to move. Afraid to blink or breathe too loudly. Where was Casey? These people were certainly going to kill them. No idea what they were saying. She waited in the concrete warehouse; the moonlight pouring through the tall windows. The graffiti telling a story she didn't understand.

People did the things they did for money. That's what everything came down to. Money. Churches wanted it. Politicians wanted it. Greed and power and money. Those things merged into one. And when people like her tried to figure out a crook, or a corruption, this is what happened.

Stay away, the dark world screamed. You can't save anyone.

She closed her eyes for a brief moment, afraid to move. Then someone grabbed her by the front of her shirt. Steven Mollett, his big bald head shining from the moonlight. "Someone wants to talk to you." His nose bloodied, his face swollen with purple bruises. He dragged her out and down through the concrete maze. When they came to a room in the back, Steven threw her down to the ground like a piece of trash. Casey lay on the ground, blood on his shirt. He didn't move. She thought he was dead. The concrete floor was wet with blood and water. A garden hose was off to the side.

"Get up," an unfamiliar voice said, with a Hispanic accent much like Lorenzo's. Sidra turned over and looked up to see Nacho Marquez standing there. Nacho looked to his left, to Dani Cameo, who was leaning against a wall.

Dani Cameo walked over, grabbed Sidra by the hair, pulled her up, and then shoved her into a chair.

Sidra looked down at Casey, a lump forming in her throat. He wasn't moving.

Nacho Marquez said, "He's not dead. He like family to me."

Sidra looked up at him. Family? That's how he treated family? Nacho and Lorenzo were similar, but

Nacho was thicker, dark hair and eyes. Mean. This was the man that was the face of the Marquez family.

The drug dealer disguised as a philanthropist. An average-looking man that could walk into anywhere and no one would know a damn difference.

Steven brought over a second chair, slammed it down on the concrete, the sound echoing through the warehouse. He gripped the back of the chair, his knuckles white, as he looked at her and then at Casey, proud of what he'd done. Casey should have killed him when he had the chance.

Nacho motioned for him to move, then sat down. He said, "Me and you, we have a problem, you see?"

"What problem? Me trying to find a missing little boy you kidnapped and Lydia Desmond? That problem?"

It was Cameo that spoke. "How about he talks and you listen?"

"I don't work for him."

Cameo knelt down at the same time Steven grabbed Sidra's hands, and she flicked on a lighter, waved it in front of Sidra's face like she was about to do a trick. Oh, she did a trick all right. Cameo held the flame to Sidra's braid. Hair burns fucking fast. Sidra bucked against Steven, tried to kick Cameo, and missed.

"What the hell is wrong with you?" Sidra said, frantic now that Steven let go. The scent wafted up her nose, four inches of her hair gone as she yanked out the burned ponytail holder and put out the singed parts.

"You no ask questions." Nacho leaned forward, his elbows on his knees, and Sidra thought about kicking him in the face. He looked at her for a long minute, time passing by like waiting for someone to get off of an airplane. Nacho leaned back in his chair, nudged Casey's foot. Nacho looked at Steven, Steven shrugged.

"You put your nose in my business," Nacho said. "I don't like that."

"I don't give a fuck what you like," Sidra said.

"Tanner Wells say you have criminal photographs."

That's what this was about? "*Incriminating* photographs. Not criminal." She flinched when he raised his hand to slap her, but that's not what happened.

Steven walked behind her, tilted her head back, and held her down. Cameo turned on the water hose. She held the water over Sidra's face for what felt like hours, her nose filling as she tried to hold her breath. She slapped at Steven, her mind losing focus on everything while he held her head back. When he let her go, Sidra coughed it out until she fell to her knees, trying to catch her breath.

Cameo grabbed her by the shirt. "The next time, your head goes in a bucket until you stop breathing." Then she shoved her into the chair.

Nacho, calm like nothing happened, said, "You get me the photos. Everything okay." He wiped his hands together like he was wiping off dust. "No problem with you. No problem with your family."

"I don't have the photos."

"Yes, yes, yes, you have. Tanner Wells does a lot of work for me. I give him what he needs. Casey Lincoln tell you what happen to his wife?"

Sidra swallowed, afraid to speak. Hot tears stung her eyes.

"We kill to survive," Nacho said. "I provide good money. Work. People who do wrong to me and my family? Have no place. What you do is between you and God. We have a problem here. You bring me the evidence or I will get it myself. You choose."

They'd set her up. Getting hit by the car. Steven parked across the street. It was either to lure Casey out, or they were just going to go into Shackelford once they realized Steven was in trouble.

"Even if I give you what I have, digital photos don't go away. How can you be okay with what Tanner Wells does to these women?"

"Tanner Wells is mariposa. A butterfly with little colorful wings. I don't care. Let me show you something." Nacho looked at Steven. Steven walked out of the room and came back in, dragging a blue body bag, and Sidra's heart sank. Steven pulled it toward her, unzipped it, and she almost threw up.

"You also kill to survive, eh?" It was Edgar Burke. She couldn't handle the smell, and swallowed down bile, the acid coming up like a wave. The reminder of what she'd done was right in front of her. The decay made him gray and nearly unrecognizable. Steven unzipped the bag further, the stench taking up the entire room. "You go in with him," Nacho said.

"What?"

Steven grabbed her, and Sidra pulled away, but his grip was tight, and she remembered the way Lorenzo's guys put Edgar Burke in the body bag.

"Remember when you kicked me in the balls?" Steven said, and shoved Sidra's face close to dead Edgar Burke, so close their noses touched, and she tried not to breathe, but it was almost as if she could taste it. Tears welled up, but she forced herself not to cry in front of these sick people. Steven was almost pushing her face into Burke's, and Sidra threw up, mostly spit and stomach fluid, but once it started, she couldn't stop.

Cameo laughed.

Sidra pushed back and nearly fell on Casey, who still wasn't moving. "Okay," she said. "I'll get you whatever the fuck you want. Just leave me alone."

"Now," Nacho said. "We see eye to eye."

# Chapter 24

**When they walked** out and she heard a car leaving, multiple cars she now realized, Sidra moved to Casey and felt for a pulse. It was there, and still strong. He was breathing. Scared to touch him, she put her head on his chest for a moment.

He was wet from the water, blood coming from somewhere. She didn't know if he was shot or what. As she tried to assess him, he said, "Leave me."

"Oh, God."

He opened his eyes, and she touched his face. "You need to go to the hospital."

"No. I'm okay."

"You're not okay. What did they do to you?"

His face was swollen and turning purple. Blood oozed out of his mouth and dripped down to his split ear. His hands looked raw and bloody from trying to fight back. Sidra lifted Casey's shirt. He winced. From his chest to his belly and sides, he was red from getting punched, but they'd turn into nasty bruises soon. That was if he didn't have any major internal damage and he survived.

"You can leave me here."

"I'm not leaving you," Sidra said, and stood up, the stench from Burke unbearable. She zipped up the bag and noticed a small tear near the zipper.

She heard, "Hello," and spun around fast. A haggard old man stood there. He had a dirty gray beard and eyes that had seen too much pain. All of his teeth were missing.

He said, "Sometimes they leave booze behind."

"What?"

"I sleep here sometimes," he said. "And sometimes I find booze. Did they leave any?"

"No. We'll be out of here soon. I need to find a ride."

"Why don't you use the one out front?" he said. "Key still in the ignition. I would take it, but I got nowhere to go."

She walked to the front and spotted Casey's Explorer sitting in the parking lot, the front end damaged from where they hit the tree. The keys were in the ignition. Her purse and gun lay on the seat. What kind of game were these people playing?

Between what Sidra and Casey had in their wallets, she came up with one-hundred twenty dollars. She backed up the Explorer close to the entrance.

Inside, she found the old man snooping around. He said, "No, they didn't leave any behind."

"How well can you lift?"

"I lift it up to the Lord every day. Jesus is going to take all my problems away. If you read your bible, good Lord Jesus can lift you too."

How endearing. "If I pay you a hundred dollars, will you help me move something into the back of that vehicle?"

"If you pay me a hunert dollars, I'll do a back flip. And," he said, digging in his pants pocket. "You can have this for free." It was a torn page out of a bible.

"You keep it," Sidra said. "A hundred dollars. No questions asked?"

"Sure thing, Missy. Let me see the money."

Sidra handed him money out of her back pocket.

"This ain't a hunert."

"You'll get the rest after you help me."

He put the money in his pocket. "This'll do anyhow. Pay went up from back in my day."

"Pay for what?"

"Moving bodies," he said. "Don't think I can help you with the big fella, though. He ain't dead yet, is he?" Then something must have dawned on the old man. "You ain't gonna kill me, are you?"

"Do I look like a murderer?"

"Murderers look like a lot of different people." He slid his tongue over his top gum.

Casey tried to sit up, groaned, then lay back down.

"Guess he ain't dead. So what's this about?" the old man said.

Cold from the water, she really wanted out of here. "The guy in the bag tried to kill me."

"Yep, yep. That's usually what it is. I helped this old colored fella a long time ago. Paid me forty dollars to bury a man raped his sister. I didn't kill him, just helped him, you see? Well, let's get to it so I can catch some shuteye."

Sidra grabbed the bottom of the body bag and dragged it through the warehouse, the smell following along with it. The bag wasn't light, but this was the best way. The old man had followed her to the door. Sidra had to step outside for a second to catch her breath. She said, "I just need help getting this in the back. Can you manage?"

"I rightly think I could. Sure you want to ride around with that?"

She didn't have any other choice. "What's your name?"

"Eugene Mason the third," he said, and smiled.

"Nice to meet you."

The old man proved to be stronger than he looked. He hefted his side of the body bag and helped Sidra get it in the back, the sound of it crinkling like a tarp.

"Whew," he said, and stepped away to take a deep breath.

A minute later, she said, "The big guy? You think you can help me get him up?"

"I reckon," Eugene Mason said.

Moving Casey was a struggle, even though he tried to help himself. When they finally got him to the car, he opted for the back seat so he could lie down.

Sidra handed Eugene Mason the rest of the money.

He said, "I hope the good Lord helps you with whatever's bothering you, Missy."

"Thank you for your help," she said, and drove away with him standing there.

***

The fire Casey had been watching when he spoke with her on the phone had burned out, the faint glow of embers still smoldering. She got Casey inside and into the twin bed in the living room. Sidra took off his boots and wasn't sure what else to do for him.

Lying there, his face all busted up, he looked dead. She looked for a first-aid kit, found peroxide and gauze, cleaned his face and ear, careful not to cause any more pain. Two times he asked her to stop touching him, but she'd taped up the split ear without hurting him further. He also had a cut on his head and probably needed stitches. All she could do was put a bandage on it.

Sidra backed the Explorer as close to the fire pit as she could. The lid was off, and she found a bag of marshmallows sitting in a nearby chair, along with a couple of empty beer bottles.

Looking around, she tried to remember what she saw the first time she was here. The pit was dug about three feet into the ground. Not knowing exactly what to do, Sidra opened the back of the Explorer and pulled the blue body bag out, and let it drop to the ground.

Without the tear near the zipper, the bag would have contained the smell, but it didn't and it was sickening.

How far would the scent of a burned body travel?

She got the body inside the pit, put some logs on top, and then noticed the metal rods near the cabin. They weren't heavy, but a good forty-five pounds each like a barbell. She lay those on top of the logs.

She moved the vehicle.

Poured gasoline on the fire pit.

Lit a match.

Watched the flames go up.

Sidra sat down in the chair, stretched out her legs, and didn't feel relieved about what she had done.

*\*\**

Sidra went back inside the cabin sometime around six o'clock in the morning. Dad had texted her, asked if she was okay and what the hell was going on. All she could say was that she was fine, and she'd tell him everything later.

Then she crashed on the sofa like a pile of bricks.

She woke up to Casey throwing the front door open. "What's wrong?" she said, panic setting in as she jumped up to follow him.

"I gotta piss." He stood at the edge of his porch, pissing a bloody stream, groaning a sound of pain like a wounded animal. She wanted to cover her ears. He walked back inside, threw himself on the bed, and didn't move.

It was nearly noon.

Sidra changed his bandages and assessed the damage. He didn't look good at all. The gash on his head wasn't oozing blood, but the cut looked deep.

"I'm okay." Casey swatted her hand away.

"You need medical attention." He didn't say anything. She needed to get out of there and get those photos back to Tanner. "I have to go, okay?"

He nodded.

"I don't want to leave you but I have to."

He opened his eyes.

"I have to return those pictures I stole."

"I didn't know where they were," he said.

"Why would—Jesus." They were beating on Casey because Sidra had the photos. She put her face in her hands.

"They said Brandon's dead."

"What?" Sidra looked at him.

"I'm done," Casey said. "I can't do it anymore. I need to get out of here before Nacho and Lorenzo go to war with each other."

Sidra wiped away some tears. That feeling when it was all for nothing. The weight of the regret weighing down on her. She could feel herself swimming to the surface, but something wouldn't let go of her.

No, Sidra told herself. No more.

Brandon was dead? How could they?

The image of Edgar Burke came to her mind, his gray dead face inches from hers, and she couldn't get it out of her mind.

Sidra went to the Explorer to get Casey's cell phone when she remembered the bag he'd shoved under the seat, and reached underneath for it. Casey must have cleaned out the vehicle, because there were scraps of notes, receipts, and a copy of his vehicle registration inside, along with a crumpled photo of Sidra.

Back inside the cabin, Sidra handed Casey his cell phone. "I'm going to call you every hour. You better answer it."

He nodded and reached for her hand, gave it a light squeeze before he let go.

Sidra called the Shackelford office, knowing Mom would answer. She said, "I need someone to pick me up."

"Where are you?"

"I can share my location with you through the location app."

"Hold on," Mom said. Then Sidra heard: "Talk to your sister."

"What?" It was Daley.

"I need you to come get me. I'll send you my location."

"Why don't you call Uber?"

"Just come get me." Sidra sent him a request so they could connect. "You should have it now."

"Got it," Daley said. "All the way to Monticello?"

Like it was so far. Sidra tracked him from Fayetteville. When he got closer, she started walking down the gravel driveway through the woods because he wasn't going to find the entrance. Casey didn't have a mailbox. Thankfully, the driveway wasn't a mile long like Daley's and she made it to the highway in three minutes.

Daley passed her once, turned around, then pulled into the opening covered in pine needles. Sidra hopped in his truck, his pride and joy, and he said, "What the fuck? You stink like—"

"Can we go, please?"

"Were you rolling around on top of a dead skunk?"

Sidra looked at him. "Casey almost died last night. My life was a little iffy too."

Daley backed out and rolled down the window. He said, "You look terrible. Like a bear ate you and shit you out whole."

Sidra shook her head. "It was all for nothing. Tanner told the Marquezes I got the photographs, and they came after me. He had the dead guy I shot at my house. They burned my hair." She could feel the tears coming. "They beat the shit out of Casey. They killed his son. None of it matters anymore. Tanner and the gang bangers win. We lose. And they get to continue doing all the illegal shit they want as long as people like Tanner Wells are on their side."

He leaned his head a little out of the window. "Don't forget, you were nearly sold into human trafficking. Hit

286

by a car. Took your innocent niece to a drug dealer's horse ranch. Your life sounds like a terrible Chick Flick to me."

She looked over at him, and wanted to shove him out the window.

\*\*\*

He drove her to Shackelford because that's where Sidra's van was. Daley started wiping down his leather seats immediately and spraying the whole truck with Lysol. Sidra noticed Steven Mollet's black Mazda was no longer in the parking lot across the street.

Back in her own house, the bare spot of carpet suddenly meant something to her now. All she saw was Burke's face. She'd shot him, but hadn't really felt like she'd killed someone. Maybe because when they'd put him in the body bag, he was still alive, and when she saw him last night, he wasn't.

How did Nacho Marquez end up with Burke's body?

Because they were family.

But now they had a problem because Nacho knows Lorenzo is trying to take out his people.

Sidra called Casey. He answered, his voice groggy from sleep. "Just checking," she said.

"I thought you were joking. Are you really going to call me every hour?"

"Yes. Goodbye."

In the bathroom, she hung her head over the trashcan and cut off all the burned ends of her hair. The cut wasn't even, but it would do for now. Since she was young, her hair had become her identity. Such a frivolous attribute, she knew and understood that, but it was who she was. Of course it would grow back. But that bitch burned her hair. In a dark part of her mind, she imagined Tanner and Cameo in the fire pit, burning to death.

She looked at herself in the mirror. Took a deep breath and tossed the scissors in the sink. The clothes she had on were going to have to be burned, she'd never get the stench of death out.

She took a shower and used half a bottle of shampoo in her hair and tried to think this through. Didn't Tanner Wells understand all she had to do was delete the files on her laptop? And even then they wouldn't disappear? *Bring me the photos*. This didn't make sense. But that's what she'd do.

When she got out of the shower, she made a turkey sandwich, then called Casey again.

"Are you okay?"

"Still pissing blood, but I've been worse," he said. "Call in two hours next time."

Casey hung up.

Sidra looked through the bag again. He had receipts from various restaurants. A receipt from Wal-Mart caught her eye. It was dated almost five months ago. Boys' SpongeBob underwear. Boys' size 4T shorts.

Socks. Pajamas. Transformers toothbrush, and various other little boys' clothing. A Mega Bloks set and play doh. Sidra set the receipt aside.

There was a scrap piece of paper crumpled into a tiny ball with five addresses. A note scribbled on top said: *Every 3 days*. The addresses didn't list cities, just numbers and street names.

841 Renzi Way
520 White Tail Plains
664 Denver Court
315 Marble Drive
173 Winnipeg Drive

A quick search showed all the addresses were within ten to twenty miles of one another. There was also a Denver Court in Marietta, but Sidra didn't believe the 664 was that far north. Therefore, two addresses were in Clayton County and one in Spalding, two in Henry.

Back to the Tanner problem, Sidra picked up her cell phone and took a long look at it. She called him on his cell phone. Of course, it went straight to voice mail. She didn't stop calling for ten minutes. Called the District Attorney's office, spoke with Jolene Pike, who assured her that Tanner Wells was in his office. Would she like to speak with him? "Yes, please."

Minutes passed before Tanner picked up the phone, said quietly, "What?"

"I got your message." She squeezed her fist at the sound of his voice. "How do you want this done?

Because I'm not meeting with the fucking Marquez crew again."

The noise he made wasn't a laugh, but it was something of a triumph.

She said, "I'll put the thumb drive with the photos in your mailbox."

"Hold on." Tanner hung up on her. A second later, her phone rang. He called back from his cell. He said, "I want whatever devices you saved the photos on as well. We both know it's never erased—"

"Where do you want to meet?"

"Will you be alone?"

"Absolutely not." Must have lost his mind.

"I'll be done here by five—"

"Then I'll meet you in the parking lot of the government building. Hopefully, it's still safe."

Sidra hung up the phone and breathed until her hands stopped shaking. She called Woolsey. "Can you put a virus on a flash drive?"

"Is it possible, yes."

"Can you do it?"

"That's above my expertise. Call Mr. O."

She should have thought of that. "Thanks, Woolsey."

Sidra called Amy to make sure it was safe to come over. Inside, she asked for Ian. He was in a downstairs office that looked like something out of national security. There were two TVs on the wall. Eight computer monitors and hard drives everywhere. Their entire basement was *O'Brien Creative Design*, a code writing and digital consulting business. Ian had five employees on his team, grinding it out from here and their own home offices.

The two guys working with him paid Sidra no mind. She said, "Can you put a virus on this?" and handed him the flash drive.

"Can I what?" Ian pushed his wired framed glasses to his forehead and rubbed his eyes.

"Mr. O'Brien, lad," Sidra said. "It's important. Didn't Amy tell you about the pictures?" Sidra sat down in a rolling chair next to him.

He said, "Don't tell her this, but I try to ignore her when it comes to family drama. I mean, business, sorry."

Normally, they'd banter back and forth, but right now, she didn't have time for anything funny. "Ian, seriously. It's important. Can you do it without it tracing back?"

Ian adjusted his glasses. "What's the story about it?"

In the condensed fashion, Sidra told him. He nodded, knew some of what was going on. He said, "Well, as you like to do, let's get sloshed first and then get to work. How about it?"

Ian was a great boss. He had a full bar downstairs, and when someone took a shot, they all took a shot. The guys, she didn't even know their names, stopped working to take shots. Whatever got them through their day.

By the time Ian finished, he had a virus code imbedded into the files. When a photo was opened, it would fuck something up. On top of that, he piggybacked another virus to attack if the files were actually downloaded. The beauty of it was that no one would know there was a virus attached. Ian also spent forty-five minutes removing everything important from Sidra's laptop, put the virus on there as well.

Sidra said, "Ian, you're the best. I wish I could find a husband like you."

"Oh," Ian said, "you're not really wife material. You just need an Irish drinking buddy."

She wasn't sure if that hurt her feelings or not.

# Chapter 25

"**I don't think** we're the best ones to do this," Sidra said to Dad as he drove to Griffin. "We both want to rip his throat out."

Dad kept his eyes on the road. "It's not too late to go to the authorities."

No, it wasn't too late, she just didn't think this was enough evidence to take him down.

"There are people I trust, Sidra. Bailey Flex works for the GBI. We put the bug in their ear and they'll watch him."

"I just need a bit more time."

"I've seen a lot of bad stuff in my life, Sidra. No matter what I think I understand, the people who prey on other people are different types of monsters. They can't be understood. Their minds are messed up. And Tanner? I thought he was a good guy. He comes from a good family. And I'm really surprised about him."

They pulled into the parking lot at the government building at 4:30. She thought they'd sit and wait, but Dad said, "Give me that," and pulled the laptop out of her hands.

"Dad," Sidra tried, but he got out and slammed the door shut.

She followed behind him into the building. Through the metal detectors. Left their names at the first floor desk. Took the elevators to the third floor. Dad pushed through the heavy wooden doors, looked at Jolene Pike, whose smile faded when Dad walked right past her.

Dad had been doing private investigative work with criminal defense attorneys for years. He thought highly of Tanner as a budding prosecutor and had become comfortable with him because he knew his father. Maybe that was a mistake. Just like Sidra made the mistake of trusting him because of who he was.

The office door was open, and Tanner stood when they walked in. Dad threw the laptop at him like a boomerang where it hit the shelf behind him and knocked off some photo frames and a couple of plaques.

Dad said, "If you ever come near my daughter again, I will kill you."

"Don't threaten me, Harvey. I'll have your license."

Sidra wanted to grab Dad and get him out of there before he got arrested. She didn't feel victorious with him on her side; she wanted to run and hide. But that's how people like Tanner Wells wanted her to feel.

Jolene Pike had walked down the hall, and Sidra made eye contact with her, begging her to just give them a minute and they'd be gone, out of this office forever. Jolene Pike put her head down for a moment and when she looked at Sidra again, those eyes said something to her. But then she turned around and walked away, her perfume wafting behind her.

Did she know something?

The DA's office wasn't quiet. People were hustling around and Dad wasn't being quiet either. He said, "You won't be able to hide behind that desk forever."

"Verbal assault. Destruction of property. Cocaine charges. Murder. You think I don't know about your family's indiscretions?"

Murder?

Was he talking about Edgar Burke?

That would make sense if Nacho told him about it.

"Doesn't give you a right what you did to her. You go ahead and tell them I broke your picture frame. Make sure to show them what's on that laptop when you do."

On the way out, Jolene Pike looked at Sidra as she stopped in front of the desk. Jolene seemed genuinely nervous about something. Did she know the things Tanner did? Was she covering for him? Sidra started to say something, but Jolene shook her head and turned away because another assistant was looking at them. Sidra reached into her pocket and tossed the flash drive on Jolene's desk.

When they got in the car, Sidra stopped Dad from leaving. "Just wait," she said.

"What for?" He gripped the steering wheel like he was holding the car in place.

"Let's just wait, okay?" A minute passed. She said, "Thank you for standing up for me." Knowing he would have risked everything for her even when he spent half his time disappointed with her choices. When he smiled at her, it took everything she had not to burst into tears.

He squeezed her leg. "If the investigation business fails, we can always reopen the ice cream shop."

She smiled at that and squeezed his hand.

A minute later, Tanner Wells left the building in a hurry. "Follow him?" Dad asked.

"No. I'm waiting for Ms. Pike."

"Jolene? Oh," Dad said, and nodded. "She's a nice lady. She comes from a good family."

"Yeah? So does Tanner Wells."

A few minutes later when they spotted Jolene Pike exiting the building, Sidra started to get out. "Let me work my magic," he said. He walked up to Jolene Pike, who didn't stop walking, kept her head down and didn't give Dad the time of day.

Some magic.

He got in. "She'll meet us at Crappy Hill."

Sidra gave Dad a sideways glance. "Didn't even look like you talked to her."

"That's part of my magic."

\*\*\*

Hill Street café was a little hole in the wall cafeteria that looked like it was straight out of the fifties. Worse than Clemmie's. Hadn't been updated since Griffin was officially incorporated. All the vinyl seats on the chairs were torn, and it scratched Sidra's leg through her jeans. The place smelled like mothballs and grease, reminding Sidra of an ancient school cafeteria. Crappy Hill didn't have any waitresses because it was a cafeteria-style restaurant. When they sat down at a table, a man from behind the serving station said, "Y'all gone eat?"

Sidra felt bad for thinking so poorly of the place when she knew the food was cheap and they served a lot of low-income and homeless people. Dad got up, asked for three waters and handed the guy a twenty.

Jolene Pike sat across from them, the floral scent of her perfume overpowering the scent of disinfectant. She took her straw out of the wrapper, then stuck it in her glass of water. Took a long drink then said, "Are y'all gonna tell me what happened in there?"

"That depends," Sidra said. "I need to make sure nothing leaves this table."

"Well, I'm not like your Mama, honey. I know when to keep my mouth shut."

Sidra nor Dad said nothing to defend Tilda's gossiping.

"You looked like you wanted to say something back there," Sidra said.

297

"Maybe I do need to tell you something." She slid her glass of water away and looked between the both of them. "I've been working for the District Attorney's office for thirty years. First in Clayton County, now Spalding." Jolene tapped a painted fingernail to her nose. "My little nose smells things, you understand?"

"And that's what we'd like to know," Dad said. "I've known you for a long time, Jolene. I just learned that—" He looked around. "Tanner Wells is not a good person."

"Well, I know that," she said. Jolene dug around in her purse and came out with a compact, checked her face, then snapped the compact shut. "Everyone heard the glass break and the shouting. What happened?"

Sidra decided to take the lead. "Tanner Wells asked me on a date and he did something to me."

"What do you mean?"

The question wasn't meant as though she didn't believe her, she could tell Jolene Pike was curious. Other than drugging her and taking the photos, Sidra didn't know what else Tanner had done to her. She said, "Ms. Pike, he drugged me. But I don't have any proof of that."

Jolene Pike's eyes grew wide. "My great niece said the same thing."

Sidra leaned forward. "What are you talking about?"

"My great niece, she's actually my goddaughter. Her name's Shelby Jane McElroy. Her mother married John McElroy out of Atlanta. Do you know them?"

They didn't.

"Anyway, Shelby met Tanner a couple of years ago, and I guess she played a little hard to get, you know, because he was a little older and she had already had her heart broken once before. But after the second date—" Jolene leaned in real close, said above a whisper, "Shelby thinks Tanner raped her." Then, back to her normal tone again. "But she didn't have any proof. She felt real guilty about the whole thing. Well, I asked him a couple of times about it, and he said it was none of my business."

"Did they date for a while?"

"Oh, no. Shelby Jane didn't want anything to do with him after that. I didn't blame her. She wasn't like—" Jolene Pike took a deep breath, then took a drink of water. "It wasn't like what you'd think. She wasn't beat up or anything like that."

Sidra knew exactly how Shelby Jane felt. "Did she go to the police about it?"

"She did," Jolene said. "They questioned Tanner about it, and guess what?"

"Nothing happened?"

"Shelby lost her job. She was working at the Museum of Art, and had been in school trying to get her MFA. She lost her scholarship, too. It was just terrible."

299

"How can you work for him?" Sidra said. "I mean, how can you stand to be around him all day?"

Jolene grabbed a tissue out of her purse and dabbed her eyes. When she finished with that, she looked in her compact mirror again. "The one side of it is that my niece claims this, and I believe her, I do. The other is that I look at him working and all the good things he does. He doesn't seem like he's got an evil bone in his body."

Sidra almost snorted. "I'll tell you what Tanner Wells does, Ms. Pike. He takes innocent women on dates. Drugs them. Then he dresses them up in lingerie and takes pictures of them."

"I told you to keep your eye on him," Jolene said.

"You weren't very specific."

Jolene rolled her eyes. "I can understand the shouting." She reached into her purse and took out the flash drive. "What's this? Pictures?"

"Yes."

"What do you want me to do with it?"

"Whatever you do, do not plug that into a personal computer. It's got a virus on it." Sidra took a drink of her own water. Let a minute pass. "He's also involved with the Marquez family. I'm sure you know all about them. Can you tell me anything more?"

Jolene shook her head. "I see his emails and correspondence every day. Stuff comes up with their names but nothing that red flags. In fact, he spends a lot of time convicting bad guys."

"They're probably feeding the system with little fish so the big fish can own the ocean. I think he knows where Lydia Desmond is."

"The girl missing from the ranch?"

Sidra nodded. "The night I had my date with Tanner, Lydia was there. She's the one who took the photos."

"Well, if what you say is true, then he has something coming for him. Who needs to see this?" She held up the flash drive.

"Slow down," Dad said, and held up his hand. "You need to understand who you're messing with here."

"Oh, no," Jolene Pike said. "I'm a little old lady. Tanner Wells doesn't know who he's messing with. What do I need to do?"

\*\*\*

Later that night, she drove back to the cabin to check on Casey. She pulled up, and the fire was out. Was Burke gone? Burned down to ashes? Nope. Sidra flashed a light and saw what looked like something out of a CSI. Shit.

"You didn't do it right." Casey's voice startled her. She spun around and he stood there barefoot, wearing only jeans. "You have to put the top on. It makes the fire hotter. It's a makeshift crematorium."

"I couldn't push it on, it was too heavy."

Casey sighed heavily. "Me neither." She noticed the bottle in his hand.

301

"You shouldn't be drinking right now. If you have a problem with your kidney's that's only going to make it worse. Have you eaten anything today?"

Casey sighed heavily again and looked inside the firepit. "Who is that?"

"His name was Edgar Burke. He's the guy that I shot. Didn't seem to bother me until I saw him in the bag. He was alive when they put him in there."

"First ones are always hard."

"I don't plan on killing anyone else unless it's Tanner Wells. Or Dani Cameo."

"See how easy it is?" Casey took a drink. "Get swept away in it like the ocean in a bad storm. You're just a ship trying to sail through and it reaches up and takes you under. They killed my son."

They stood there in silence for a moment. Casey looked at the burned body. Sidra looked at Casey. "Can you help me finish this?" she said, talking about the fire.

Casey got the death pit back up and running, flames about a foot out of the pit. He added more wood, got the iron rods nice and hot, and then, together, they pulled the cover on top of the pit.

Casey stepped away to catch his breath, and for a moment Sidra thought he'd fall over. He picked up his liquor bottle and sat down in the chair, took another drink.

"They killed my son."

Sidra got a plastic chair from his front porch. This wasn't much of a sight to watch. Looked like one of those BBQ smoker pits buried in the ground, the smoke coming out of the slats.

Sidra put her hand out. Casey handed her the bottle.

Cheap vodka.

They sat there for hours, mostly in silence, yet talking about random things that crossed their minds. Tried to keep the chat away from everything that had happened, because it only made the anger worse. But the thoughts were there, they wouldn't go away, they came and went like those ocean waves, and when she thought about what they did at the warehouse, shoving her face next to Burke's, Sidra felt like she was in the storm and she could never get out.

Casey said, "I'm not a good person. I couldn't protect my wife. I couldn't protect my son. He was four years old. And I did this to him. Did he suffer? What happened? I don't know."

He talked like that for what seemed like hours. All the things he'd done that made him a bad person. Can't erase those things. He tried so hard to take care of his sister after his mother passed away, and now he's lost Lexi too. She can't stand him. She won't even let him see his own niece and nephew. He deserved it, he wasn't a good person.

"What are you going to do, Casey?"

"Hell, I don't know."

"Can we go inside? I brought food for you and I'm starving."

"You're going to eat the food you brought me?"

Sidra grabbed the bag out of the van. Leftovers she'd grabbed from Shackelford when she'd dropped Dad off. Inside, Sidra found plates and warmed up chicken pot pie. When she sat down to eat, she could barely taste the food.

They squeezed in at the small table in the cluttered kitchen. Various tattoos covered his chest and forearms that Sidra could get a good look at now. A hodgepodge of various phases in his life. Imprinted over his heart, she stared at tiny baby feet, the detailed lines of the print, and Brandon's name written over it. Joanna's name was on the other side, written in a swirly script. There was a Celtic Cross on his back. His arm had a skull, the eyes were covered and the words *See No Evil* across it.

She said, "I'm serious. What's your plan? You can start over, you don't need to get mixed up in illegal crap anymore."

He dropped his fork like she'd said something offensive. "You expect me to just forget about them? My wife and son, and just start over? That's easy for you to say. Someone like you, everything just laid out on a nice, pretty table for your choosing. No hard decisions to make. You and your perfect family sitting around the dinner table singing kumbaya."

"We're more of a *Crazy Train* kind of family."

Casey started eating again. "I'm not going to do anything right now," he said, his tone softer. "I just want to be alone."

"Okay."

"You don't have to go, though." When he reached for the bottle of vodka, Sidra took it from him.

"I'm a little worried about you right now. Mentally and physically."

Casey didn't say anything else, just ate his food, then opted for a shower. While he was in the shower, Sidra took a closer look around. He had wallets and driver's license in a drawer in the kitchen that belonged to various people. Car keys. She'd seen these before, but now she knew where they came from. Envelopes were piled up with other people's names like he'd stolen mail. She didn't recognize any of the addresses as the ones she'd found on the list in Steven Mollett's car.

The photos of his wife and son were still sitting in the box on the table. She looked through them, seeing now how young Joanna was. She was a pretty blonde and their son had the same light hair. They made a cute family. Joanna was small. Casey, big and strong. Brandon adorable.

Was he really dead?

Casey dropped the soap in the shower, the sound loud because the bathroom didn't have a door, and she heard him curse and groan as he tried to pick it up.

Looking through Casey's pictures felt like she was peeking into a part of his life he didn't want seen. There were some photos of him with other friends that she could only assume were drug friends. A picture of him and Cameo caught her attention. They had their arms around each other, their heads so close their cheeks touched. Another picture of them together with guns in their hands. They were older photos. Casey was young, looked almost like a teenager. Cameo had a head full of dark brown hair, her face was younger, too.

Something dark crept up inside her, an anger and a desire for revenge that, if left to stew, couldn't be contained.

Sidra shoved the photos back in the box and put the lid on. When Casey emerged from the shower, he looked exhausted and out of breath.

"Get in bed," she said.

He complied, pulled the sheet up to his chest, and was asleep within five minutes. Sidra washed the dishes and stacked them on the drainboard. There were clean pots and pans stacked on the counter. The cabin was so small there wasn't a place to put anything.

The thought of driving home was daunting. So instead, she curled up on the sofa and fell asleep for a few hours. When she woke up, it was two o'clock in the morning. She left and didn't tell Casey goodbye.

# Chapter 26

**The next morning** at Shackelford, Sidra sat at a computer trying to get information on the houses when Dad walked in. "Mom has you on the schedule for a job today. Some basic investigating that a kindergartener could do."

What was he trying to say?

"I can't right now."

"How long are you going to be on vacation, Sidra?"

"Today," she said. "Just until today, I swear."

Dad walked out of the office with his coffee mug in hand. She wasn't doing anything to earn any employee of the month awards right now. She sat down for thirty minutes and gathered any information she could on the properties, printed it all out, then left Shackelford, her van packed up with gear for a full day of surveillance, and drove to Clayton County.

Today's plan was simple. Go to each location, do surveillance for about an hour and take photos.

Steven Mollett lived in a nice house in a bad neighborhood, and it looked like he took pride in his property. Amazing what trafficking money could buy. There was a wooden fence around the backyard and a large mixed-breed dog ran around. She wanted to burn Steven's house down and kidnap his dog. But she stuck to the plan and did nothing.

She drove to the next location. White Tail Plains was the closest, so she started with that. This was the part of surveillance she didn't like. Not knowing the lay of the land and going in cold, hoping no one paid attention as she got acquainted with the place. This particular house was a rental property owned by GTPM. What a surprise.

While the house wasn't pricey, it was in a decent looking blue-collar neighborhood. Split-level ranch where all the houses looked alike. Easy cookie-cutter houses they put up in less than a year, and voila a full neighborhood.

The house was yellow with white bricks around the garage. The yard was open, with no fence, with the neighbor's house about forty feet away on each side. She didn't have a great place to park except on the street in front of another house. The houses here looked to be taken care of. The grass was cut, bushes trimmed.

Around 8 o'clock, the garage door rolled up and a blue truck exited, the driver a Latino, and he was alone. Sidra snapped some photos in rapid fire and jotted down notes in her notebook. An hour later, the house and neighborhood was quiet.

She moved to the next house, about eight miles east, in a neighborhood that was much the same as the first. This house was also a rental owned by GTPM. Neither of these first two houses looked like what someone would suspect a human trafficking house to look like. But that was the point. Sidra took more photos and made more notes. She'd feel a lot better once she gathered her information.

Marble Drive in Spalding County was thirty minutes away, and it was a shitty old house in a shitty part of Griffin. This house belonged to a man named Pete Jackowski and his wife, Geraldine. Sidra's van stood out only because it wasn't dented, or have any bullet holes. Geraldine, Sidra presumed, sat on a sofa on the front porch yelling at a chihuahua that was taking a dump too close to her flowerbed. There were three more scrawny, shaking chihuahuas running around. A chain-linked fence surrounded the entire house.

Sidra snapped photos of the two vehicles in the driveway, of Geraldine and the dogs. The woman sat smoking a cigarette, her bony body swallowed into the sofa, and Sidra could see her teeth looked like kernels of corn in her gums. Geraldine answered a phone call and one dog wandered off to the backyard.

So many things she could do right now, but she remembered Burke, and the threat Nacho gave her, and Sidra settled back down.

This is how they instill fear.

*Okay, Nacho. You win.*

As Sidra watched Marble Drive, people walked by, the dogs started barking like alarms, and when the walk-bys leaned against the fence, Geraldine would step off the porch and say hello. When this happened two more times, Sidra realized they were definitely selling drugs out of this house. Those little dogs letting them know when they had business.

"Shut up," Geraldine yelled at the dogs. Think they'd be used to all this activity by now. Geraldine paced in and out of the house, and finally Pete came out. He walked around a little bit like he was nervous. He smoked a few cigarettes, his hand shaking like the chihuahuas that ran around his feet. He left a little while later, came back with McDonald's and shared the food with the dogs.

They took more phone calls.

Five people stopped by in one hour.

Lord, where were the police?

Oh, that's right. Maybe they were friends with Tanner Wells.

Twenty minutes later, a shiny black sedan showed up. This was interesting. Sidra snapped photos and took video with a camcorder at the same time. Learned that two hands better be working when something was happening. The guy that got out was Green, Mikey Alverez's brother, Tito. The little dogs went berserk. Geraldine hollered at them while they lost control like pissed off hornets at his feet.

Tito side-stepped around the dogs, walked inside with Pete, then came out carrying a small black duffel bag. Change of plans, Sidra thought, and followed Tito to the warehouse district in Griffin. Okay, it wasn't really a district. More like a street. But it was filled with nothing but abandoned warehouses with broken windows and overgrown grass.

Tito blew the horn, and minutes later, Cameo came out. Sidra felt her pulse quicken at the sight of her. Cameo walked over, leaned into the car window for a minute, then Tito was gone.

*You have to gather the information*, she told herself and followed Tito. They were five minutes away from the Griffin-Spalding airport, a tiny airport for private aircraft. Tito parked, went inside the office, then drove through a gate to a hangar. He was there less than ten minutes, either to pick up or drop off.

Sidra wasn't sure if she was burned, but Tito didn't go anywhere directly. He drove around in circles, so Sidra gave that up really fast and drove to Henry County, even though she desperately wanted to know what was going on inside that warehouse.

841 Renzi was an apartment complex off of N. McDonough Rd. It granted easy access to I-75. The entire apartment complex was owned by Omega Holdings, the parent company of GTPM. It was a nice complex that offered a pool, car washing station, and a playground. Renzi apartments was busy. People coming and going from the nearby shopping centers.

311

Sidra was surprised the complex wasn't gated, but this wasn't Atlanta. The crime in McDonough was minimal in this area. Safety was an illusion, though. She snapped photos from the driver's seat, not bothering to conceal herself. Whoever lived here, she would not find them without recognizing a vehicle or face, or knowing which apartment she was looking for. The police would need a warrant to get a list of everyone who rented from here.

The house on Winnipeg Drive was in a beautiful subdivision across the interstate, about ten minutes away. A long time ago, this was the kind of neighborhood she imagined herself living in with Brady, two kids, and a dog named Charlie. All the houses were red brick, some one-level, some two. Perfectly landscaped yards, each one giving the house a unique look with various flowers in front. The mailboxes were brick, the driveway's pristine.

173 Winnipeg was also owned by GTPM. There was no for sale or rent sign out front. Why would Steven Mollet have a house like this listed? It was a stretch from Pete and Geraldine's house. Were they using this house to transfer money and drugs as well, or were they keeping women here?

By mid-afternoon, the sun blazed outside with a fury. Sidra snapped photos of the house, sweating her ass off by now. She wasn't going to be able to sit here long in a neighborhood like this. It wasn't a busy neighborhood, but people noticed stuff like this. And sure enough, she spotted a guy walking towards her van. Sidra had been in the back of her van, the curtain pulled.

He was a middle-aged guy, wore sunglasses that hid his eyes. She climbed into the front seat. The guy knocked again, but not angry. Sidra started the van and rolled the window down just enough so they could hear one another.

"What are you doing?" he said.

"I'm in the market for a new house."

"Let me guess which one you've got your eye on." He nodded toward 173, with its beautiful irises along the front. "Are you a cop?"

Harvey Shackelford's Rule # 1 to good surveilling was to notify the police first, so that way, when someone called them, it was easy to explain.

Rule #2. Get out when you're burned.

"No," she said. "Didn't mean to cause any problems. I'll be going now."

"I know what you're doing," he said. "You're watching the house. I don't blame you. There's something always going on over there."

"What do you mean?" Sidra rolled her window down just a little further. "Who lives there?"

"That's the thing. No one really lives there. Less than a month ago, a young couple moved in, but it's still the same thing. People going in and out all the fucking time. Shady people, too. I live at 170, been here for four years," he said, and nodded behind him.

313

After everything that had happened, she didn't feel trustworthy, but she told the truth, and said, "I'm a private investigator looking into Lydia Desmond's disappearance," and gave the guy a few more details.

The guy stood there in gym shorts and a sleeveless shirt. He had keys and a cell phone in his hand. He nodded, recognizing the name. "I don't know how it connects. The young couple that lives there has a little girl. People go in, and five minutes later they're out. This goes on all day."

Sidra looked over at the quiet house.

"Believe me," he said. "Some days are quieter than others. But something is going on. My name's Roger Bristol. My neighbors are the Thiessens. You can park in either of our driveways. They won't be home until about six, but I'll give them a call."

Sidra handed him a business card. "Thanks. If you think of anything else, let me know."

When Roger Bristol left, Sidra parked her van in the Thiessens' driveway because it gave her a better view of the house across the street. She sat in the back of the van and felt hidden enough to keep an eye out.

Sidra sat there for over an hour and got nothing. No movement whatsoever in this house. The way Roger Bristol described it, the house was a drug house like the one Pete and Geraldine operated. This house was another way to conceal the crimes, because no one ever expected drugs to come in and out of a house like this.

Then finally, a white Infiniti pulled into the driveway. The garage door rolled up and the Infiniti pulled in. Crap, she was going to miss whomever was in that vehicle. Sidra snapped photos. A good-looking blonde guy got out. Who is he? Where had she seen him?

Sidra's brain was in overdrive.

He helped a little girl out. Blonde hair, that's all she saw. Sidra was so focused on trying to figure out where she'd seen the guy, all she could do was snap photos. He walked to the mailbox, looked around, checked the mail. Nearly beating herself upside the head as she scrolled through her memory bank.

Where have I seen this kid?

Because that's what he was. A college looking kid. Oh, God. It was Tyler Honeycutt, Abi Marquez's husband. The wedding at La Sombra. They were living in a beautiful house owned by Nacho Marquez's company. Of course.

Did Tyler have a daughter?

She didn't remember seeing her at the wedding.

The kid ran back into the garage. Tyler shut the garage, and they were gone. What the hell was going on?

Sidra scrolled back through the photos. She didn't get any good pictures of the girl's face because she was so focused on Tyler. She had blonde hair to her shoulders. Had on blue jean shorts, a red t-shirt, and flip-flops.

Could this be Brandon?

No, Sidra thought, Nacho said—

But it didn't feel right. Could this be the break she was looking for?

Sidra continued to watch the house. Abi arrived around five p.m. Sidra recognized her immediately. She drove a black BMW, pulled it into the garage without a look across the street. The Thiessen's arrived home promptly at six, gave Sidra a little wave, parked in their garage and then she didn't see them again. Roger Bristol was true to his word and must have called them. Thankfully, they were letting her work.

Shortly after that, what Roger told her was true, just like he'd said. Cars would pull into the third garage, then leave within minutes. It wasn't until Sidra spotted Tito in the shiny black sedan that she knew what was going on. These people had been picking up money all day and dropping it off here. No one suspects the nice house in an expensive neighborhood to be a money drop.

Sidra left at ten o'clock when the lights shut out.

# Chapter 27

**The next morning,** the house on Winnipeg was quiet until late morning when a blue truck pulled into the driveway. It was the same blue truck from the house in Clayton County. The guy didn't go into the garage even though the garage door rolled up. Instead, Tyler came out holding the little kid's hand. He handed the kid off to the man in the blue truck. The man put the little kid in the back seat, took a minute to buckle the car seat. Within minutes they were gone, the garage door rolling back down. Worried that maybe Abi was watching from the window, Sidra waited a minute before she left, and hoped she could catch the blue truck at the house where she'd seen it yesterday.

There were so many ways to get there. But sure enough, she caught up to the blue truck driving down Tara Blvd. It pulled into the driveway, driver got out, walked around to the other side and got the kid out. After they went inside, Sidra didn't see anything from them all day. Not even a peep outside the window curtain.

Three days later, the man moved the kid to the other house in Clayton County. This time she got good photos. When the kid got out, convinced now it was Brandon, Sidra's heart slammed into her chest. The man walked him up the front steps and handed the kid off to another guy, who wore loose jean shorts to his calves.

Dad had been on her for the last three days about the job she'd missed, her swearing to him she was getting somewhere with locating Brandon. When he called her, she thought for sure he was going to scream at her. Instead, he said, "Have you seen the news?"

"No."

His voice was light when he said. "Check the news."

Sidra grabbed a cell phone, not sure what Dad wanted her to search for without giving her any clues. But it was everywhere. Nearly fifty people in government received an email with photos of Tanner Wells dressed in women's lingerie. While they suspected photo manipulation, the media mocked him once they got ahold of the pictures. Tanner Wells didn't have anything to say on the matter. It seemed the email had come from his very own office computer.

Don't worry, she wanted to tell them. More will come out soon.

Dad said, "Sidra, I don't know what you're doing but you need to be careful."

When they moved Brandon to the drug house in Griffin, Sidra thought she was going to die. Geraldine took him by the arm and ushered him inside, the sadness on his face as he watched the man who'd dropped him off leave.

Geraldine called him BB, told him to get inside. The dogs nipped at Brandon like they wanted to play, but one of them bit his finger and he started to cry. Once inside, Sidra didn't see him again until the next day when he was allowed outside to play with the dogs, and Pete and Geraldine continued with business as usual.

Sidra thought about calling the police.

What would she say? How could she explain that drug dealers kidnapped this little boy, yet there was no information about that? His mother was murdered, and yet there was no information on that either. If the Marquez family had fake papers made for Brandon, then how was she going to prove anything?

The paper with the address said every three days.

They were moving Brandon in a rotation throughout the houses.

Sidra wanted to pull him out of there. He'd been gone for five months now. They'd established a routine, and she didn't want to fuck with that just yet. But all it took was a second and they could change that routine. One second and he'd be out of the country. One second and he could really be dead.

Another stranger came to pick him up. This time taking him to the apartment. But instead of keeping him locked inside of Apt. 26B, Brandon was allowed to play on the playground and go swimming. He was with a man who looked to be in his late twenties. And even while Brandon was in the pool, the guy was on his phone, not really paying attention.

Maybe this was her way in.

But there were cameras everywhere. She couldn't just go in and take him. Sure, she could explain to the police why she took him and they'd believe her after a while, but it was getting there that was the problem.

Brandon was obviously traumatized. He was skittish and apprehensive of anyone who approached him, including the other kids at the pool. He'd scream if Sidra grabbed him. And she had to remind herself that these people were drug dealers. That was clear when she noticed the guy at the pool carried a gun with him. Every one of these people was told to protect this kid.

Sidra needed to go to the police.

No, first she needed to confirm it was Brandon.

Casey took one look at Sidra's camera, and he was confused.

"Is it him?" she said.

They sat at Casey's tiny kitchen table and he put his hand to his mouth. "How did—" Tears started.

Sidra said, "If that's him, he's alive."

"He's so big." He wiped away the tears. "And his hair is so long."

Sidra lifted the lid on Casey's photo box, took out some photos of Brandon. Definitely the same kid.

"Where is he?" Casey started to stand up.

Sidra put her hand on his arm. "You are in no condition to do anything right now. For now, Brandon's okay." After two weeks of watching, she'd learned a lot. "He likes this guy the most. Probably because he gets to go outside." It was the apartment. She showed him Abi and Tyler Honeycutt's house. Pete and Geraldine's place. There was a good picture of Brandon holding one of the dogs as he carried it around the yard. "He likes the dogs even though they bite him."

The emotion of it all hit him. Like trying to reach for something that disappeared only to come back again. Casey cried, a deep sob that took Sidra's breath away. She couldn't bear it any more. She got up and walked outside, took a deep breath, and tried to come up with a game plan.

*** 

Dad took the reins on this. Told her she was absolutely going to the police. "Not the police, sorry," he said. "This is too big. I've already called Special Agent Bailey Flex with the GBI. Would you like me to go with you?"

No, she didn't. Sidra drove to Atlanta, to the Georgia Bureau of Investigations, where Bailey Flex waited for her in the lobby.

"Agent Bailey Flex?"

"That's me."

She was not what Sidra had expected. The woman in front of her had to be in her fifties. She wasn't overweight, but she wasn't thin. Gray hair had been pulled back into a ponytail that was as long as Sidra's. "Flex?" Sidra said again.

"Yeah. If you take jabs at my name, I'll put you in a headlock like I did with your daddy thirty years ago. Come on."

Sidra smiled and some of the anxiety evaporated. After a couple of stops at security, they took the elevator to Bailey Flex's office.

Her office was a cubicle. With no privacy. "Isn't there anywhere else we can talk?" The room wasn't jam packed like a police station, but they were within earshot of everything.

"Well, sure." She hefted herself out of the chair, and they ended up in a warm, stuffy conference room.

"I don't know where to begin," Sidra said, "so here's the dilemma. A four-year-old boy's been kidnapped by drug dealers and I know where he's located."

"Okay," Bailey Flex said, leaning forward, her face suddenly serious. "What's his name? When was he reported missing?" She grabbed a yellow legal pad and pen from the center of the table.

"That's the problem," Sidra said. "He wasn't reported missing. His dad is... *was* working for the Marquez family. He stole some money from them and they kidnapped his son." Sidra closed her eyes for a moment and wanted to tell Bailey everything, but she couldn't and thought about what cards to play. *Dad said I could trust her.* "So much has happened in the last month. We've got to get this little boy out of there. His name is Brandon Lincoln."

"I can't just go about anything cold, I need details. We have to get it through the proper channels."

Sidra started from the beginning and told her everything except the part about Edgar Burke. She said, "I hit him with a bat and called Lorenzo Marquez to come and get him." Everything Sidra said, she felt the judgment. Getting involved and not calling the police with information she had. Not reporting anything. Bailey's eyes snapped to Sidra's when she told her the parts about Tanner Wells, but Sidra again lied and left out the part about Jolene Pike and the flash drive.

Bailey said, "Along with the nudie photos of himself, appears Tanner Wells accidentally forwarded some emails to the Governor showing a history of illegal activity between himself and Ignacio Marquez. This stays in this room. We just got a warrant to confiscate Tanner Wells's office computer."

That was good news. Sidra said, "We have to get Brandon out of there. *Right now.*"

"Now hold on a minute. All that and you still haven't told me who this guy is?"

"It doesn't matter," Sidra said. She pulled a stack of 5X7 photos out of her bag. "Brandon has to be back at this location right now. This is where they keep the money. I don't know where the drugs come in, but I followed this guy, Tito Alverez, to the Griffin-Spalding airport. But we can go right now and get Brandon. He doesn't need to be in that drug house."

"Doesn't work like that. I have to contact those counties, they have to put together a team, we need to do our own surveillance. It's got to go up the chain. We can make it happen, but it has to be thoroughly investigated."

"I did investigate it," Sidra said, feeling her temper flare. "For four weeks I've been investigating this."

"And you can't expect us to put our lives on the line based on your information. You should have reported this information as you gathered it." She tapped her pen on the notepad where she'd circled a couple of question marks. "Why are you protecting him?"

Sidra sighed. Put her head in her hands for a minute. Why was she protecting him? She had no ties to him. No loyalty. He didn't mean anything to her. They weren't involved.

"His name's Casey," she said. "Casey Lincoln."

"Give me a second," Bailey said with a nod. She stood up and left the room.

Sidra started to panic. Did she just send Casey to his fate? And why wouldn't Bailey Flex do something right now about Brandon? To pass the time, Sidra looked through the photos again, took a glance at Bailey Flex's notes. Where did she go? What's she doing?

She couldn't stand it anymore.

When Bailey returned, she had a stack of papers in her hand. She sat down, said, "His name is Clarence Wyatt Lincoln. Born in Phoenix, Arizona. Did some time in Texas." Bailey flipped through the files. "He got a Georgia driver's license ten years ago. There was a house sold to Clarence and Joanna Lincoln. Wife, I presume?"

Sidra nodded.

"The good news," Bailey said, "is that I don't see any warrants. The bad news is that his name has come up numerous times in connection with drug activity regarding three prominent drug cartels from here to Texas." Bailey tapped the papers with her finger. "This is how we mess up as law enforcement. Clarence Lincoln gets left alone because he seems like a nobody. Then when the reports get stacked together, they show a better picture of what's going on."

"Is he going to go to jail?" Casey was going to kill her for going to the police.

"I don't know. We have so many files on the Marquez family, and the police catch their mules and their little shop dealers, but it's never enough. For every bad guy they catch, there are five more right behind them ready to make some money." Bailey looked through the papers again, shuffling them like she was going to find something new. "Where is Joanna Lincoln in all of this?"

"Nacho Marquez murdered her."

Bailey shook her head. "What?"

325

"I don't know what to do," Sidra said. "They've threatened me. Kidnapped me. Burned my hair. And yet I'm willing to walk out of here right now, go knock on that door and get Brandon Lincoln myself."

"Don't do that," Bailey said. "Leave it to the professionals."

If Casey ended up in jail, who the hell was going to take care of his son?

***

Sidra was irritable, and when Mr. Elbert knocked on her door, she snapped, "What?"

"You had thirty days. Why have you not moved out?" Took one look inside the house. "You haven't even packed anything."

"Can't I have a little more time? I'm in the middle of work right now. I don't have time to do anything else."

"No," Mr. Elbert said. He held up a copy of the papers. "I gave you a thirty-day notice, okay? And in your rental agreement that you signed, you said when the time came you'd be ready to move when you got the notice." He spread his arms wide. "I don't see a mover's truck. You know what's going to happen when you're not out by tomorrow? You lose your possessions because I'm going to bust down this door and start renovating."

"Mr. Elbert, please. One more week. That's all I ask."

"If you're not out by seven o'clock tomorrow morning, the police will remove you. You better start getting this stuff packed up right now."

He shoved the papers at her, and when he walked away, Sidra slammed the front door. This could not be happening right now. Sidra balled the papers up and threw them away. What was she going to do? All she thought about were the horror stories of landlords throwing their tenants' belongings out on the street. She had approximately eighteen hours to move out.

Shoot her now.

Sidra didn't even have a single box to pack up a single thing. In her bedroom, she put her personal stuff in a suitcase. More personal stuff into duffel bags. Grabbed a roll of trash bags and started shoving her towels and bed sheets in there. Moving so many times in the last ten years, Sidra didn't own a lot. She'd learned her lesson a long time ago. The less shit she acquired, the easier it was to move.

She called Mom. "I'm getting kicked out of my house. I'm going to have to stay at Shackelford, okay?"

"You mean for one night, right? You can't move back in. I can't do that again."

"I guess I can sleep in the minivan." She tried to lay the guilt on thick.

"Well," Mom said. "If you park it here, at least you'll have access to running water." Mom laughed. Actually laughed.

"I'm homeless, Mom."

327

"Let me see what I can do, Sidra, Jesus, this is why you should have gone to college," Mom said, her voice full of exasperation.

Sidra kept packing. Threw everything in trash bags and pillowcases. She had to say she'd done a pretty damn good job in such a short amount of time.

Her cell phone rang.

"Hey, Val."

"Hey, girl. I have that apartment—"

"I'll take it." Sidra tossed a trash bag near the sofa.

"It's small, but the—"

"I'll take it. How much a month? Can I get in today? I have to be out of this shithole by tomorrow morning."

"The window unit's—"

"Valerie Wiz*nudes*ki—"

"Um, it's Wisnewski."

"I'll take the apartment."

"I warned you," Val said. "I'll be home in a couple of hours. Do you remember where I live? Don't get lost."

Val didn't live far, and no one could get lost in Fayetteville if they tried.

At four o'clock, Sidra drove over to Val's place. It was off of South Jeff Davis in a decent area mixed in amongst some businesses. The main house was a small two story, with a detached garage and an apartment above it. This would work for a little while.

Wooden stairs stretched along the outside of the apartment. Inside, the stifling heat felt like an oven, and the damp air stuck in her lungs like glue.

"The window unit doesn't work," Val said. "So it's hot as balls in here. You'll have to buy a new unit if you want air. And the bathroom sink leaks. Right now it's shut off."

Sidra stood there with a box in her arms, sweat already dripping down her back. Time was ticking, she thought.

Val started rambling as she showed her the tiny apartment. "Fridge and stove work. That smell is from the last renter, he was a mechanic. There's a hookup for a washer and dryer in the garage, but it doesn't come furnished. I don't care what the hell you do with the place, just don't go having any loud parties late at night. I work almost every day from 4 o'clock in the morning until the afternoon, and I'm about to go to bed now. Rent's five-hundred a month."

Sidra looked at her. This tiny apartment was half the size of the house on Tulip. And that place was less than a thousand square feet and her rent was the same price.

"I think it's fair," Val said. "If I had time to fix this place up, I could double that. Here's the key. The good news is that I bring home a lot of leftovers. So if you're ever hungry, let me know. Sorry about the heat, I gotta get out of here."

For now, Sidra needed to unload everything. When she finished, she sent out a text message to her brothers asking for help with furniture. They said no at first, but within two hours, they had her bed and dresser inside the apartment, along with the sofa, table and chairs. Each load had someone cursing about the heat.

"You're going to sleep in here?" Daley said.

"No, she's going to die in here," Mitchell said.

"I bet," Woolsey said, sweating the worst of them all, "you won't even make it until dark in here."

Daley popped open a bottle of vodka. He took a sip and smiled. "I bet she won't dehydrate."

And just like that, they moved Sidra into her new home.

# Chapter 28

**A task force** from each of the counties where each of the homes were located was put together, along with help from the GBI. Two nearby counties offered the help of their SWAT teams. They were going to hit each of the homes at the same time. In the past, every one of the houses had been visited by police for some reason that was associated with some kind of drug activity. That's the only reason they moved on this so fast. GTPM owned the houses, and the business was under watch because of the whole Diane Hutchinson deal. Not to mention a four-year-old's life was on the line. They were ready to do this. The brick house that Abi and Tyler lived in didn't have any prior activity and wasn't even on the police's radar.

Geraldine was out on bail right now because of a drug charge, and here she was back at the same thing. After two days of work, no-knock warrants had been issued on each of the houses.

Sidra had still spent two days with her eyes on the house in Griffin. It's where Brandon was. Although she didn't know exactly what the task force's plans were, Sidra was under the impression they were going to raid the houses in the middle of the night. But not last night. When Sidra arrived at the house on Marble Street, the place was lit up like a blue and red sideshow event. Police cars lined the street.

Sidra parked her van, but the police officer wouldn't let her walk over there. She didn't know what was going on. Then her cell phone rang.

"We got no kid." It was Bailey Flex. "We got drugs. Money. Guns. Needles. Little yappy ass dogs, but no kid."

A cold sweat crept down her spine, and her hands shook. "What?" The police officer blocked her. "He has to be at another house then."

"No one's found him."

"Can you tell this cop to let me through? I'm on Marble near Washington."

A minute later, the cop spoke to someone on his radio, Sidra anxiously waiting to know what happened. Where was he? The house on Marble Street was Brandon's last known location, she'd watched him here yesterday.

"Go ahead," the cop said.

Sidra ran down the sidewalk, then slowed down when her approach put some other cops on alert. She found Bailey Flex in a bulletproof vest, not looking like the same person she'd met in the GBI office.

Bailey Flex circled her finger in the air. "This is great, but no kidnapped kid. A lot of people in play for this. What happened?"

"Is he not at one of the other houses?"

"No," Bailey said. "They hit pay dirt at the house on Winnipeg. Close to three million."

"Jesus."

"Geraldine Jackowski is dead. She pulled a gun when they told her to get down. More worried about her ankle-biting dogs than anything. Found a guy here with two out-of-state warrants. I'm not in charge here," she said, "just filing the reports."

"Are you sure he's not in there?"

"They're tearing the walls down as we speak."

"Fuck." Sidra walked off.

"Hey," Bailey said, and Sidra turned around. "Still want to talk to your friend. And don't even think about driving to the other hot spots."

***

The paintball warehouse was empty except for Mr. Eugene Mason the third. He was in one of the smaller rooms, sitting against a wall, eating Vienna sausages and drinking something from an old tin can.

"Hey there." He gave Sidra a wave.

"Has anyone else been here this morning?"

"Not that I'm aware of. Fella used to live in Kentucky left here in the middle of the night. Know anything about the shootout this morning?"

"Geraldine Jackowski is dead."

"Oh." Eugene Mason took a sip from his can. "That's a real shame. I'm real good friends with her sometimes."

"Have you seen a little boy around here? Specifically, one with long blonde hair?"

"Boy with long blonde hair?" He raised his eyebrows. "No. You got any change?"

Sidra went to the van and scraped up what little change she had, then dumped it in Eugene Mason's dirty hand. "God bless you," he said. "Hope you have a nice day."

Why'd they change Brandon's schedule? She looked around for a moment; the place bringing back too many bad memories. The blood from where Casey had been beaten up—looked like someone dumped the bucket of water over it. The floor was dried now, the red blending into all the spray-painted graffiti. She wanted to pick the whole warehouse up and throw it. Turn everything upside down until little Brandon tumbled out.

This is what Casey felt like when he hit the drug houses after he got word of Brandon's whereabouts. Slapping Cameo out of a chair. Burning people to get rid of evidence. This was the emotional place he'd been in for five months now.

Brandon could be stuffed in a body bag right now, sitting on Casey's front porch. He could be halfway out of the country. A needle in a haystack. Kids go missing every day and they are hardly ever in situations like this. It's usually custody disputes.

Of course there are sickos who take kids and do horrible things to them.

Sidra was starting to think Brandon wasn't any better off right now. She'd try one other place, then run over to Steven Mollett's house just in case he was there.

The warehouse where Tito had stopped was on a street with other abandoned warehouses. Broken windows. Empty, damaged crates. A stack of chain-link fencing. A homeless man was asleep in a sleeping bag on top of a stack of pallets, a white cat curled up around his neck.

There weren't any cars in the parking lot, and Sidra parked past concrete blocks, hoping the van wouldn't be spotted. She grabbed her Glock and made her way to the warehouse. The whole place was quiet until she got really close. Voices echoed from the inside, and she heard arguing and found a hole in the metal side, but she couldn't see anything.

"I hope your cousin does a better job than your little brother."

Cameo. That was enough to keep her moving. Up metal steps to get a look through the tall windows, she saw Cameo and Tito arguing near a black SUV. The whole warehouse floor had pallets wrapped in plastic. More vehicles. At the top of the stairs was a door that had been chained closed, she could try to slip through the gap but it would result in giving herself away.

Back down the stairs, careful in her movements, she moved to the back of the warehouse where the grass was waist high. There were a couple of windows back here that flipped open. She looked through one of them before stacking some pallets and opening the window. Ducked quickly when she spotted Steven Mollett.

Jesus. The sound of her heart pulsed through her ears.

She'd shoot him second. Right after Dani Cameo.

Sidra squeezed herself through the window, trying to be as quiet as possible. The window was about eight feet from the floor. She dropped down onto some boxes and something to her right fell on the concrete floor, echoing like a motherfucker.

The room was filled with metal shelving, boxes stacked on a lot of them. She ran to one corner, then out through another door. This room had dirty windows along the front. She hid for a moment while she heard—who she thought was—Steven Mollett, checking things out. When Sidra felt safe to move, she crawled over to the windows and peeked out to the floor.

Tito was gone, replaced by some other guy who was on his cell phone. Cameo stood at a door, smoking a cigarette. The garage door lifted, and a vehicle backed out. Garage door closed. And then Sidra's heart started pounding. Thought she couldn't breathe. Through a window four feet off the floor, Sidra spotted inside the office, a little blonde head. The tip of it. She couldn't be certain because the height of the window was taller than the possible head she'd seen.

Sidra ducked down and breathed for a minute to gather her thoughts. At this point, she wanted to go out shooting whether or not she saw Brandon, but if he was in that room, his safety was the most important thing.

Weighing her options, she decided to find out if Brandon was in the room, then call 911. And while she wanted Cameo and Steven dead, she was going to avoid them at all costs. But her gun was at the ready, just in case.

Listening carefully, she made her way past rusted out stairs and crouched down behind a stack of pallets. She didn't know if there were real sneakers in these shoe boxes, or if it was money or drugs, but everything was wrapped up really tight.

Just as she made her way to the next set of pallets, she heard, "Hey," right behind her and turned to see Steven Mollett. He reached up and Sidra fired the gun, the bullet hitting him in the right shoulder. He stumbled back a step, wasn't far enough away for her to take a good aim, but when she fired, she hit him in the upper cavity. He knocked the gun out of her hand, kicked her in the stomach, and Sidra fell back on her ass. As she tried to scramble to her feet, Steven grabbed her by the hair.

He was bleeding pretty badly.

Cameo ran over. "What's this shit? Oh, look who it is. Our little friend who don't listen." She took one look at Steven and said, "You're going to pay for that." When Cameo took a couple of steps toward her, Sidra punched her in the face.

"Bitch," Cameo said, and threw her own punch. It landed on Sidra's left cheekbone, and Cameo didn't back off. She swung again, and Sidra blocked. Sidra punched her in the stomach, and Cameo got Sidra in the kidneys. There was no hair pulling or wide swings. Cameo knew how to street fight. Sidra grew up with relentless brothers. Jabs followed every single blow each of them took to close the distance.

When Sidra was close enough, she took advantage of her own height, pretended to punch with her right, and caught Cameo in the throat with the left. Cameo bent over, and Sidra kicked her hard, then Cameo came at her, wrapped her arms around Sidra's waist and shoved her back into a pallet. The corner. Fucking hurt.

Raising her knee, Sidra tried to push her off, but Cameo was stronger than she looked. After a few more minutes, Sidra was getting worn out and started to get sloppy, but so was Cameo. She pulled Sidra forward and tried to throw her to the ground. Sidra kicked her again. Then someone grabbed Sidra from behind. Not Steven. He was gone. Sidra lost her advantage. She couldn't take two of them. It was Tito. A scrawny little shit with a fresh start. As soon as he pulled Sidra off, Cameo punched her in the stomach. Then Cameo grabbed Tito's gun and said, "Do you want to die? You fucking want to die, don't you?"

Tito had Sidra around the neck, something she could escape, but the damn gun was on her. Cameo had a busted lip. Blood dripped from her eyebrow. Bruises on her face. Sidra was sure she looked the same. Sidra spotted her gun halfway under a pallet. And then Tito dragged her into a small room filled with cleaning supplies.

A cell phone in her hand, Cameo dialed while she gave Tito instructions. He ducted tape Sidra's hands together while Cameo spoke on her cell phone. Some Spanish. Some English.

"I'm moving the kid now. What do you want me to do?... Oh. Si. Cinco casas? That bitch, Sidra is here... Si. Yes. Yes." Cameo looked at Sidra. Tito taped her hands to a metal shelf bolted into the wall. When Cameo hung up the phone, she said to Tito, "Go get my kit. And my lighter."

Tito left for the zip ties, and Sidra pulled at the duct tape. Cameo put the gun to Sidra's temple. "Nacho's coming for you." She slid the gun down Sidra's cheek like she was drawing in the blood. Then, with her left hand, Cameo squeezed Sidra's breast. "Oh, you like that?" Cameo stepped closer, close enough that Sidra thought to head butt her. Cameo groped Sidra again. "I heard you like to get drunk and let people take photos of you."

"Fuck you."

This made Cameo smile. She grabbed Sidra's hair and pulled her head back, let the gun barrel ride along the front of her chest. With the duct tape stretched enough, Sidra threw her weight at Cameo, her hands coming free of the hold, and the shelf nearly falling over. And then she went at Cameo again. Sidra kicked. Punched. Shoved Cameo into the wall. When Cameo tried to take aim, Sidra moved low and rammed her. The gun fell to the floor.

Sidra grabbed Cameo by her hair and kneed her in the face, certain this time she broke her nose. Threw her down and grabbed the gun.

This time, she didn't hesitate.

Put two in her chest.

And Sidra wouldn't feel an ounce of guilt about killing Dani Cameo.

Cameo's eyes blinked, her mouth gasped. That cruel human being would never hurt another person again.

Sidra didn't look back once. On her way out of the cleaning room, someone shot at her. She ducked behind a car and tried to find the source. Probably Tito.

"Put down your gun." Sounded like Speedy Gonzales. Definitely Tito. Not knowing whether he was a good shot or not, Sidra moved behind a pallet. More shots at her. She looked up and fired a couple of rounds to the top floor, ran until she made her way to the office. The door wasn't locked, but when she went inside, there wasn't anyone here.

"Brandon?"

A pillow and a wet blanket were on the floor behind a desk. Some goldfish crackers and a chocolate milk. When Sidra looked out the window, she spotted Brandon walking up the metal stairs. "Shit."

As soon as she exited, Tito fired. She spotted him at the front of the warehouse, making his way towards her. He was on his cell phone. Jesus, backup would be here soon. Sidra pulled out her own phone and dialed 911 as she moved. "Shit," she told the dispatcher. "I don't know the address of my location. It's the strip of warehouses a few blocks behind the Piggly Wiggly. Hurry up." And then she hung up.

Going up the stairs would make her an open target. Brandon was gone, which meant she'd have to find him somewhere and do it fast before Nacho Marquez's people showed up. Maybe the police would show up first.

Time to move.

Sidra took the steps, knowing Tito calculated her movements as he shot at her, the bullets pinging off the metal and into the wall. When she got to the top, she threw herself down on the floor.

Perfect view of Tito now, she fired at him three times close to his head, then took off down the open walkway into a room where she thought Brandon had gone.

"Brandon? It's okay, I'm here to help you."

Silence.

341

She found him hiding behind some boxes, scared shitless. Still in pajamas, no socks or shoes. They must have moved him right before SWAT showed up. Brandon pushed himself further away from her. Her beat up face must have been scaring him. Sidra put the gun away and held up her hands. "I'm going to take you to your daddy, okay?"

"My daddy died."

Sidra reached for him and he scooted away. "Brandon, we don't have a lot of time. You have to come with me before the bad guys get here. I'm not going to hurt you."

"I wet my pants."

"That's okay. Come here."

Sidra took his hand and pulled him to her. He smelled like pee and the stink of not having a bath in days. She picked him up and went to the door, listened, and then opened it an inch and stepped back. Nothing. Used her foot to swing the door open. Tito was not in the position she'd last seen him, which left her antsy. There were so many hiding places down below. Sidra had the gun out again as she ran to the door that she'd hoped led to the metal stairs on the side of the building. No bullets this time.

Sidra knelt down, stuck her head out the chained door. Looked clear. "Go through the door and I'll be right behind you."

"No." Brandon started to cry.

Sidra smoothed back his blonde hair. "Don't cry," she said, her shaking hand cupping his face. "I'll go first, but I need you to come right behind me, okay?"

As she squeezed through the door, she kept a tight grip on his arm as she also tried to keep an eye on the outside. Once outside, she carried him down the metal stairs and heard a car door slam shut. She held her finger to her mouth for him to be quiet. Just get across the parking lot. The van wasn't far. Sidra moved low, past some pallets. Past the chain-link fences.

To the right, she heard loud voices. Spanish. Nacho. If he caught her now, surely he'd kill her. No questions asked this time. He was going to be pissed when he found out Cameo was dead. Past the chain-link fence was a stack of tires. She moved there and felt safe enough to run. Ran as fast as she could and held onto Brandon.

Bullets. Go! Go! Go!

Then a sharp pain hit her. She cried out as a hot searing pain shot through her arm. She needed to move Brandon to the other hip. Two guys ran behind them. When she moved Brandon, he screamed. The van was right there. Almost there.

"We'll make it," she said, but Brandon was screaming. She looked down and saw blood. He had blood all over his shirt. Two guys were behind them. Sidra dropped the gun, looked down at the boy. He had blood on his side. His face was pale.

Not looking behind her, she cradled him in her arms and took off running again. A police car came down the street. He stopped and opened his door. Sidra ran to him, too scared to let go of Brandon. He'd been shot.

Why couldn't she save him?

# Chapter 29

**The hospital wasn't** equipped to handle Brandon's injuries. After stabilizing him, they rushed him to a hospital in Atlanta. Sidra remained at the hospital in Griffin because of her injuries, and she was thankful to get away from the warehouse. The bullet that hit her arm wasn't exactly a graze and required stitches to close up the wound and about an hour's worth of treatment. Sidra was okay. Brandon was not. No one here knew the extent of his injuries. They gave her a scrub shirt to put on, and she'd washed her arms, but she still had blood on her in various spots. Her blood. Brandon's blood. They mixed together and showed no difference. Sidra sat in a hospital room, her left arm in a sling, and had given her statement to a sergeant with the Griffin PD. Then to a detective that couldn't for the life of him understand why she hadn't called 911 sooner. Agent Bailey Flex came in for a statement, told her, "This has turned into a shitshow, honey."

"When can I go home?"

"The media is already outside." Bailey sat down on the bed.

"Do you have a cigarette or a scotch or something?" Her arm was numb for now, but that shot would wear off soon. Sidra looked at the blood on her hands. "Am I in trouble about anything?"

"I don't think so."

"My gun is in the warehouse."

"I have no idea if or when you'll get it back, it's got to be sent in as evidence."

Sidra took a deep breath and swallowed back the tears. It was all hitting her at once.

Bailey said, "Four houses and a warehouse full of drugs. That's some work. You found the little boy. And all this shit with Tanner Wells. You're as tenacious as your old man. You should be proud of yourself."

When Dad walked into the room, Sidra lost it. Like a geyser. She jumped up and threw her arm around him.

"You found him," Dad said, and hugged her tight.

"He got shot. He was in my arms and they shot at us."

"It's okay." He held her and patted her back, pressed his cheek to her head and she'd only ever felt like this as a little girl. He'd fix anything.

She said, "What am I going to tell Casey? Did the police get Nacho?"

"No," Dad said. "Looks like they took out a couple of their own guys, though. A little shrimp had a bullet in his head."

The thought gave her chills.

After she was finally discharged, she picked up her van and drove to Fayetteville, smoking a cigarette to calm her down because drinking and driving was illegal. She couldn't do this anymore. Hold all of this guilt inside, smothering her without a chance of relief. It was killing her. That's why she drank so much, because of the guilt, and she wanted it to go away, to numb her brain so she wouldn't think about it anymore.

Sidra needed to see Brady.

*** 

It didn't surprise Sidra to find him in his office in front of the TV playing a video game. "Hey," he said, barely glancing at her as she stood next to the television. A joystick and buttons attached to a pad sat on his lap so he could play the game. He had headphones on his head.

"I need to talk to you."

When he looked at her, he flinched at the busted-up, bruised face, the scrubs, her arm in a sling, remnants of blood on her. His smile quickly faded when he realized she'd been crying.

"Can you turn that off?"

"Just a second."

How many fights did they have over this when they were dating? Don't bother him when he was in the game zone.

347

"What's wrong?" he said and had to let his character die to get out and save his game. He set the game pad down on the coffee table and tried to roll away. She stepped in front of him.

With shaky hands, Sidra handed Brady the photo. She wiped away tears. "You have a son. I don't know anything about him. His name. Where he lives. Nothing."

Brady took the picture. The one where she smiled with the baby in her arms. It was a good one of his face. His eyes were open. "What?"

"That's where I was after your accident. I didn't run away from you. You'll probably never talk to me again, but I needed you to know."

Brady stared at the photo for a long time, his bent fingers wrapped around it as he tried to balance it between his hands, and mentally absorb what she was saying.

"Say something," Sidra said.

"*Say something?*"

"Brady." She swallowed hard to keep from crying. "I've been living with this guilt for a very long time. This secret. And I don't think I made the wrong decision. Neither one of us was prepared for that."

"You don't get to make that decision," he said, with a calm fury in his voice.

"Do you remember what you said to me that day?" She could tell by the look on his face that he did. "But

348

you were so caught up in rumors that nothing seemed to matter."

"I thought you were lying about being pregnant."

"Why would I lie about something like that? You told me to have an abortion, and that you didn't care about me. It was like you wanted me out of your life for good."

Brady pressed his lips together trying to think of something to say to keep the blame on her and that was fine, she'd been living with this for years.

"I said I didn't mean those things I said to you, Sidra."

"No one was there for me. I almost died, and no one was there. Because you were too much of an asshole to let shit go. I told you, Brady. I told you my period was late, and you called me a fucking whore because you were convinced I'd been with Jesse Gallop. What was I supposed to do?"

The look on his face? She was glad he couldn't get out of that wheelchair because he looked like he wanted to hurt her. He looked at the picture again. "Are you serious?"

"I almost died today. And a little boy I tried to save... I don't know, he's hanging in the balance right now and I'm at a loss with what's going on. My family doesn't know about this—fuck Brady, I thought this would be easier."

"You should have told me this years ago," Brady sat leaning forward. He hadn't shaved in days, his face looking more sallow than usual. "You drop this on me and what am I supposed to say?"

Sidra looked away. "I was gone for months. You didn't even think anything about that."

"When was I supposed to think about anything other than the fact that I would never walk again? Huh? Months in the hospital. Two surgeries and over a year of recovery. When was I supposed to notice anything other than you abandoning me when I needed you the most? Do you think I deserve this?"

"Of course not."

"I don't think you really ever loved me."

"Don't you dare say that."

They stared at each other for a long time, his face and sad eyes full of nothing but confusion. If Brady were in a different condition, he'd be partly to blame for her decision. But he wasn't. He was a disabled man, and therefore, this was all Sidra's burden to carry. A choice she made that she'll live with for the rest of her life.

"I can't move on, Brady. I'm just stuck—"

"I don't want to see you again." He held the photo out to her. "I mean it. I don't ever want to see you again. Take that with you."

"No, you keep it."

***

Sidra found Casey at Bingo's. He sat at the bar nursing a beer. The look on Bingo's face told her it wasn't good.

Sidra sat down, and Casey took one look at her and shook his head. "You could have washed my son's blood off before you came to see me." She got up and went to the bathroom.

She looked terrible, and her body started hurting everywhere. For the life of her, she couldn't scrub the blood out of her fingernail beds.

Back at the bar, she sat down next to Casey. He drank his beer in silence, and she could tell he wanted to explode. Maybe even slap her out of her chair.

Bingo set a glass of something in front of her and Sidra threw it back, nodded for another.

"I should have called you and told you what was going on," she said.

"You called the police."

"That's what you're upset about?"

"No, goddammit! I'm upset because my son got shot because you wouldn't tell me where he was. I don't know if he's okay. I can't go near the damn hospital. He had a bullet in him, Sidra."

"It could have been you getting him out and he still could have been shot."

"No," he said. "Because I would have walked in there and shot them first."

"You got me into this. I'm sorry you don't like the decisions that I made."

351

Sidra threw back the second drink, and they sat there in silence. It was late afternoon, only a few people were in the bar. Of course they were listening, but no one really cared. There wasn't anything else she could say to him, she didn't understand why he was upset with her. She got Brandon out of the hands of his former boss, that's what mattered most. If he needed someone to be mad at, then fine, she'd take it.

A minute later, the door opened and two uniformed police officers walked in. Casey turned his head, saw them, then looked down at his beer.

"Casey Lincoln?"

Casey looked at Sidra. "You brought them here?"

She didn't answer him. Agent Bailey Flex wanted to talk to him. So, yeah, she technically brought them here.

The officers stood behind them. One of them said again, "Casey Lincoln?"

"Yeah?"

"I'm going to need you to come with us."

"Am I under arrest?"

"No."

"Then fuck off." Casey had the beer bottle between his finger and thumb, turned the bottle around a couple of times. Sidra reached over and took the bottle out of his grasp so he wouldn't do anything stupid.

"I'm sorry, Mr. Lincoln, but we have orders to bring you in. We'd like for you to make this easy on everyone."

Casey shook his head, looked down at his hands, and for a moment the tension was a little unnerving. She felt the officers move behind her and she turned, held up her hand.

"Casey?"

He looked at her, something desperate in those eyes. "I just wanted my son back. Where's he going to go now?" When he spun around, he tried to push through the two officers. They each grabbed an arm, patted him down. They cuffed him even though he wasn't under arrest. Casey turned around to look at her.

All the fight in him gone.

***

Back in the apartment, she took a shower and scrubbed herself clean, but nothing seemed to get rid of what she felt right now. When she got out, the place was so hot; she was sweating. Couldn't breathe type of sweating. She packed a light bag and drove to Shackelford to spend the night.

Although she wanted to crash, she walked into the office and found Mom at the computer checking email. She took off her reading glasses when Sidra sat down.

"You okay?"

"No."

"I'm sorry," Mom said. "I know it's hard. Everything's in the good Lord's hands now."

"Yeah?" Sidra said. "Was everything in the good Lord's hands when Brandon's mother got shot in the head? Was it the Lord's hands when Brandon got a bullet in him too, or was it in *my* hands?" Sidra took a breath. "I'm sorry. Life's just shitty."

"Yes, it is sometimes. I'm waiting for a phone call about the little boy's condition. I'll let you know as soon as I hear something."

Dad walked in with his cell phone up to his ear, a smile on his face, and Sidra could hear Bailey Flex's voice on the other end. When he hung up, he said, "She wants all your notes on everything. Photos. Locations. Interviews. Everything. Either turn them over or they'll get a warrant. It's pretty serious. They've been hit-and-miss on the Marquez family for a long time, but this is something else."

Sidra turned to the computer and began looking for Lexie in Arizona. Took her about twenty minutes before she found a Lexie McDermott, formerly Alexis Lincoln. She was thirty years old, married with two small kids. Searching through some social media photos, Sidra found an old photo of one of Lexie's birthday parties as a child, and she was certain the older boy standing next to her was Casey. But she couldn't be certain.

Sidra asked Dad about a contact in Arizona, and he told her to get in touch with Wesley Swain. After speaking with Wesley for five minutes, he said, "Tell me specifically what you would like for me to do?"

"Locate and confirm that Lexie has a brother named Clarence Lincoln in Georgia. To the best of my knowledge, she wants nothing to do with him, so she may hesitate."

Sidra explained a few more details with Wesley, who said it may take a couple of days. She understood this, she'd had to locate people herself, but she left the frustration out of her voice and was very thankful for his help.

What Sidra wasn't expecting was a phone call from Lexie four hours later. She was in tears and left behind the same kind of life Casey was living when she'd gotten married. For four hours, Sidra talked on the phone with Lexie, who seemed like a really sweet person.

It was going to be a long night

\*\*\*

Early the next morning, Mom and Sidra drove to the hospital in Atlanta to check on Brandon, who seemed to be stable and had woken up sometime around two o'clock in the morning. Alone, without a familiar face around him.

Kid must have been scared out of his mind.

Mom said she'd stay with him for however long it took him to recover. She was good with things like that. What Sidra wasn't expecting to find was a handful reporters outside of the hospital, or Casey Lincoln

355

sitting in a chair down the hall from Brandon's room. There were three police officers, along with Agent Flex.

Casey spotted Sidra, and said, "I don't want her anywhere near my son."

"What's wrong with you?" Sidra said. "I'm the one who saved your son's life."

"Really?" He stood up.

Bailey Flex put her hand on his arm to stop him. She looked at Sidra. "You probably need to go."

Mom said, "Excuse me but I'm not leaving."

"Who are you?" Casey said, being a real jerk about this. He was going to be really pissed when he found out his sister was going to be here in the next day or so.

"My name is Tilda Shackelford, and if there is anyone in the world that you need right now, it's me. Now you can quit being inconsiderate and accept some help from me for your little boy, or I'll do it without your permission. I know a lot of people, young man."

Casey sat back down. "When they let us in, I'm going in there first."

Nacho's people told Brandon his dad was dead, and when Casey went in there, she couldn't tell who was crying louder; father or son.

She couldn't take it anymore.

Sidra went outside to smoke a cigarette. She looked up at the sky said, "Yeah, well, I don't see you making any good decisions right now, either."

An hour later, Sidra spotted two police officers and Bailey Flex walking Casey through the parking lot.

Sidra walked the aisle over as they reached an unmarked car next to a police cruiser. Not in cuffs, but those two officers were ready if he ran. Casey looked like hell, his face red and blotchy.

Sidra said, "What happens now?" mostly to Bailey Flex.

"Can I have that?" Casey gestured to her cigarette. Sidra hesitated a moment, then gave it to him.

Bailey said, "We're not sure yet, we're still working out details."

"They want me to testify against the Marquez family," Casey said. "Put me in protective custody. No jail time. My son also goes into protective custody, but not with me."

Bailey shrugged. "We're working out some details."

"Is Brandon okay?"

"Yeah," Casey said, rubbing his hands over his face, cigarette ash dropping to the ground. "Long road ahead of him, though. But he was smiling." He wiped away some tears. "He was smiling. Likes your mom already."

She tried desperately not to cry. Felt like she'd betrayed him, but this was for the best.

"We need to go," Bailey said.

"Can I take another cigarette?"

Bailey said, "You're not smoking in my car."

# Chapter 30

**A cop stood** outside of Brandon's room, and Sidra had to show him her license, and for a minute she thought he was going to deny her entry. Once inside, Mom sat next to Brandon's bed. He was wide-eyed but looked weak and so pale against the white blanket.

"Hi," Sidra said. "Do you remember me?"

He nodded, looked away shyly. But he smiled at Mom, who rubbed his nose with the stuffed dog she'd brought him.

"You're a brave boy," Mom said. Sidra sat down across from her, wiped away more tears. "Are you going to be okay?" Mom said.

"I'm just mourning or depressed. And Casey's pissed at me and I don't understand why."

She put on her Mom face and said, "Go wash your face and knock it off. We have other people to worry about right now."

"Yes ma'am," Sidra said and did what she was told.

\*\*\*

They decided Mom would stay at the hospital with Brandon, and Dad would pick her up later. When Sidra pulled into Shackelford, she nearly had a moment of panic. She barely parked before she jumped out at the sight of Bruce Zeller. He leaned against the back of a black sedan parked in Mom's and Dad's driveway on the left side of the house.

Sidra stared at him. He paid her no attention.

She was ready to call 911, but when she walked inside, Nacho and Lorenzo were on the leather sofa. Dad sat in the armchair across from them. Daley leaned against the office door frame, and Mitchell stood behind the sofa with his arms folded.

Dad turned when Sidra walked in. "We were just talking about you."

"You fucking asshole," she said to Nacho. "You don't care who you have to hurt, do you?"

"I do nothing," Nacho said. "The people who work for me sometimes do bad things." He held up his hands in self-defense. "I sometimes know nothing what they do."

So that's how he keeps his hands clean, and he'll kill his own people to do it.

Nacho said, "We come to discuss a truce."

"What's that supposed to mean?"

He leaned forward. "You hurt a lot of my business. I'm sure the police will want to talk to me very soon. And what do I say?"

359

She was stunned. "A little boy is in the hospital right now because of you. And he's just collateral damage. For what? A couple hundred thousand dollars? Did you come here to threaten us?"

"No," Nacho said.

Sidra turned to Dad. "This is the man who was going to zip me up into a body bag with a dead guy."

Dad didn't seem too uncomfortable. Almost like they'd had a discussion without her and none of this mattered.

Nacho said, "Let's just say we even."

"No, not even. To be even, we'd have to be playing a game. I'm not playing a game with you or your fucking family." Sidra put her foot up on the coffee table and leaned into them. "I'm well aware of what you're capable of, Señor Marquez. With the amount of money you have, you can take each one of us out like children in a drive by. But I'm not going to live my life in complete fear of you."

"No fear," Nacho said. "I want you to leave my family alone. My business alone."

Sidra wanted to laugh. The big-time *Businessman* wanted her to stay away. "Then you make sure to tell your people that we're off limits. Do you understand?"

"*You* understand?"

Sidra looked at Lorenzo, who sat there looking a little unsure of himself, almost uncomfortable. She said, "Maybe all your problems are gone, Lorenzo, and you get your family back in town." He eyed her coldly.

Nacho stood up. "Next time, Sidra. You have problem, you come see me. First, you come see me, and we have no problem." He gave a nod to Dad and walked out of Shackelford. Lorenzo stood up, smoothed back his silver hair, paid Sidra no attention as he walked out as well.

*** 

Brandon spent a week in the hospital and was then moved to a Children's hospital for more specialized care. Mom didn't leave his side the whole time, and he was getting better every day. Casey knew his sister was going to take Brandon back home with her to Arizona. They were trying to decide what to do with Casey, who really just wanted to go to his own home, to hell with protective custody. The police didn't think that was a good idea.

Nacho Marquez claimed he wasn't at the warehouse the day Brandon was shot. He claimed that multiple people who worked for him in his restaurants had acted on their own in Brandon's kidnapping, and that they were selling drugs on their own accord. He had nothing to do with it. His niece Abi and her husband Tyler were innocent bystanders in the raid, as they didn't know that Dani Cameo and Steven Mollett were using the house to store drugs and money.

Isn't that something? And the Marquez family was left to continue business as usual.

361

The evidence was stacking up against Tanner Wells. Now that he had been charged, women were coming forward, but they'd only found four women who he'd taken sexual photos of. They still didn't have the names of all the women. They wanted Sidra to testify. What she'd been through seemed like a small price to pay to open up all the criminal activity Tanner Wells was up to. She still honestly had no idea what happened that night other than the photos. But Tanner Wells missed one thing that night he drugged Sidra. He forgot to wipe Lydia Desmond's fingerprints off of his Canon.

Sidra spent the last two hours digging around Casey's cabin. She moved the trash bag filled with wallets, cell phones, and keys into her van. Anything that she could find that didn't look like it belonged here, she took it. Then she ransacked Casey's bedroom. Boxes stacked to the ceiling. It wasn't like she was going to find little lunch boxes with stacks of money in them. But that made her think twice about the toy box in the corner of the room. Sidra lifted the wooden top, pushed aside a baby comforter, and found a toy box full of cash.

She sat down on her butt and let out a laugh. This wasn't a couple hundred grand. This—good God, Casey had been skimming money for years. The Marquezes probably didn't know the half of it. How the hell was she going to get all this money out of here?

***

She still had nothing new about Lydia Desmond, which was what Sidra was looking into when the knock came. Two detectives stood there, flashed their badges and asked to come in.

She knew they wouldn't stay too long because of the heat. "Don't mind the mess."

They introduced themselves, said they were with the Macon Police Department.

Sidra nodded. "What can I help you with?"

One of the detectives, Morten or Martin, took out an evidence bag with a gun in it. "We were wondering if you could tell us how your prints got on this gun."

Sidra's prints were on file with the state because of her P.I. license.

She recognized the gun, not because it looked special, but because she only ever handled one gun with a silencer. Edgar Burke. "I don't know," she said, well aware that the detectives stood three feet away from the trash bags full of evidence she'd pulled from the cabin. "If you've seen the news you'll know I just spent a month tangled up with some bad guys."

The other detective, Floritchovitch or something, wiped his forehead with a handkerchief he'd pulled from his pocket. "Sure is hot in here."

"That it is," Sidra said.

"Took a while to find you," Morten or Martin said. "Your address isn't correct."

363

"I just moved a few weeks ago." How convenient, she thought, that the house she'd shot Burke in was getting renovated. Her prints on a gun meant nothing. They had no body, no crime. "I don't know," Sidra said, and gestured toward the gun. That's all she could say. Why offer the police information that would only lead to more questions.

Whenever they found Edgar Burke's body, they'd have their answers.

Keep in touch at:

http://www.kristyroland.com

facebook.com/Kristy-roland

Thank you for reading!

Made in the USA
Columbia, SC
13 January 2022

54071563R00224